I0636026

GUN FOR WELLS FARGO

A JOHN POPE WESTERN

G. WAYNE TILMAN

WOLFPACK
PUBLISHING
— EST 2013 —

WOLFPACK PUBLISHING
— EST 2013 —

Gun For Wells Fargo

Paperback Edition
Copyright © 2020 G. Wayne Timan

Wolfpack Publishing
6032 Wheat Penny Avenue
Las Vegas, NV 89122

wolfpackpublishing.com

Paperback ISBN 978-1-64734-067-4
eBook ISBN 978-1-64734-066-7

GUN FOR WELLS FARGO

ACKNOWLEDGEMENTS

Thanks to Beta readers Denise Kearns,
Rebecca Thomas Payne, and Susan Stecker.

DEDICATION

This book is dedicated to the brave men, driver's (*Jehu's*), shotgun messengers, and detectives, who moved and protected people, mail, goods, and money for the Wells Fargo Company in the Wild West and beyond.

And, to my fellow writers at the Western Writers of America who continue the Western genre in the finest tradition of
Zane Gray and Louis L'Amour.
I salute you, my friends!

CHAPTER 1

The man in the black suit and matching derby could have been a young banker or undertaker's apprentice. Until you looked at the set of his eyes and the sternness of his face. That look would have said "policeman" at about any place or time in history. The badge, two Smith & Wesson Number Two .38 revolvers in shoulder holsters, a black jack and pair of hand cuffs, all hidden under his coat, would certainly have confirmed his occupation.

San Francisco detective John Pope sat nursing a beer at a saloon overlooking San Francisco's busy port. The docks were busy, even now, at midnight.

Pope had a tip from one of his squealers. He was now watching for one Dave Neal. Neal was supposed to be robbing an express man carrying bank money in a chest on the Bay Lady steamer. The Bay Lady was to leave its berth, circle Alcatraz Island and steam on to Saucelito, as the town was currently spelled on this August night in 1881.

Half of a ham sandwich lay on his plate, the bread getting stale. The beer had not been cold an hour ago. The barkeep knew who he was and did not bother him for a refill. He was there to watch, not to eat.

Pope watched stevedores, sailors, passengers and tradesmen for another hour.

Then, he saw someone he reckoned was the mark coming down the street. He seemed to be headed to the dock where the Bay Lady was berthed.

Pope left a dollar on the table and slipped quietly out the door. He stood in the shadows, watching, his body coiled and ready to move.

The express messenger was pulling a dolly with a wooden chest on it. Pope could not see the details, but knew it would be a wooden box strapped with iron and secured by a padlock in its hasp.

Two men approached the messenger. They could have been acquaintances or, robbers. One pulled a sap and hit the messenger a glancing blow on the head. The other grabbed the dazed man and walked him to the side of a wagon and set him down. The other began to wheel the dolly back in the direction from which it had come.

Pope stepped out fast and forcibly. He pulled the Smith and Wesson from his left shoulder holster in a cross-draw.

"Detective! Throw up your hands! Do it right damn now!" he ordered in a voice to be taken seriously. Apparently the two men were not intelligent enough to recognize how they should respond. One did the stupid thing.

The man beside the semi-conscious messenger drew a small gun. Pope saw it out of the corner of his eye and swung the .38 in his direction. The man was already moving, gun pointed at Pope.

Pope cocked his .38 and sent a bullet into the man's torso. The man jerked and stood still in surprise for a minute. Then, he fell off the pier into San Francisco Bay, notable for its cold, dark water and fast currents. The other man was running with the dolly, which Pope knew to contain a thousand dollars in gold coin.

It took Pope less than five seconds to get close enough behind him to swing the black jack against the back of his head. The man fell as if he had been pole-axed. The lock box fell off the dolly and rolled over on its side, but remained secure.

Pope dragged the suspect to a gaslight pole and handcuffed his hands around it, guaranteeing he could not flee when he regained consciousness.

Keeping one eye on the box, he peered over into the water. There was no sign of the man. His body was probably heading out towards Alcatraz, maybe even eventually making it out the Golden Gate. If the sharks didn't get him first.

Pope took a silver police whistle out of his vest pocket and blew it three times.

He went over to the dazed messenger.

"You alright?" he asked. The man rubbed his head and nodded.

"I am. My head hurts like hell. Did the one you shot get away?"

"I couldn't find him in the water. I guess he's dead or dying and floating out to sea. If you are okay, I'm going to sit on your treasure chest and protect it until reinforcements show up."

"Thanks, detective. I'm not quite in shape to provide all the protection Wells Fargo requires right now, but I'll back you up from here," he said, drawing his large revolver and holding it in his lap.

Pope touched him on the shoulder of his jacket and walked over to the green wooden box with a purported thousand dollars in gold in it.

He sat on the lock box and waited, the revolver in his hand, but out of sight under his jacket. The messenger was becoming more alert, rubbing his head.

In five minutes, he saw two men in suits coming towards him at a fast walk. A couple of uniformed police officers were a block behind them, coming faster. Detectives, Pope thought, though he did not know them.

He holstered his revolver after reloading the spent cartridge and pushed his lapel aside so his badge would be prominent.

"Well, detective! You seem to have done our work for us tonight!" the older man in a suit said.

He stuck out his hand.

"Jim Hume, with Wells Fargo. Did one get away? Our information was two robbers were going to hit."

"Kinda," Pope said to a man he knew to be, along with Allan J. Pinkerton, one of the two most famous detectives in America. He was the former sheriff of El Dorado County, California and Wells Fargo's chief detective.

"The other pulled a gun and I had to shoot him. He went off the pier into the drink. I looked for him, but no sign. He's either dead on the bottom or floating faster than a steamer out to sea."

"It appears our treasure is intact," Hume said, looking at the box Pope was sitting on.

"Yessir, it does appear to be. I see your partner is tending to the messenger. I saw the hit he got on the head. It did not seem too hard. He never was completely out. Shame the other thug got stupid. I'd rather have cuffed him than shot him. But, he made the decision and got his dues."

"That's the only way you can look at it, son," Hume said.

"Excuse me a minute, sir," Pope said and he motioned the two policemen over.

"Would one of you get Detective Sergeant Howell here? He needs to sign off on one of his detectives shooting somebody." One policeman rushed off to the station to get the senior detective summoned from home or the so-called Jenny Lind Center where the detective offices were.

"Where's the shot fella?" the remaining officer asked.

Pope pointed to the water.

"How about get some boat hooks and poke around for the body. Get dock workers to help. He fell in close to the shore. He needs to be looked for right away to have any chance of recovering him. I doubt you will find anything, but we still have to make the effort."

Hume had his accomplice right the lockbox and then he and Pope put it back on the dolly.

Hume retrieved the bill of lading for the money and delivered it to the other Wells Fargo man, who wheeled it up the Bay Lady's gangplank and prepared to deliver it across the Bay.

Soon, the Bay Lady sounded two whistles and left its moorings, the Wells Fargo detective aboard with the lockbox, en route to its final destination at a Marin County bank.

"You saved my company paying a thousand dollars reimbursement to the bank over in Marin County tonight, detective. There will be some reward money in it for you," Hume told Pope.

"I'm not sure I can take it, sir," he responded.

"Sure you can. I spent my career, up until eleven years ago, as a police man. I know for a fact SFPD is lenient on conflicts of interest. A number of your fellow detectives work part-time for me right now. Maybe you should to. Maybe even full-time."

"That's good of you, Mr. Hume. But, I like being able to arrest the people I investigate. Your folks can't do arrest anybody."

"We can, but it varies with politics. Currently my senior detectives and I have special police powers in San Francisco. But, they come and go with changes in mayors and chiefs. I'm working with the state, but nothing has happened yet. Pinkerton runs the biggest detective operation in the US without arrest powers, but I guess we can beat them!" Hume said.

"Better than Pinks, sir?" Pope asked politely.

"Oh, their detectives are good and they are well-trained. But, some of their activities have been extra-legal. Ours never are. I see to that!"

"This is all interesting, Mr. Hume. What have they done illegal? Not arguing the point, just trying to learn, mind you."

"The best example was the ill-advised attack on Jesse and Frank James' mother, blowing up her house, hanging her husband and causing her to lose her arm. It was illegal and just plain wrong, no matter what criminal low-life's the James boys are."

"I was not aware of the story," Pope said. "If you'll excuse me, I need to see what progress the uniformed officer and dock hands are having recovering the man I shot. And, I need to interview your original messenger. It looks like he is in good enough condition now for me to talk with him."

"You go ahead, son. I'd like to sit in on the interview with my man. I won't interrupt you. I just have to make a report to my higher-ups, too," Hume said. Pope nodded his assent.

"Any luck on hooking a body, officer?" Pope asked.

"No, detective. It gets real deep not far from the bulkhead. Even if he moved ten feet, we could not hook him with these boat hooks."

"Thanks, officer. Let me get your name for my reports. I'll say you were a big help." The man shook his head in thanks, but said nothing.

Pope added the name to his notebook and he and Hume walked over to the Wells Fargo messenger, now fully awake, but still prudently sitting up against the spoked wagon wheel.

"How are you doing?" Pope asked.

"My head still hurts, but it's clear now. Howdy, Mr. Hume."

"Glad you are all right, Murphy," the senior company detective said.

"Let me ask you, Mr. Murphy—especially since Chief Detective Hume and the other detective were on the docks at midnight. Did you have advance knowledge there would be a robbery attempt here tonight?" Pope asked, writing the man's name in his notebook.

"Let me address your question, Detective Pope. Yes, we had a tip. Detective Hackney and I were on the way with time to spare, but the Geary Street cable car ran over a pedestrian and we had to hoof it half the way. So, we got here after you did, what we were going to do," Hume said.

"Did you get a name? We will interrogate the man cuffed to the light pole, but I always like to know the answer before I ask a suspect a question," Pope explained.

"You have good instincts for such a young detective, Pope. I fear I was much older before I figured out how to really, effectively question suspects. We had the name David Deal," Hume said.

"My source said Dave Neal. Pretty close. Let's see what we can get from the other suspect over at the gaslight pole," Pope said. He took a few more minutes filling in blanks from Murphy and noting his comments. Then, he and the Wells Fargo man walked over to the suspect handcuffed around the gaslight pole.

"Comfortable?" Pope asked pleasantly.

"Not much," the man growled.

"Well, it's gonna get worse for you very quickly if you don't answer some questions."

The man, clearly a hard case with no love for the law, said "I ain't got nothing of benefit to either of you," he said.

Pope got right up in his face and spoke quietly.

"I'll be the one who determines what the benefit of everything you tell me is. First off, what's your name?" Pope said.

"To hell with you!" the man said.

"Fine, Mr. To Hell with You. I'm going to unhook you and move you out of public view to question you. You get my drift?"

Pope unhooked the nippers and frog-walked the man to the wagon wheel Murphy was leaning against.

"Got some company for you, Mr. Murphy," Pope said.

Murphy got up and began to black out. Pope and Hume grabbed him and supported him between them until he regained his balance.

The suspect, re-cuffed started to run off, but Hume tripped him. As he got up, Pope decked him with a roundhouse to the jaw.

He was out like a light.

Pope dragged him over to the wagon wheel and cuffed him uncomfortably against the tall tread so his arms were stretched to the limit while sitting. They finished talking with Murphy while the suspect began to regain consciousness.

"You ready to talk with us now? Or, do you want to be obstinate? If you do, I will question you a bit here and a lot back in a cell," Pope warned.

"Now, what is your name?"

"Zack Beedle." Both detectives were busy copying.

"Your friend who I shot?"

"Dave Neal."

"Where did the two of you get the information about the shipment tonight?" Pope asked.

"Dave got it. I don't know where. That's all I'm saying until I find out what's in it for me," Beedle said.

Pope backhanded him across the mouth, drawing blood.

"Maybe that's a little sample of what's in it for you. A real little sample. You realize with Neal gone, you stand to take the whole charge for this robbery and assault?" Pope said.

"Let me add a little something on behalf of Wells Fargo. You answer *all* of the detective's questions and give us names of associates, I might see my way clear to hire a defense attorney for you. But, it better be worth my while. Otherwise, you are looking at a lot of time in prison. A whole lot!" Hume said.

Beedle seemed to get serious and gave the offer some thought.

"Okay. I'll give you everything I know just, not here. Too many people know me on the docks. Seeing me spill my beans to a couple of suits with guns will get me killed as soon as the steel door closes. How about hit me to make it look like I ain't answering and drag me off to jail. I'll talk there in front of your lawyer."

Pope and Hume looked at each other. Hume nodded. Pope slugged the prisoner with a blow rendering him unconscious again. Nobody gave a look. All walked hurriedly on, considering it was what it was. Police using standard 1880's techniques with a prisoner.

Several other uniformed officers had arrived and were watching the first officer and a couple stevedores fish for Neal without success.

Pope hailed a couple over and had them take custody of Beedle and call for a wagon to transport him to the lockup.

"I'll meet you at the lockup tomorrow around eleven with a lawyer for this ruffian," Hume said. "You want breakfast? Or, to go home and sleep until it's time to go question Beedle?"

"I think breakfast. I have to hang around for my sergeant to take his shooting report."

"It'll be quick. My recommendation helped get him promoted to detective sergeant," Hume said. "I saw everything. It was from a bit farther away than I might testify, but I did see it. My man on the Bay Lady did, too."

"Thanks, Mr. Hume. I think it was a righteous shooting."

"No question about it. Now, let's get something to eat. Mainly, let's get coffee."

They walked back across the street to the saloon where Pope had done his surveillance and ordered breakfast.

Pope noted during breakfast Hume asked a lot of questions about him. The questions stopped when they saw Detective Sergeant Howell approach the crime scene. Hume stepped outside and waved him over and led him to the table.

"Where's the fella you shot, Pope?" was the first thing out of his sergeant's mouth.

"In the drink Boss. Either on the bottom deeper than the boat hooks will reach, floating past Alcatraz Island, or popped up out of sight and got away. I really don't know which," Pope answered.

"What's your best guess?" Howell asked.

"Floating past Alcatraz," Pope said without hesitation.

"What happened?"

Pope told him.

"I saw it all, Hank. It was a clean shoot. Just as Pope said," Hume added.

Howell finished his notes and looked up.

"In that case, we have no reason to delay eating." He motioned the bartender over and ordered a large breakfast, knowing the tall older man who had promoted him to detective fifteen years ago was flush and would pay.

******

An hour and a half before, Dave Neal felt the .38 bullet hit him. The hundred forty six grain lead round nose penetrated his jacket, his vest, his dirty shirt and his skin. Half of the short lead bullet stuck out. The other half was between two ribs of his skinny chest, but did not puncture his lung. Nor, did it bleed much through his several layers of cotton and wool. Which was a good thing due to a very large, hungry shark population in the Bay.

He bled more from his hands, as he cut them on razor sharp barnacles, as he moved from piling to piling to get away from where they would be searching for him.

Dave Neal was not the sharpest pencil in the drawer. But, he was a survivor. Living where and how he had all his life and doing what he did for a living — constantly breaking the law — had honed well-tuned animal survival instincts.

Four hundred yards away, he was hypothermic and exhausted from the cold and the exercise. Neal found a ladder up the bulkhead and climbed it painfully and slowly. It was an empty slip and nobody saw the wet man reach the top. He eased across the street and into an alley. Taking off all his clothes, he proceeded to wring them out and replace them. He took off his shoes and emptied more of San Francisco Bay from them than he thought possible.

Somewhat drier and a degree or so warmer, Neal began the trek to his room atop a saloon ten blocks away. He dragged along due to the weakness from the onset of hypothermia, but the exercise helped raise his core temperature. Neal did not have a clue about any of this, but kept pushing along because he realized he had to or would die. He could enter his room unseen by a rear outside stairway and looked forward to seeing to his wound, stoking the coal stove and warming up.

Somebody had squealed on him. Was it Beedle for money? He could hear Beedle being captured from several docks away. Beedle was one of the few people who knew where he lived. The bastard would bring the police directly here as part of a deal. He had to die and fast.

Changing both clothes and plans, Neal headed to the jail.

He racked his brain, trying to think of who he knew inside awaiting trial or transport to San Quentin Prison.

He came up with one name along the way. Taking out a pencil nub and scrap of paper he brought for the purpose, he wrote a terse note to the man. Because of honor among thieves, he thought he could trust Josiah Yoakum to kill Beedle. Yoakum owed Neal big time. He would know if he denied the request, Neal would arrange for him to get a homemade knife in the back at San Quentin.

Neal knew from personal experience at the San Francisco jail prisoners were in an open area. Sleeping was done in cells, usually unlocked. It was a scary, violent place, even for the most seasoned and toughest of prisoners.

Neal got to the jail at his planned time. Shift change. He stopped a guard heading in and gave him the note to Yoakum and a silver dollar. The money was a significant sum to the guard. Neal knew Yoakum could read. He had no idea if the guard could read, but decided to chance he couldn't.

Neal left immediately and returned to the stove and hot food he so desperately needed.

By dawn, Neal was asleep. Before falling asleep, he determined he would get the one who shot him and pay back Wells Fargo for its detective shooting him and the loss of the money he had already mentally apportioned to facets of a new life. He underestimated the detective force at SFPD and assumed Pope was Wells Fargo.

******

When Pope got home to his tiny downtown apartment, he trudged up the steps and unlocked the door. There had been robberies in the area, so he kept his right hand near his gun. It proved to be unnecessary.

He did not bother with his stove or food. He just stripped to his underwear and lay across the bed on top of the wool blanket. He was asleep in very few minutes after a twelve hour work day. He had thought about the reward from Wells Fargo. It would be nice. Maybe he could put it towards a small house.

His grandpa, who raised him, always said land was the way to build wealth. Grandpa had a lot of land. Hundreds of acres in Alameda County, near the small town of Oakland. His land had rolling hills with poplars, willows, elms and sycamores scattered across the landscape.

It was land upon which the old man taught him wood-craft and, tracking. Something he would hardly use in San Francisco, but would find helpful anywhere else in the West. How to cut sign, build a low-smoke fire pit. Hide from pursuers. Kill game anywhere. Kill men anywhere.

Grandpa at sixty-five was still the deadliest man Pope knew. He had proven it over and again. He was the youngest mountain man at the 1840 rendezvous on the Green River in Wyoming. He had fought wild animals, hostile braves, crooked whites and unbeliev-able weather. And, not only survived, but reveled in it. Both genetically and by example, he had passed that drive and skill set on to his only grandchild. They were the only two surviving Popes since the young detective had been ten.

During his tenth year, Pope's parents and sister had been killed in an Indian raid. The boy had fired until his father's musket was too hot to touch. Only the appearance of neighbors on horseback, riding and shooting, caused the war party to retreat.

His, grandpa Israel Pope had responded to the wire and ridden to Kansas from California. He showed the ten year old how to identify the tribe from the arrows a few of the braves had used.

Then, they rode. A man in his early sixties and a boy of ten. By the time the senior Pope had arrived, there was no chance of tracking. So, they went for the village. They watched patiently, being bitten by bugs they could not slap, urinating where they lay, chewing jerky and drinking only canteen water for days.

Then, it happened. A war party of young braves assembled. From observation, it was clear these were the only ones of war party age in the village.

The two Popes crawled the mile back to their horses.

They began to follow the party. It was heading to an outlying ranch. The Popes set up on a hill overlooking the ranch. They were close to the young braves.

As the party circled on their horses to plan their attack strategy, Pope senior took the leader off his pony with a .54 slug from a Hawkins rifle. He dropped the big single shot and he and the boy opened up with repeating Henrys from close range. In the melee, braves dropped as did ponies inadvertently hit.

When the Henry's ran dry, the Colt's began. And, then there were no more braves standing.

The Popes reloaded and approached. They took no prisoners. Man and boy head shot each survivor. The boy did not flinch. These people killed his mother, father and sister.

"Vengeance is mine, sayeth the Lord." And, the Popes, said the Popes.

Riders from the ranch rode out to find the bloodbath. There was nothing for them to do but bury the dead.

Without a word, the Popes rode off.

The boy was stoic about his baptism under fire. The older man had prepared him and continued for the next eight years until he made the short ride to San Francisco and enlisted with the San Francisco Police Department.

******

John Pope did not know anything about modern policing or investigations. Nor, did he know anything about city life. What he knew was logic and survival and how to shoot both rifles and revolvers. It quickly appeared those skills were quite enough to excel at the SFPD and he rose quickly off the streets and into a suit.

Pope wondered about the effect of his .38 on the man he knew as Neal last night. It did not seem to hit him very hard. Did it have enough power to stop a fight when someone was shooting back or coming with him with a knife?

Uniformed officers were now carrying the big break-open S&W's in .44 caliber. But, they had long barrels and would be hard to conceal and heavy to carry. Especially, if he continued his practice of carrying two guns. Pulling a second gun was a lot quicker than reloading the first one when the chips were down, so Pope did not plan to change the practice of carrying two.

Pope had not shot to kill since the fight with the war party with his grandfather. He had shot several armed prisoners at a jail riot when a patrolman. And, he had drawn his duty weapon many times. But as a policeman, it had been his brawling abilities and truncheon which had served him best so far. But, last night brought him back to the reality of his job. Kill or be killed was a rule which could surface at any time.

He needed to give some more thought to what firearms he was going to carry. Maybe a piece of the reward from Wells Fargo would let him choose whatever he wanted.

He washed hair and body, using the pitcher and bowl in the room. He heated the water on the coal stove. Pope selected a clean white shirt and brushed the black suit, derby and shoes.

He stopped at a restaurant on the way to the jail and had a quick breakfast.

As planned, Pope got to the jail a few minutes before the scheduled meeting with Jim Hume.

Hume greeted him on the hour and they went in. At the iron-barred wall where they had to check their weapons, they saw a lot of activity and yelling on the other side. Something was amiss and badly so.

"What's going on?" Pope asked the jailer at the desk.

"There's been a stabbing. Fella's dead," the jailer responded.

"Got a name," Pope asked.

The man looked at his log book where new prisoners were entered. He traced ten names down to a name with an X by it.

"Zachary Beedle."

Pope and Hume looked at each other with disgust.

"We need to speak to the jailer investigating the stabbing," Pope said. "Right now damn it!"

The jailer looked like he was going to say something regrettable.

Pope held up a finger stopping him, just as Detective Sergeant Howell walked in.

"Boss, somebody in there stabbed and killed our robbery suspect from last night. We need to find out who and why. Was it over cigarettes or something? Or, maybe a hit. If so, who put it out?"

The sergeant demanded the man summon the jailer who had found Beedle and questioned other prisoners.

The inside jailer was beyond worthless to their investigation. His only usable information was knowing which prisoners were nearby when Beedle was found, including his cell mate.

There were five in total.

"Put them all in holding cells and advise them not to talk with each other or they will get another charge. Impeding a murder investigation. Tell them that will mean San Quentin time for sure," Pope said, making it up as he spoke. He saw the look on Howell's face fade from disbelief to understanding.

The men were moved to separate holding cells. Pope planned to interview from outside the cells, so the detectives kept their assortments' of revolvers, saps, knives and brass knuckles.

They questioned the cell mate first. He claimed to be asleep until he felt something wet dripping down on him from the upper bunk. When asked if he saw another prisoner in or leaving the area. He looked around like a scared rabbit and said "No."

The detectives all saw him look several cells down as he answered negatively. They could not tell which prisoner the cell mate wanted to be sure heard him hold back identification.

"What are you in for?" Pope asked, changing the subject to one less worrisome to the prisoner.

"Drunk and disorderly."

Pope whispered something into Howell's ear. Hume was able to hear it and nodded imperceptibly.

"Jailer! We're done with this worthless piece of garbage. He has nothing for us," Howell bellowed out.

When the jailer came and unlocked the lockup door, Howell followed them out.

Instead of going to the open incarceration area, Howell directed them up to the detective's bullpen and had him handcuffed in an interrogation room to await further questioning without the probable murderer listening.

Pope and Hume jointly questioned the other four, including a big thug who was inordinately uncooper-ative. Pope noticed a spot of blood on his sleeve. When he saw the detective looking, he put his hand over it and scowled. Each was asked if they knew Beedle's place of domicile and any of this associates. None did. Both detectives believed them. Beedle had not been in long enough to establish confidences with anyone.

Pope knew Hume had seen it too and noted his name for a further interview before he was transferred to San Quintin later in the day.

Before going to the detective bullpen, Pope made another stop and arranged to have a post-mortem photo made of Beedle's face. There would be no autopsy, but the photo might help at the docks in determining friends and hence, perhaps, accomplices. He also had a department artist draw a sketch of Neal and print ten of them.

Two of the three detectives entered the interrogation room where Tom Spicer, Beedle's short-term cellmate was handcuffed. The third, Howell, watched through a slot. He was there to observe reactions to various questions, body language and quirks the two across the table might miss.

Hume suggested a deal and a strategy to the SFPD detectives before the interview.

"Alright, Mr. Spicer. Here's the deal. We think you saw something. We also think the killer was in the lockup area listening to us question you. That's why we said we were taking you back and brought you up here instead," Pope said.

"Now, you tell us something we need to close this murder of Beedle, which is related to a Wells Fargo robbery attempt and I will pay your drunk and disorderly fine and give you a ticket to anywhere reasonable you want to go away from here. Wells Fargo will also include enough spending money to get you there well-fed," Hume offered.

Spicer nodded and Pope picked up the questioning.

"What did you see when Beedle was knifed?"

"I saw a shadow and felt somebody come in the cell where we were both sleeping. I thought they might be coming after me, so I cracked one eye open. But, he went for the new guy in the top bunk. I heard a sound like somebody killing a hog with a big knife, then a groan. The blood started real quick," Spicer said.

"Who did you see?" Hume asked.

"It was the big man a couple cells down just now. Yoakum."

"There's no question in your mind?" Pope asked.

"Nope. It was him. He keeps a shank under his mattress. I bet it's there right now."

"You don't think he ditched it?" Hume asked.

"Naw, big and ugly as he is, he's chicken. He has to have an edge. The knife is all he's got. He's going in for hard time. Fifteen years."

Howell immediately sent two burly detectives from his squad down to the jail to search Hosea Yoakum and his bunk for the murder weapon.

It took both two hundred pound bulls and a couple of jailers to restrain the murderer, but they found the homemade knife with blood on it and removed his shirt with the blood stain for evidence and brought both back to the bullpen.

The detective sergeant called Pope and Hume out of the interrogation room and told them what had happened and pointed to the evidence laying on the table.

The three sent for a deputy assistant attorney and met with him. They discussed their findings and showed him the evidence. It was agreed, given the bloody knife and shirt, Spicer could give a signed, notarized affidavit and not have to appear at the trial.

That was done with the prosecutor's guidance. Hume paid the fine and gave Spicer forty dollars. The two big detectives escorted Spicer to the train station. They watched him buy a ticket and get on an eastbound Santa Fe train. They did not bother with the destination. They just did not want to have him murdered on their turf.

"Well, we solved a murder, but did not contribute much to the Wells Fargo case," Pope said to Hume as they walked back to the jail to pick up the ten photographs Pope had ordered of Beedle's face as well as a sketch of Neal's face, as well as Pope could remember and tell the artist.

"No, we didn't. But, maybe the pictures of Beedle and sketch of Neal will help us find an accomplice. It strikes me either there's a third man in this robbery, or the man you shot, Neal, has come back to life," Hume said.

"I keep getting the same feeling about Neal. Beedle wasn't in jail long enough to have an argument with Yoakum. There was no evidence they knew each other at all. So, somebody was worried about Beedle ratting them out. Giving an address, friends, whatever. That had to be Neal or an unknown. I wonder how they knew about the transport of the gold coins to begin with," Pope said.

"I hate to say it, but we might have an internal problem. I have no evidence and no suspects, but just the same, I put a couple detectives in the office where the shipment started. They will see who works there, for how long, what the level of trust is and the like," Hume added.

He went on to give an example.

"It's like when I was a detective in your shop. If we had a wife murdered, the first suspect we looked at was the husband. Similarly, we are pretty close to the vest about our shipments of gold coin. Had it been five thousand dollars, I would have understood it better," Hume said, still hoping it was not an inside job at Wells Fargo.

They looked at the photographs of Beedle and sketches of Neal. "Despite being a bit pale and dead, it's a good likeness" Pope noted. Hume agreed, grinning sardonically at the younger detective's comment. Pope gave Hume five of each and kept five. Of his, he gave four to Howell to give to other detectives working the docks and wherever leads took them. He kept one for himself. Pope really wanted to solve this one. Not SFPD, not Wells Fargo. Him. He just feared Neal was not shot properly and had gotten away. His mantra was his grandfather's. "Shoot the bastard 'til he cain't get up. Then, shoot him one more time for luck." The young boy had asked "Whose luck, Grandpa?" The answer was understandable.

"Your luck boy. It ain't lucky if he gets back up or even rolls over, gives you the evil eye, then shoots you. Put his ass down for good, boy. And, you'll live to be an old codger like me."

Pope knew it was gospel. His grandfather had said it. So, it had to be. And, he believed it to this very day and it bothered him he may not have done what his grandfather had said.

Hume shook hands with Pope and headed back to Wells Fargo headquarters to distribute the photos of Beedle to his detectives and try to track down the source of the information about the shipment from criminal associates of the dead prisoner. They agreed to keep in touch and share any new leads or developments on old ones.

Pope checked his pockets for silver dollars and some five dollar gold pieces. He may have to spread some wealth around among San Francisco's seedier citizens today. Maybe tomorrow.

He wanted to know where Neal lived and, where Beedle lived also. He would search both dives for clues. He hoped to question associates of both men for information about the two deceased ones and anything on their plans after the robbery. That might give Pope an idea where Neal, if he was still upright and wasting California air, may head to escape San Francisco. Pope wanted to bring him back with nippers on or across the saddle. And, he did not much care which.

He hit his regular snitches first and spread some dollar coins. A dollar could get a pretty good meal, a room, a few minutes with a lower class soiled dove, or a couple of drink of rotgut or hits on the *pin gon* pipe at a Chinese opium den.

The regulars offered nothing of use and he considered the five dollars an investment for future crimes.

Pope then started working dock workers, sailors and deliverymen in the dock area. The Bay Lady was in, so he went aboard and spoke with the purser and captain about what they knew of the prior night's shipment. They knew nothing, so thinking the information might have come from a crew member was invalid.

Pope stretched his area of concentration out several more blocks.

He met one street person who claimed to recognize Beedle. The man did not know Neal. He said Beedle lived "somewhere over that a way," pointing northeast. "Mebbe three blocks, I don't know," earned the man a dollar.

Pope walked in the direction of "that a way" and, after several blocks, began to question street people. None wanted to talk.

Though young in his early twenties, the detective was tall and powerful. Nobody who dealt with him ever made him out to be a pushover. The combination of money and threats worked as he got nearer and nearer to where Beedle lived.

The room was described to be a third floor room in a flophouse one street over from Popes current location. He found the place and walked up to the third floor. All the doors were closed. Though it was mid-morning by now, he heard snoring from behind one of the doors. He rapped on the door.

On the second set of knocks, he got a "Go the hell away!" in a raspy, cigarette and gin voice.

"San Francisco police. Open the door! Do it now, or I'll kick it in!"

As trained, he said this from beside the doorframe to avoid any bullets which may precede the door opening.

He held one of his .38's in his hand.

Pope thought he heard bare feet padding towards the door and stepped further aside and back.

A bearded, wild-haired older man pushed the door open.

Revolver held available but out of sight by his right hip, Pope used his left hand to flip his lapel back and show the badge pinned to his vest.

"Detective Pope. I need your help with a couple easy questions. Then, you go back to sleep. If the answers are real helpful, you might go back to sleep a little richer."

That seemed to get the man's attention. He had breath smelling like an unmucked stall, so Pope continued staying back.

"See this man?" he asked, flashing Beedle's photo.

"Which of these rooms is his?"

"307," the man said, emitting an odoriferous invisible cloud.

"Anybody live with him?"

"Naw. Nobody's put up with that piece of crap," sweet breath said.

"How about this man? Ever seen him with him?" Pope asked.

"Nope. Never seen him with him or any kinda way."

Pope flipped him a fifty cent piece and told him to go back to bed. He hoped the man would use it for a brush and some tooth powder, but seriously doubted it.

As soon as the door was closed, Pope, revolver still in hand, walked down to 307. He tapped on the door. Nothing. So, he kicked it hard and it flew open.

He scanned the room, looking over the sight groove of the revolver.

Not seeing a threat, he walked in and closed the door. It closed but the shattered lock did not engage.

Pope searched the room thoroughly. He found and pocketed a cheap Allen & Thurber .32, a pocket knife and a length of iron bar. He was sure the latter was used for head thumping during robberies. Beedle had a threadbare winter coat and some worn gloves. No extra clothes or shoes. There was a pitcher and bowl, but no sign of soap for washing or shaving.

Worse, there were no addresses. Not of Neal or associates or next of kin. There was literally nothing to help Pope solve his case.

He went out, fully assured the room would be picked clean before the sun set. He could care less. Anybody who would take that stuff needed it. It surely had no market value, even in this depressed area of town.

*****

Neal laid low the whole day. He was a night stalker. When he laughed, seldom as it was, it was when he realized the sun hurt his eyes. He could see better at night.

He figured sleeping during the day would keep him out of sight of the police anyway. He was having some chills still from spending too long in cold San Francisco Bay. But, he chalked it up to being damp in cool night weather. He had no clue hypothermia frequently led to pneumonia and organ damage, especially when no efforts were immediately taken to bring core temperature back up quickly.

Neal got up in the afternoon, still shivering and dressed. He went to see his source to cut a deal. He found out tomorrow the safe would have twenty thousand dollars in it. Five for the source, who would be protected and fifteen grand for him. It would be his ticket to ride. Ride out of San Francisco and to Arizona or somewhere with a silver or gold mine and nobody looking for him. A nice suit and a train trip.

Neal needed to work fast. He had to pick up a gun and, more importantly, some dynamite. Dynamite would be tough to find in downtown San Francisco. He could get it at about any rural feed or farm store.

Neal took his last cash out from a loose board in the floor and hired a horse for the day. He rode to near the Millbrae Estate and found a farm store. He bought six sticks of dynamite and a fuse. Neal told the owner of the store he needed to blow up a stump. The man told him one stick should be fine, two at the most.

For the job Neal had in mind, more would be better, he thought.

"How long does this fuse take to hit the dynamite and blow the stump?" Neal asked.

"About ten seconds. Should be enough, what with stumps being out in the open. You can light it, run a hunnert feet and hide behind something. It'll work just dandy!" he said.

He rode back and returned the horse. Neal knew from his inside information the twenty thousand would arrive in the morning and ship out the next morning. Tomorrow night would be his only night to break in, blow the safe, and make off with the money. He bought a knapsack. The office was near the docks. He could take the midnight departure of the Bay Lady.

His inside man was going to leave the rear door unlocked.

Wells Fargo was serious about their locks and he had neither the knowledge nor tools to pick one.

Neal did not know the disposition of the money. Was it gold coins? Paper currency? Would it be loose? So, he figured scoop it all up and dump it in the knapsack, sling it on his back and walk unseen down to the docks. Should be a piece of cake. He could blow the safe, get the money, slip out the rear door and nobody would be the wiser. Except for his inside man, who would meet him in the alley and be paid his cut. Or, maybe just die of a gunshot wound. No! A knife would be better. It would be quiet. Even in the confusion after an explosion.

Neal, getting more tired as the day wore on, wiped his sweaty forehead with his sleeve and returned to his room. He hid the explosives under the loose board, skipped eating because he did not feel well, and went to bed.

*****

The next day, the Wells Fargo dock area office cashier was nervous. Two company detectives were hanging around the office. Even Hume had been there. They knew something was going on. Somebody had told Neal about the shipment on the Bay Lady. In the muck-up, they thought Neal was killed.

He checked in the shipment by counting the currency and some gold coins, logged it in to the register and placed the money in a canvas sack in the safe. It was tagged with the amount, sender, and destination.

When Neal appeared during the afternoon, it had scared him, Boris Kirov, half to death. It was like a ghost had appeared. Neal walked right in, head down, past the two detectives.

Kirov nodded to the back alley. Both men went there separately. Kirov told Neal about the new, big shipment and was promise a vague amount equal to "a year's salary" out of the take.

All he had to do is leave the rear door open when he closed and wait hidden in the alley for his cut. Easy enough. He had been promised a couple hundred out of the botched robbery the other night. But, he knew one of Hume's men had already delivered it to Saucelito.

He also told Neal it was a San Francisco detective who shot him, not a Wells Fargo detective. Kirov thought Neal was surprised, but could not tell for sure since the robber was acting funny. Kirov was a former Moscow embezzler who started over clean once he had come to the States. His good English and knowledge of financial matters got him hired quickly at Wells Fargo. They had no way to check his record back in Mother Russia.

Kirov's living clean changed about a week ago. Neal sought him out and bought him drinks at a local saloon. They had vodka. Neal had bought him a lot of it, including a bottle to take home.

Now, he was back in his element, though working for one of the best-run companies in America. One almost as famous for its detectives as for its red stage coaches.

"Well," he thought, "there will not be anything to point in my direction. It will be over tonight and I will hide my money for later and just go ahead working like before."

******

Pope continued to work the streets of San Francisco, trying to find an address for Dave Neal. He was almost out of snitch money.

His grandfather taught him to track at night and how to do surveillance at night. He told the boy few people, Indians included, expected a white man to be after them after dark. Most would expect a pre-dawn attack on their camp, but not a tracker after them all night.

Popes night activities were assisted by a new device employed by the SFPD. It was a kerosene fueled Dietz police lantern. What made the police lantern different from regular oil lanterns was the ability to shoot a longer range beam into the dark instead of merely lighting the immediate area around the lantern itself. He did not always carry it at night, but had found it often made a big difference in solving cases or seeing evidence at night.

Pope was like a bulldog on the trail. He just did not want to give up. He skipped lunch, made himself eat dinner and knew he would be sunrise getting back to his room. He brought the lantern with him when he left late in the morning and had it in a leather evidence bag slung over his shoulder. The bag contained the small lantern and a metal bottle of kerosene and his notebook, the pictures of Beedle and Neal, gloves, a magnifying glass, a knife, a charcoal pencil and a sketch pad.

He went back to the scene of the crime and started over. Spotting a bench, he set the bag on it and sat down to observe. He was working for free at this point, but did not care a whit.

******

Neal dragged himself out of the bed. He thought he might feel a little better. He was not shivering. He put the dynamite and some wooden matches in his knapsack. He included some socks, a rolled up union suit, his Bowie knife and a Colt .38 rimfire caliber conversion of an 1852 .36 cap and ball revolver. He would duck in an alley before the robbery and tuck it into his waistband. Maybe the Bowie, too, to take care of the Russian.

Neal knew he needed some food to fuel his body after the rough couple days. He shouldered the knapsack and left his room forever, never looking back.

He stopped at a restaurant and treated himself to a steak and potatoes and some apple pie. All the heavy food was a mistake and he knew it right away.

Neal paid for it and walked into the alley and lost it all against a wall.

Back on the street, he looked at the clock on top a bank building. He had half an hour before meeting the Russian. It would take most of it to just walk to the Wells Fargo office. He wanted to get there early to make sure there was not anyone waiting to ambush him. Neal did not trust his mother, who he had not seen for thirty years. He was nervous about the Russian. What if the detectives broke him? What if he told them about the plans for tonight? He would be a sitting duck.

Neal smacked himself against the right cheek. He was getting jumpy over nothing. The Russian was tough and would not break.

Twenty minutes later, he reached the area of the office. He held back and watched, leaning against an alley wall. He was partially hidden in the shadows.

Nothing seemed out of the ordinary. He crossed the street and walked away from the office. At the next corner, he turned left, then left again into the alley which ran behind the office a half block down. He proceeded slowly and stopped long enough to stick the Colt into his waistband in the dark.

He slowed even more as he approached the rear of the Wells Fargo office. He saw a dark, squat figure moving back and forth around the door. It was the Russian.

Neal walked up and nodded. The Kirov looked nervous, but it was to be expected, Neal thought.

The Russian nodded towards the door and shook his head, probably indicating it was unlocked.

"I'll wait around the corner here for you to get the money and give me my share," he whispered his accent strong and voice hoarse.

Neal nodded and went in the rear door. He pulled the Colt in case Kirov's nervousness was over a setup.

It did not seem to be. Neal knew in advance from Kirov where to find the safe.

He had never blown a safe. He eased the fuse down between the sticks, all of which were bound together. He propped the bundle against the inside edge of the safe door and struck a match to it.

Neal ran as fast as he could towards the front of the office and squatted down behind a desk. The manager's glassed in office was in front of him. He ducked his head and put hands over his ears.

Before he heard the blast, he felt the wall of super-heated air knock over the desk he was behind, bowl him over and implode the building.

Dazed and temporarily blinded and deafened, Neal lay on his back and the second floor collapsed on top of him. He could not even feel the glass shards from the manager's office sticking in every part of his body. He was able to crawl out from a section of the ceiling which had fallen on him. His first thought was the money.

One look at the room where the safe had been convinced him it was useless. The building was starting to burn. Fast! He needed to get out and right now.

Neal pushed himself and made it across the debris to where the rear door had been. There was not even a wall there anymore. As he stumbled onto the alley, he tripped over Kirov's body. He turned right and went the long way down the alley he had come in so few minutes ago.

*****

Pope was sitting on the bench observing the flotsam and jetsam of dock people when the nearby buildings were rocked by a big explosion. At first, he thought it was a major earthquake. Then, he smelled the burning and reckoned it was too soon for earthquake-spawned fires. Not within seconds, he thought.

He grabbed his bag and shouldered it as he proceeded at a fast walk towards the smoke and confusion. He heard multiple three-blast police whistles. Whatever it was, it was big.

Within minutes, Pope walked into hell. It was the Wells Fargo building. Or, rather it had been the Wells Fargo building. Now, it was rubble.

He could hear the fire brigade coming in the distance. Uniformed officers were beginning to walk into what was the front of the building.

Popes first thought was to stop them. A roof could collapse. But, there was no roof. Then, he thought of evidence. Probably destroyed in the explosion.

His mind raced. Gas leak explosion? Robbery gone bad?

Pope entered the rubble of what had been a fine building.

"Any bodies in here?" he asked of the two police officers.

"No, detective. None yet. This area seems to have the most damage," one observed.

"That probably means dynamite and an attempted robbery. This is where the big safe was. My guess is gold coins flew through the air like buckshot."

Pope got his magnifying glass out and walked over. He did not want to kneel in his black suit with nothing but ash on the floor, so he squatted and studied the floor. He saw a couple tiny bits of currency.

"Hey, detective. I got blood over here. Somebody was in here!" a policeman yelled.

Pope went over and studied the floor.

There were spots of blood all over. And, a clear place almost in the shape of a man on his knees. Someone, probably the bomber, had tried to hide from the bomb here. And, not been anywhere near as protected as he thought before the explosive ignited.

Pope followed a light blood trail to the back. There was no back wall. He walked out onto the debris-filled alley. He tripped over Kirov's body too and recognized the cashier at once.

"What the hell is the cashier doing here this late at night?" he asked himself. "And, why was he outside in the alley?" There was no conclusion he could reach without having Kirov as a conspirator. The rear door was relatively intact. It was laying in the far side of the alley where the concussion had blown it.

Pope lit the Dietz police lantern and turned the door over. He wanted to see the lock and see if it had been jimmied.

There were no scratches on the lock plate. The person who entered had a key or the door was left open for him. He had to have entered from the rear. There was too much traffic to go in the front without notice, even by patrolling policemen.

"Was Kirov waiting here after letting the robber in?" he thought aloud. That seemed a logical assumption to Pope.

Pope focused the pencil beam of the Dietz on what used to be the rear doorway.

With the powerful light he saw a bloody footprint.

Withdrawing the sketch pad and charcoal pencil, he drew a size and shape approximation and noted a chip on the right side of the heel and several broken threads on the edge of the sole. There was the beginning of a hole in the center of the sole. He added that, then compared his drawing to the actual print. It was pretty close. The angle looked like the wearer of the shoe was walking to the right down the alley, so Pope went right and showed the light on the alley. The cobble stones did not show any more footprints, but specks of blood were present.

Pope got the impression the man had a hundred small bleeding wounds instead of one big one. "That has to hurt!" he exclaimed aloud.

He followed the blood trail to the end of the alley and across the street. He shined the Dietz on the street and lost it for a while, but picked it up further down.

He saw it on the steps of a rooming house and went in. Following it up the steps with the shine of the lantern, he stopped where the blood trail led down a hall instead of up more steps. He came to a door. It was partially open.

Pope drew his gun and nudged the door open with his foot. He saw a man on the floor, face down. He recognized Dave Neal even from behind. Pope nudged him with the .38. No movement. He rolled Neal over. His eyes were locked open in an unseeing stare.

Pope had found his bomber and his robber from the docks. There was no need to handcuff him.

Dave Neal had died minutes before his pursuer arrived.

Pope leaned out of the window and blew his whistle three times for backup.

He sat on Neal's bed and waited, thinking about the timeline. About the suspects. All were dead. Neal, the ringleader. Beedle, the co-conspirator. Kirov, the inside man at Wells Fargo.

Pope would do something new for SFPD. He would make a murder board and diagram with lines and photographs to tie all the events together for the brass and Wells Fargo.

Pope would place the sketch of Neal from the robbery beside a post mortem photograph showing the two were the same person.

He would add the photo of murdered arrestee Beedle at the jail.

And, a photo of the Wells Fargo office and of cashier Kirov's body outside the rear of the blown-up building. The time line would show Kirov dead there well after closing time. Why else would he be there? The board would depict all the important aspects of the case in one place.

The next day, word came down from the chief to the chief detective to Howell for Pope to prepare a summary presentation for a meeting hosted by the chief and senior representatives from Wells Fargo and City Hall.

Pope called it the "perp walk of the dead," but understood the political need for the chief to hold the meeting and show off how his department had solved two crimes in several days. Actually, how Detective John Pope had solved them. Pope was beginning to understand politics and did not even expect a "well done" out of the deal. But, it would just be another feather in a hat starting to look like a chief's headdress.

CHAPTER 2

The Wells Fargo case summary with the brass was held five days after the first robbery attempt.

Pope knew he was expected to put on a stellar performance. He was confident with both his facts and his methodology.

He used his murder board to tie the times and people together and his audience was convinced his summary was correct by the time he finished. Hume was thinking a couple steps ahead of him and arrived at the same conclusions sooner than the rest of the police and bureaucrat audience.

Pope had solved the Bay Lady attempted robbery, caused the arrest of Beedle, arrested his jail house murderer and logically proven Neal was behind it, identified the inside man at Wells Fargo and tracked the culprit in charge of the Bay Lady attempt and the botched dynamite attempt at the Wells Fargo dock office. All within several days. While he considered it just part of his job, he realized it was a good piece of police work.

The chief got up and took full responsibility for the success of the quickly solved investigations. Nobody but him bought a word of it.

Hume caught up with Pope on the way down the hall from the meeting room next to the chief's office.

"Got time for lunch? There are a few things we should chat about," the older detective said.

"Always a pleasure, Detective Hume. Let me drop off my exhibits first and I'll be right with you," Pope responded.

They went over to California Street, to the Tadich Grill and ordered pot roast and mashed potatoes.

"I listened closely to your presentation, Pope. I was looking for investigative reasoning, instead of just getting leads from snitches. Your use of photographs and sketching the shoe print and following the blood trail and using the Dietz police lantern immediately instead of waiting until daylight were of interest to me. I'd like to think it's how I would have proceeded," Hume said.

"Thank you, sir. I just followed logic. My grandfather taught me how to cut sign and track it. He also said to follow a trail while it's hot. He taught me night can be your best friend and your quarry's worst enemy."

"Was he a lawman?" Hume asked.

"No, sir. He is Israel Pope. A mountain man."

"I know of him," Hume said. "The last of the mountain men. Known tracker. Never boasted like the rest. But, if he got on your trail, you were done. He's a legend, but I expect you've known for a long time."

"I knew right off he was a hero when I was ten and he took over caring for me. The legend part I figured out later. We still write every week. I try to get over to the ranch at least once a month."

"I bet he's proud of you," Hume said.

"I believe he'd be proud of me no matter what I did. Whatever I am, good or bad, is due to that old man, Mr. Hume. He was my ma, pa and best friend. And, always will be."

"A fine legacy for a man to leave, Pope," Hume said. "How do you think he'd feel about you becoming one of my detectives at Wells Fargo?"

"He'd be rightly proud of me for sure. He knows, as I do, there's no more respected detective force in America than yours. It's a badge any man would be honored to wear."

Hume mentioned an annual salary to Pope. It was not exorbitant, but still considerably more than a SFPD detective with several years' experience made or, would make as a sergeant.

Pope reached across the table and proffered his hand. Hume shook it as the meal was delivered. The deal was consummated over really tender and flavorful pot roast, its gravy captured in a nest atop the mashed potatoes.

Pope was to give two weeks' notice to SFPD, take a week with his grandfather, and join Wells Fargo three weeks hence.

In lieu of the reward he had spoken about, Hume gave Pope a starting bonus. It was a draught for three hundred dollars.

They were near the Wells Fargo headquarters building. Hume took Pope in and showed him where his desk would be and introduced him to the cashier downstairs who cashed the draft.

They parted and Pope went back to his office and wrote out a letter of resignation and presented it to Howell. The sergeant had already been warned by Hume of the upcoming offer. He hated to see the kid go, but did not blame him at all. In fact, he was a little envious. He suspected the money would be better, though he had no idea how much better. There would also be the power of Wells Fargo and its affiliated majority ownership of American Express Company. It was a heavy badge worn by men capable of living up to the expectations which came with it.

The next two weeks went quickly. A couple of strong arm robbery arrests and one manslaughter of a friend by another friend, both drunk outside a bar on Geary Street.

He was still conflicted over replacing his guns. The wounding shot on Neal to an otherwise fatal location was disappointing. Had Neal not fallen overboard, he could have returned fire and killed Pope.

There was a famous gunsmith in San Francisco and Pope went to see him at A.J. Plate & Company on Market Street.

He outlined the need for dependable knock down power, dependability and concealability.

The Colt shopkeeper or sheriff's model led in dependability and feel in the hand. The Smith & Wesson was faster to reload, but seemed slower to cock and fire. The Merwin & Hulbert Pocket Army was like a Swiss watch in its workmanship. It even had changeable barrel lengths. It only took seconds to change them. Its problem was the tight fitting of the cylinder for the black powder era. Six shots and it had to be cleaned thoroughly. Six shots were probably all right for a detective in town, especially backed up by a second gun. On the trail or the plains where there was an outlaw gang or hostile war party, he knew it would not suffice. But, with an identical twin backup, he felt it would be a good choice.

Pope settled on a pair of five inch barrels in .44 caliber. He ordered the gunsmith to reduce the barrel length to three inches and add new front sights for the blued revolvers. He was fitted for a double shoulder holster. To make them more concealable, he specified thin ivory grips smoothed down even thinner. The man at A. J. Plate promised them by two days hence. Pope added four boxes of cartridges. He would practice at his grandfather's ranch after his two remaining weeks at SFPD were up.

His next stop was a haberdashery. He chose dark gray and navy blue vested suits to go with his current black one, some black Florsheim shoes and a pair of Western rider's boots. His black derby hat was in good shape and a periodic brushing kept it new looking.

During lunch, he had asked Hume if he would be on the trail much, or mainly in town. Hume said both, probably split equally. His first assignment was to be a swing detective working out of Wells Fargo headquarters in San Francisco and responding to robberies and passenger kidnappings within a multistate region. He would mainly be taking trains and stages to get to the crime scene, then hiring a horse for the trail. When he got a long-term assignment to a regional office, like Denver, he would secure a horse and more permanent living arrangements. Hume said the "when" would be defined by events.

The week with his grandfather was good. The mountain man still retained his vitality and endurance. They rode, hunted and camped in the hills. It gave Pope an opportunity to refamiliarize himself with skills he had not used in the city. Skills he found he missed very much and would be using on the trail of stage and train robbers. He showed the old mountain man his Dietz police lantern and promised to order one for him upon his return to the city.

By plan, the ranch only had a couple horses and heads of cattle on it now. Pope senior wanted to save his energy to walk and ride on his land instead of spending too much of every day doing ranch work. After his years on Wyoming, Idaho and wherever the beavers drew him, he still had a hard time sleeping under a roof. He spent more than a few nights on a treed hilltop sleeping in an open front lean-to.

The two men parted with the promise to continue writing weekly and trying to visit monthly.

Pope reported to duty early on Monday morning.

During his first month, Pope was assigned to shadow several assigned senior detectives. This would expose him to the Wells Fargo way of doing things.

He learned rapidly and began to add more tools to his investigation kit. Different size cotton sacks to put evidence in, tweezers to pick up small items, a better magnifying glass, binoculars and the Wells Fargo Confidential Cipher Book with its codes for both letters and telegraphs. Part of his lessons was in locks. He learned what determined a good lock and how to pick any lock. A small picklock set came with the training. The detective armory had a variety of handcuffs, saps and firearms. The only thing he would envision checking out was a double barrel shogun and box of buckshot. He already had a Winchester carbine in .44-40 caliber to match his twin Merwin & Hulbert revolvers.

At the end of the first month, Hume summoned Pope into his office.

"How's it going, Pope?" the famous detective asked.

"I think well sir. But, I guess what really matters are the reports you are getting back from the men I am shadowing. What do they think, if I might ask?"

"You can always ask me whatever is on your mind. Occasionally, I may not be able to answer. But, this is not one of those times.

My senior detectives said you already have a good base of investigative skills. They said you are a fast learner and picking up Wells Fargo style readily. Ha! Both even said they had learned a few things from you! I know what SFPD's training for detectives is. Nothing! So, you may be creating some technique as you go. I'd like to think I did the same as a young deputy, then sheriff.

Before I give you, your first alone assignment, let me tell you a bit about our stage and express business.

Most of our stages now are our own, in the past we were an express company and used other companies' stages. Ultimately, we bought many out.

Our stages are built by Abbot-Downing & Company in Concord, New Hampshire. That's why our red stages are referred to as Concords. Our drivers are the best in the business. They are called *jehu's* after King Jehu in the Old Testament who drove his chariot like a bat out of hell, or *whips* for obvious reasons. The reins are referred to as *ribbons*. A jehu with a standard six-horse team will be handling twelve reins or ribbons. Our guards, many of whom serve like detectives when called upon, are called *shotgun messengers*. We often refer to the assets we transfer for other people as *treasure*. The treasure is usually transported in heavy green wooden boxes strapped with iron. They have good padlocks and are further often locked onto the stage, either under the jehu's seat or under the rear seat inside the stage. The stages carry a maximum of twelve passengers. Eight can squeeze inside and up to four can ride on top, holding on for dear life as the stage flies around dusty curves at top speeds.

I am going to send you off on your own earlier than most. It's a dangerous one, Pope. I hope your shooting skills are as good as your investigative ones.

We've had two Concord stages hit by robbers in the past week and a half.

They have occurred on the run between El Paso and Van Horn in Texas. The robberies are violent and passengers are being beaten. A woman was molested, but not raped.

What I am going to do is to put you in the coach, heavily armed with a Texas region detective. We will have a top shotgun messenger up top with one of our best drivers, or *jehu's*. The lock box will have rocks in it. So, the robbers are going to be pretty mad with any survivors if they get as far into the robbery as opening the box.

If you don't have a shotgun, check out a sawn-barrel one and a couple boxes of shells."

"Mr. Hume, who are the robbers? I have a small familiarity with that area. It's real close to the Rio Grande and Mexico isn't it?" Pope asked.

"Over half the run is parallel to the Rio Grande. Mexico is literally yards away. Then after about two-thirds of the trip, the road turns northeast and away from the river. With the turn comes some pretty tough mountain country. My detective questioned the *jehu* who had the ribbons on both robberies. He miraculously survived. Neither shotgun messenger did," Hume said.

"I have train tickets to get you from here to El Paso. The special Concord will leave in the morning three days hence, so you will have plenty of time to get there and make your acquaintance with Detective Raymond Smathers. You'll like him, Pope."

"Sir, what about accents? Mexican or American?"

"Both. One robbery took place on the part near the Rio Grande. The *jehu* heard both accents. The second one was on the mountainous stretch. Same thing. I think it's a gang. Does it operate out of Mexico and duck back across the river each time? Mebbe. That's for you to find out and tell me. You and Smathers, that is," Hume said.

"Here's an envelope with train tickets both ways, expense money and a good map of the area. Smathers will introduce you to the whip," Hume said, "once you get to El Paso. He was talking about having the

US Marshal lend a couple of deputies to ride along. A good shotgun messenger up top with four good guns inside would be a nice surprise for a gang.

Pope, I usually like to arrest and prosecute. In this case, I just want to stop the robberies before passengers get hurt or killed and more of our men die. Do what you and Smathers need to do. God speed, young man!"

Pope knew the meeting was over with those words and stood, pocketing the envelope.

"I'll be back when the matter is taken care of, Boss," Pope said and turned and left the office. He was grinning.

"Early for a first 'away' assignment, and a real good one, too," he thought. He checked his silver Waltham pocket watch and the train ticket. He had several hours to get his gear ready and be at the station.

The first thing he did was follow Hume's suggestion to check out a shotgun and some shells for it. He got four boxes of twenty-five each. He passed by the ten-gauges and picked a twelve gauge 1878 Colt with mule ear hammers and a pair of twenty-inch barrels.

Pope had a quick sandwich and coffee for lunch and went to his room.

He checked his investigation kit and put it by the door. Pope put some .44 cartridges, socks and clean shirt and one fresh tie in a sack and pushed it into one end of his carpet bag valise. The remainder of the space held a canteen, hatchet, Bowie knife, trowel, coffee pot and small iron grill. He added matches, salt, flour, coffee and lots of jerky. A small waxed cotton tarp and wool blanket completed his packing.

Slinging the leather investigation bag over his shoulder, he carried the cased shotgun in one hand and the valise in the other.

He motioned for a hack to take him to the train station.

An hour and a half later, Pope stepped aboard an eastbound train, a tall man in the black suit and carrying an obvious cased shotgun not attracting a second glance from any other passenger.

He found his seat and placed the shotgun and valise in the overhead rack. He kept the investigative kit beside him to review the map of the area of Texas where the robberies occurred. He estimated the miles from El Paso to Van Horn and Van Horn back down to Old Mexico. He noted the distances in his book and measured how far the route ran beside the Rio Grande. This gave him some perspective as well as some clues as to whether the gang operated out of Mexico or perhaps they had a hideaway in the mountains along the route. A mountain hideaway would be harder to breach for a posse.

Pope decided there was little more he could decide about the gang until he got in place. He already had his talking points with Smathers and the questions he wanted to resolve.

He leaned back and watch California fly past his window.

It took, with stops, eleven hours for the train, then a stage for the last part of the trip to San Diego. He transferred to an eastbound train.

They entered Arizona Territory and crossed the Colorado River at Yuma in the middle of the night. The train crossed the four year old railroad bridge and steamed towards Tucson.

Tucson came around dawn. The train pulled into El Paso, Texas around noon.

Detective Raymond Smathers met him at the station and they walked over to a hotel and he checked in and dropped his gear in the room.

Smathers was about forty, a medium height, muscular man with a large handlebar mustache and sharp Van Dyke goatee. One look and you could tell he was not a man to mess with.

Pope learned he had been a Texas Ranger, then an El Paso officer until joining Wells Fargo five years ago.

"I met with the US Marshal for West Texas this morning, Pope. He said he'd lend us one deputy marshal. The Texas Ranger captain offered a ranger, too. I told both the only way we were going to stop this bunch of hooligans was with superior firepower.

I think with Boxer hauling ass on the ribbons, Scott as shotgun messenger, a Deputy US Marshal, a Texas Ranger and two Wells Fargo men inside, those fellas are in for a surprise they will never forget!"

"It sounds like a good plan, Raymond. I didn't get the idea from the Chief Detective he was looking for arrests. He just wants it fixed.

It's good we only have badge toters aboard the stage and no passengers. Is it the standard Abbot-Downing stage out of Concord, New Hampshire?" Pope asked.

"It is. So, it could carry twelve passengers. With us four aboard and a six-horse team, it should be fast. Scott will have both a scatter gun and a rifle up top. Once stopped, Boxer is a good man with a six-gun. But, handling twelve ribbons, he has his hands full. Literally!"

"Sure does. What kind of terrain have the two previous robberies occurred on?" Pope asked.

"*Three,* previous robberies. We had another yesterday while you were travelling."

"Anybody hurt?" Pope asked.

"The whip was nicked in the shoulder. Drove on to Van Horn through the Quitman and Eagle Ranges. They lost a small amount in the strong box and a couple of male passengers got robbed and roughed up. One man lost a tooth."

"Whereabouts did it occur?" Pope asked.

"Just after the northerly turn and on the upgrade into the first mountain range," Smathers said

"Still mixed Anglo and Mexican accents?"

"That's what the driver and shotgun messenger said. Didn't get much out of the passengers. Some dudes from back East. Scared so bad I think one messed himself."

"Well, having a gun pointed in your face can have a real strong effect on you," Pope chuckled without much sympathy.

"Ray, are these just random? Or, do they seem to be planning around people or treasure aboard?"

"I thought about the same thing. 'Pears to be random. Yesterday had these yahoos from New Jersey or somewhere. None of them had a pot to pee in. The treasure chest was light. Altogether, not a good stage to rob."

"Hopefully, yesterday's experience will make them hungry for a big hit tomorrow," Pope said.

"And, that's what we will give them. A bunch of big hits!" Smathers added.

"Ray, you know what strikes me as wrong with this plan? We ought to have about ten Texas Rangers, maybe with two saddled horses in tow, riding a mile behind us. If we don't kill them at the spot a robbery happens, we can't chase them down. They'll get away and we will be back to square one."

"You're right, Pope. I tried to get more rangers. With the deputy marshals, you may get a helluva gunfighter, or somebody's nephew who got hired as a favor. The bosses were tight. If you and I ride a mile behind the Concord, it might work. But, it is not going to be the plan the boss laid out. He's a great leader, but you don't want him mad 'cause we didn't follow his plan. Not at all," Smathers said.

"I understand. So, we have to shoot fast and shoot straight."

"Yep. We do. I'd say an early dinner, no alcohol and get plenty of rest. The other two will meet us at the stage station at seven-thirty. Let's meet for breakfast an hour before."

******

They met the driver, Boxer, as he was checking his team of six. Scott was next, with his sixgun a Marlin carbine, and a long barrel Greener ten-gauge.

Both men struck Pope as ones to ride the river with, as Israel Pope used to say about some of his fellow mountain men.

Texas Ranger Ham Budner was known to Smathers as both a good man and fast with a gun. The Deputy US Marshal, George Echols was unknown to Smathers and was the wild card in this game.

Smathers briefed all inside the stage station and they got on the stage and pulled off.

Boxer was easy on the team. Usually, he would push a team hard, knowing the six horses would be changed within a half hour or so at the next way station. Today, he wanted to save some reserve in the horses in case they had to run without a team change to get wounded men to medical help. Help which was very sparse along most of the route.

This run did not have a schedule to meet. Boxer took his time and changed once in the first hour. They were nearing the spot along the Rio Grande where the first robbery occurred.

The shotgun messenger advised the men inside the coach at an interim pee stop they were in vulnerable territory.

About five miles later, Boxer saw a curve with aspens on both sides ahead. He thought he saw a glint of sunlight on metal. It was going to happen!

Scott reached down and knocked on the side of the door frame of the dark red Concord number 793.

Pope stuck his head out and Scott told him what Boxer saw ahead.

The men inside rechecked weapons already checked multiple times.

In the middle of the curve in the dirt road, Boxer yelled "Whoa!" and pulled back on the twelve reins or "ribbons." As the horses tried to slow the coach, he helped with the hand brake on the right side, locking the rear wheels and causing the Concord to skid and fishtail in the dirt.

Boxer was good and kept the bottom side of the coach pointed at the earth. A lesser driver on the ribbons might have flipped it.

Scott and the four men inside held on for dear life as the coach slid amidst a cloud of dust.

Three masked men jumped aside as the coach slid

by, the six-horse team almost trampling them.

The three ran towards the coach, now forty feet away.

Scott turned the Greener on them and sent the front man straight to hell with a blast of double ought buckshot.

The ranger, Budner, took out the second man as he ran by the coach. Two shots from Budner's forty-five Colt put him down. He would not be getting up. Not in this life.

They heard horses galloping from behind. The four lawmen rolled out of the stage's doors, two on each side.

Scott and the second robber were busy shooting at each other. By instinct rather than training, the robber knew to move and seek cover. He, however, moved and bumped into the third man. Together, they made a target of opportunity Scott could not resist, so he gave them both barrels for the finish.

The lawmen opened up on the riders, who appeared to number about eight.

From the short range, the shotguns wielded by the Wells Fargo detectives shot a pattern hardly more than six inches in diameter. That allowed Smathers and Pope to aim and take their men off horses without hurting the mounts.

Echols, the deputy marshal, proved his mettle by taking out two riders with his Colt.

The ranger did the same.

The remaining two outlaws turned tail and rode from this hellish reception. Shots following them did not strike either.

A surprise shot — a high velocity rifle — rang out from beyond the aspens. Scott, still atop the coach, groaned and fell to the ground hard. The lawmen outside took cover and fired a volley in the woods.

Within seconds, they heard muffled sound of a galloping horse as the sniper rode away out of sight.

Pope checked Scott. He was alive, but not for long without help.

They had a quick conference. The ranger had served in the medical corps after the war between the states. He elected to tend Scott with a bandanna and firm pressure on the shoulder wound from a high powered hunting rifle. Boxer checked his six horses. None had been affected by the shooting

The other three lawmen caught the three best horses contributed by dead outlaws.

Pope emptied the saddlebags on a paint horse and replaced the contents with his investigative and camp gear as well as his extra ammunition.

Smathers and Echols mounted and took off in pursuit of the two fugitives who had run from the fight.

Boxer slapped the ribbons and the coach took off, his shotgun messenger fading fast in the interior. Fort Rice was being established by Tenth Cavalry black "buffalo soldiers," and Boxer knew if not a doctor, they would at least have a medic or two there. He was a thirty minute fast drive away. His instinct to save the endurance of his team had been good. He turned the horses loose and they pulled the coach as fast as a Concord could roll.

******

Pope rode slowly into the woods, looking as much for an ambush as for tracks.

He found neither, as he rode leaning down, the double barrel shotgun reloaded and in his right hand.

At the edge of the woods, he began to see tracks. They were fresh. No dust or leaf matter had blown in yet. The tracks stretched out as the rider picked up speed. He knew how to avoid someone trailing him. He tried to stick to rocky areas where he would leave less tracks.

Since the man was not coming back at him and there were tall, loose rock banks on both sides, it was pretty obvious to Pope which way he was going. Straight ahead.

Pope was a little worried about the man's long range rifle against his short range shotgun.

He raised his eyes to the front instead of the trail and peered as far off as his keen vision would allow.

Following his grandfather's training, Pope blew all the air out of his nostrils and drew fresh air in. He concentrated on his senses. He smelled the aspens, dust from his quarry's trail, and a faint smell of horse. Soon, he picked up a hint of tobacco smoke.

Excellent! The fool would never light a cigarette if he thought somebody was tracking him.

That was not bad logic on this shooter's part. The lawmen he had been watching had dead and wounded to deal with. They did not have their own horses. The rational thing would be to ride to the army camp and seek medical attention, send a wire to El Paso and have the marshal or rangers or both raise a posse.

His failure of reason was in not knowing the determination of Wells Fargo detectives who would get their man, come hell or high water.

Pope knew to be patient and follow at a distance. He did not want the man to know he was behind him. Nor, did he want a rifle ball in the forehead. The man would stop eventually. And, so would Pope. Pope would take him when he was ready to.

He drank some water from his own canteen he had attached to the horn of the gift horse's saddle and chewed a couple pieces of bison jerky.

He wondered if the outlaw had food or water with him, or was confident about making it back to camp every day?

The Rio Grande was a mile to his right. The mountains were much further up and to the left. Pope was betting on the man crossing the river into Old Mexico. While Wells Fargo had offices in Mexico, Pope was not sure what reception his Wells Fargo badge, or any American badge, would get with a group of Rurales.

The Rurales were a Mexican national force of soldier police. Men who were the arresting officers, judges and executioners, all wrapped in one group in the field. Pope respected their tenacity and tracking ability, but little else.

Pope had not seen a hoofprint for a while. He was following displaced rocks, dust stirred up, the faint smell of a horse and occasional horse droppings. He would dismount and check those for heat, which helped tell him how fresh the trail was.

Now, nothing.

Pope stopped and looked left. Would the man climb a several thousand foot steep hill into the mountains beyond?

He rode the paint part way up. No visible displaced rocks. Pope headed back down, rode over his previous trail and towards the river.

As he neared the river, he began to see tracks along his own path.

The fugitive had turned to the river and was going to cross it into Old Mexico.

Once Pope rode out into the river's edge, he would be a sitting duck for a rifleman on the other side. He turned and rode back to the trail.

Following it another mile, he turned right again to the Rio Grande. Pope crossed a mile east of where the rider did. Then, Pope traveled west again along the edge of some scrubby woods. He recognized a landmark on the American side where the stage robber crossed.

Pope moved into the woods and scouted a while. No ambush. He did not even find a sniper's nest. The man likely still did not know he had a close pursuer.

Pope saw a big dust cloud in the distance. Rurales? It was obvious to Pope his quarry did not want to encounter these Mexican rangers either. Pope ducked into some trees and dismounted. He rubbed the muzzle of the paint to help keep him quiet as the company of men carrying rifles and wearing white sombreros passed by no more than a hundred yards distant. They were riding in the direction of the man he was tracking.

While it would simplify things for the detective, his professionalism did not want the Rurales to catch his man and shoot or hang him. Pope hoped the shooter laid low too, and avoided the Mexicans. He also wondered if the outlaw was, himself, a Mexican. His gut said no, but the feeling was not based on any discernable logic.

Pope waited a full half hour according to his Waltham time piece. He had not heard any yelling or shots. Either the outlaw had evaded the Rurales or joined up with them. He hoped the former was the case.

One thing was sure. Pope had to keep alert for Rurales as well as the outlaw. Pope did not have extradition papers on the man. Hell, he did not even know his name, or what he looked like. But, he tracked him directly from the scene of the crime. He reckoned he could get a solid conviction. Pope would capture or kill him, confiscate the heavy caliber rifle used on Scott and bring him in, on the saddle or over it. Pope did not care much which way.

As dusk approached, Pope began to think the man was not returning to an outlaw hideout. The trip to the stage route was too far. He may be running after four failed stage robberies.

The man's trail was fairly easy to read. The detective considered firing up the Dietz police lantern. But, it would signal his presence in this open country for miles. This was alien territory for him, from the standpoint of the law and the lawbreakers.

He decided to call it a night and make camp with his gear he had quickly put on the paint gelding before leaving the stage.

Pope considered a less-than-conspicuous fire in a pit so he could have coffee with his jerky. But, the aroma more than the flicker of flame contributed to his final vote against it. Water and jerky. Just like lunch.

The horse had a riata on the saddle. He cut off enough for a hobble and whipped the ends to keep them from fraying.

It was not cold out yet, so he put down his waxed cotton small tarp, laid down propped against the saddle and draped his coat over him and the shotgun, his blanket over all. Pope tipped the black derby hat forward and went straight to sleep. It was almost daylight before he awakened. He poured some canteen water into his hat and let the horse lap it up. It appeared from the chewed grass, the paint had eaten sufficiently during the night.

Pope rolled his gear, saddled the paint and loaded him for the trail.

The two moved forward carefully. Pope knew the fugitive was close and did not want to ride up on him and his long range rifle.

He almost immediately began to smell coffee. He would have committed murder for a cup, but rode on, scanning side-to-side.

Pope saw a faint gray trail of smoke spirally up into the sky a hundred yards in front of him.

He tied the paint to a low-hanging branch and proceeded on foot. He moved the nippers from his saddlebag to a coat pocket.

Pope stopped behind a tree and watched a tall, spare man packing up his camp.

Pope slipped the .44 out of the holster under his left arm. He quietly walked forward, gun hand outstretched.

"Morning! Just hold tight right where you are. I'd just as soon not have to fool with a smelly, leaking body all the way back to El Paso.

My name's Pope. Detective John Pope, Wells Fargo. I'm taking you in for stage robbery and for shooting shotgun messenger Scott yesterday."

"I ain't shot nobody! I been in Mexico for a week," the man protested.

"I have tracked you here directly from the scene of the stage robbery and shooting to right here at this very spot. I left to track you within minutes. A Wells Fargo detective, a Texas Ranger and a Deputy US Marshal saw me take off after you. The rest of your gang is dead. So, it looks like you are taking the whole deal for four stage robberies, and the shooting. Maybe murder now, I don't know, could be murder by now.

So, saddle up your horse mister."

The man, who Pope found out was called William Frederick Conner, would not admit to being the leader of the gang. Nor, would he tell Pope where he was going. Pope handcuffed him in the front so he could mount, dismount, handle the reins, feed and relieve himself.

The two men mounted and headed towards the Rio Grande, avoiding the Rurales along the way. They made it and swam their horses across to the United States. Upon hitting the stage route, they turned left towards El Paso.

Pope and Conner arrived in El Paso by dinner time. Pope dropped his prisoner at the county sheriff's jail and got a receipt for the .45-70 Ballard rifle and Conner's S&W .44.

He looked up Smathers at the hotel's restaurant and joined him for a non-jerky and water dinner.

"How's Scott?" were the first words Pope uttered to the other detective.

"He'll make it. Big damn hole in his shoulder. Blew a lot of meat away," Smathers said.

".45-70 Ballard rifle. Sheriff is holding it right now."

"So, you got him! Dead?" Smathers asked.

"Naw, he's soaking his heels in the county jail."

"Shoot him any?"

"Didn't have to. He's the ringleader, but won't admit it. We may have to question him vigorously tomorrow."

"Yeah, Pope. We could question him vigorously. He shot a friend of mine from ambush. I'd like to chat with him very vigorously."

"I noticed two Mexicans in the jail. They the ones you and Echols brought back?" Pope asked.

"They are. Young peasants. Got no idea in hell about the way you do this sort of robbery thing. They were just foot soldiers."

"Ray, think once this fellow Conner and your two are charged and we make our statements, are the books closed on this series of robberies?" Pope asked.

"Pretty much. Back to San Francisco for you afterwards?"

"For a while. Until Hume decides what area cannot live without me. The good Lord in Heaven only knows where he will move me."

"I hear Alaska is nice in January and February," Smathers suggested.

Pope shivered.

"Don't worry. He will probably put you in the plains and you will meet some corn-fed beauty and have a brood of blonde-haired little chubby kids."

"You just made Alaska sound pretty good, Ray."

"The good news is we work for a large, widely-respected company. The bad news is they might send us anywhere on a moment's notice. Comes with the turf, detective."

"I guess you're right. Beats following a plow behind some mule with flatulence. Maybe."

They ordered and ate. The next day, they would appear before the local magistrate and swear to the articles of arrest on two Mexican stage robbers and their Anglo boss.

And, the day after, Pope used his return ticket and boarded the westbound train, heading back to San Francisco.

CHAPTER 3

Homer Withrow was one of the troubleshooter managers for Wells Fargo. He had managed offices from San Francisco to Mexico City. He had a Webley Bulldog revolver in his pocket. The .450 Adams bullet was big, slow and deadly at close range. He also had a gold watch in a vest pocket of his navy blue uniform. It had been presented to him by Messrs. Wells and Fargo themselves back in San Francisco.

Presented for a job well done. Many jobs well done, in fact. He was very proud of it, though he never let anyone get close enough to read the inscription they had put on it.

Withrow was a modest man. Not a braggadocio by any stretch. He took his pride in doing a job as well as it could humanely be done.

That job was currently in Independence, Missouri. The Queen of the Trails. The place from which the California, Santa Fe and Oregon Trails westward emanated. Where the Missouri River steamboats had to stop.

Kansas City had taken precedence in power over Independence in later years, but it held such significance to the settlement of the West it would always be significant.

Right now, it was very significant to Wells Fargo & Company.

The long-standing office there had dropped slowly in profitability. If it was because of bad management, Withrow would solve that quick as a flash. If a change in express, stage or movement of people or goods, he would ascertain that, too. If because of employee issues, well…. nobody better to fix than the fixer.

Withrow sat at his desk studying and changing his notes. He considered them official, so he left the pencil on the desk and dipped his pen into black India ink.

He recapitulated the different sources of income for the office and compared how some were stable. More importantly, he contrasted how some had changed.

He flipped open the safe register and began to study it again. Nothing jumped out at him, but it just did not seen exactly right. No water gushing out of this rowboat, but maybe a little leak which could sink it, if unabated over time.

Withrow laid a pile of bills of lading beside the register and started to compare deliveries with entries.

They should jive exactly. And, they did.

He broke the bills of lading down by month and then got up and went to the file room.

Withrow got last year's bills of lading, already broken by month and brought them back to his desk. A comparison should show whether cash delivery business was off.

An hour later of computing and recomputing, he decided the cash business had actually grown. As it was supposed to have.

The cash records in the safe were in two books, the safe register ("other people's money" as he thought of it) and the operating cash register (Wells Fargo cash in and out in daily transaction of business.) The two were balanced daily in the safe cash count. The balances of the two registers should equal the exact amount in the safe. And, as signed off by the counter, Cashier Joseph Pack and Withrow himself, they did.

Withrow sat, perplexed. It was not as if the office had goods or products which could be filched by shoplifters or even him, the cashier or the wire operator.

Within the past month, no recipient of "treasure" as the cash deliveries were often called, reported a shortage. And, mine treasurers, banks, manufacturing company payroll managers surely counted the cash delivery immediately upon receipt.

It was perplexing to one who had spent much of his professional life reconciling such things. Withrow was not one to throw up his hands in surrender, but he was about ready to wire the superintendent and ask for a detective. He carried the records and ledgers back to the cashier's desk and handed them to him.

"Nothing, sir?" Pack asked.

"No, Pack. Not yet. But, I *will* get to the bottom of this. As sure as the day after tomorrow is the Lord's day, I will! Go ahead and close up. You've done your cash count?"

"Yessir. Two hours ago. Nothing has changed while you were going over the books. A quiet day for a Friday," Pack noted.

Withrow walked over to the wire cage.

"You about ready to turn the wire machine off for the night?" he asked the operator.

"Yessir. Nothing but orders for tomorrow. They're already transcripted. Nothing in cipher," the telegraph operator said referring to the coded messages Wells Fargo used to keep treasure shipments, investigations and events confidential.

There was a separate Western Union telegraph office in town. The two organizations used common wires with separate transmissions for confidentiality.

Withrow watched Pack secure the safe and followed the two men out of the rear entrance of the office, locking the door with a special security deadbolt.

The men parted at the street beyond the rear alley. The manager headed to his temporary home at a two-story hotel on Lexington Avenue. This assignment had appeared to be a brief one, so his beloved wife of twenty years had remained behind in San Francisco. The hotel had a small restaurant on the first floor, so he stopped there for dinner. The food was passable for three meals a day and the menu varied enough to keep from getting bored with the same old thing day after day.

******

Later that evening, Cashier Joseph Pack was in bed earlier than his boss. And, wearing considerably less than Withrow's long nightshirt and sleep cap. A woman was comfortably nestled in his arms.

Pack spent many nights with this particular woman, Hattie Jones. It cost him three dollars for an evening. Half the nights in the month exceeded his Wells Fargo salary.

"Joey," Hattie began in a syrupy tone, "when are you going to take me away from here? You know I love you. That wife of yours in Kansas obviously does not. Otherwise, she'd be here taking care of you like I do. Just not anywhere near as good."

"I know, honey. I'm within a day or two of being able to afford for us to slip off in the night. We could go down to Arizona Territory, where it is warm if you like," he said.

"Arizona is pretty wild yet. How about Denver? Chicago? Somewhere with a little life to it?" she asked.

"Well, if neither of us are going to work, it has to be somewhere we won't be found. The Wells Fargo detectives will come looking for us and have to be invisible to them. And, it has to be somewhere we can live cheap. Maybe buy a small farm to supplement the money we take with us."

"I don't want to plow fields with these hands," which she held for him to examine, "or have thirsty brats hanging off these," she said dropping the sheet down exposing her breasts.

"Now," she asked him convincingly, "Do you?"

He stared at her bare body and got another idea, which supplanted whatever answer he may have mumbled otherwise.

Later, he stared at the paint peeling off the ceiling in the brothel room. It was not a cheap place, he thought. At least they could maintain it a little better since they were making three dollars a throw.

He looked over at her. On her back, mouth wide open. Snoring like a billy-goat going to an election.

This woman. This Hattie. She occupied most of this thoughts, day and night. She wanted out of the whoring business. She had managed to neither get pregnant, diseased, or hooked on drugs. It was pretty miraculous for six months of flatbacking. She thought he was her only way out. She was probably right. It made him darn lucky.

He was kind of short and kind of bald. But, he had a great mustache and dressed well.

And, moreover, he would be rich soon. By normal people's standards.

He had run some small dollar tests. The new manager was trying to figure it out. Pack had not accumulated enough to do anything yet. But, the biggest treasure of the past several months is in the safe. He knew once he took it and ran, he would be the only suspect. He had an idea to throw them off for a bit. At least confuse them.

He wasn't a violent man. He did not even own a gun. But, he reckoned he had better get one for the getaway. After all, he would be carrying ten or fifteen years' worth of earnings.

Pack went to sleep and awoke just before dawn. He was at the office ready to work by eight the next morning. They were open a full work day on Saturday.

He slipped out at lunch to a gunsmith's and purchased a small revolver in .32 caliber rimfire. The seller threw in six cartridges and showed him how to load the break-open action.

Pack slipped it in his pocket, feeling several inches taller and inordinately more invincible.

He came back and finished his lunch at his desk, while counting the segregated cash for delivery to several locations on Monday. It was too early to count the company money paid for cash transfers by wire to banks or other payees. Between the time he finished his lunch sandwich and four-thirty, the office had ten paying customers to transfer money or buy a money order, so the till grew by a small amount.

Pack accounted for the money and added it to the money held for delivery. He showed his books to Mr. Withrow, who countersigned with him. By five, they were ready to close for the week.

The three men left by the rear door, as always and bade one another a good Sunday off. They parted company and walked in different directions.

Pack went to the brothel and had Hattie put her clothes in a valise and be ready at the door for his arrival in an hour.

He went back to the office, a large valise in hand. It had some clothes and other personal items and left sufficient room for the express money scheduled to be picked up Monday.

He unlocked the door and went in. Inside, he lit a candle and held it close to the spin dial on the safe as the turned it right, then left, then right, and back again.

The door unlocked and he placed the money in his bag, leaving the company money.

This was not out of kindness or honor. He just did not have room for the mixed small bills and coins in his valise.

He blew the candle out and put it in the bag with the currency and gold coins.

Looking around and seeing nobody passing the front windows, he left. The alley was also empty.

Pack was unknown at the livery stable. The livery-man accepted his false name and cash for rental of a one-horse buggy earlier in the day.

Walking from the Wells Fargo office, he went to the buggy tied around the corner, and got in. Valise in the back, he drove it to the brothel. Hattie was waiting, bag in hand. She scrambled in, giving him a glimpse of ankle and snuggled up beside him, happy to be going to a new life.

They drove to the steamboat dock which was the terminus for the Missouri. Pack bought tickets for Mr. and Mrs. Hosea Calkins, his maternal grandfather's name and they left the horse and buggy tied at the dock and boarded the boat heading out towards St. Louis. They would transfer there to a steamboat heading down the Mississippi to New Orleans.

******

The next day, Chief Detective Hume sent a message down to Pope to come up to his office at his earliest convenience. Which meant "right now."

Pope donned his suit jacket and took his leather notebook as he cleared the steps two at a time.

"Yessir. You wanted to see me?"

"Sit down, Pope. I have a rush assignment for you."

Pope sat across from Hume and opened his notebook and placed pencil to paper.

"I received and deciphered this wire from manager Homer Withrow. The superintendent sent him to our Independence, Missouri office recently to get at the bottom of some irregularities. Withrow is the best non-detective trouble shooter we have. He was stumped.

Last night, his cashier disappeared with the treasure in the safe. Currency and gold coin in the amount of eight thousand dollars. He left a cryptic note. It said 'I had to take the money. I am captured. Help me. Pack.' Joseph Pack is the name of the cashier. No door had been jimmied. The safe was opened by combination, which only Withrow and Pack had, except for our emergency copy here in San Francisco."

"Had there been money missing before to cause the superintendent to send Withrow there?" Pope asked.

"Yes, but small amounts. Apparently from operating cash, not express money being held for delivery. Piddling amounts. Either taken as a test, or just for pocket money. The accounts all reconciled daily."

"How long has Pack been there, sir?"

"You should find all these things out from Withrow. Your emphasis now is getting to Independence as quickly as possible. Do not take time to go home and pack. Here is a cash advance. Buy what you need along the way or once you get there. Time is of the essence. As you may know, Independence is one end of the three major pioneer trails: California, Oregon and Santa Fe. It's on the Missouri which goes to St.

Louis. There, trains go anywhere and riverboats go north and south on the Mississippi River. Pack could be hundreds of miles away in virtually any direction. Track him. Catch him and take him into custody. I will assure proper warrants are sworn when you get him. Now go, young man. And, God be with you!"

Pope arose and nodded. He closed his notebook and walked out the door, cash envelope in hand. He glanced inside as he went down the steps. Two hundred dollars. An unbelievable advance.

Pope grabbed his investigative bag at his desk. He had not worn an overcoat in this morning and he was wearing both .44's, so he walked straight out of the door and to the train station.

He booked transfer tickets to Independence, a day and half away by train. The trail would be impossibly cold by his arrival. He sent a wire from the station to Withrow. In code from his Wells Fargo black cipher book, it said "Detective Pope on way. Arrive Tuesday." The telegrapher put in the requisite "stops," and began to key the message in Morse code. Pope ran for the platform and stepped on the train step at it started to move. The conductor saw a gold badge flash on his vest as Pope grabbed the rail, muscled up with one arm and stepped inside, saying nothing.

Once on board, he showed his ticket and was pointed to his seat for the rest of the day and night.

He settled in and did not even begin to look at the

sparse notes he took in his meeting with James Hume. Pope began penciling questions for manager Withrow. After, he noted places he would go for information on Pack. His residence, restaurants, saloons, any places he might go could help with comments he may have made about places he would like to be.

He would get a good description from Withrow and check liveries, stages, trains….whatever transportation conveyances Independence offered.

Pope walked to the dining car at noon and had coffee, soup and a turkey sandwich.

There was a two-hour layover at Denver the next day before he transferred to a train to Kansas City. He stepped off the train and walked around to stretch his long legs.

Pope saw a gun shop and went in. He did not take time to pick up his carbine at his room or a shotgun at the Wells Fargo armory. He saw a rack of shotguns and pointed out a short-barreled one to the counterman. It was a British Greener ten-gauge with shortened barrels. The action was tight and the barrel release lever properly off-center.

Pope bought it at a good price and negotiated two boxes of double-ought buckshot in the deal as well as a leather carrying case designed to also serve as a saddle scabbard.

He trotted back to the station carrying his shotgun, investigations bag and valise in time to board the Kansas City train.

The next day, Tuesday, he arrived in Independence and walked to the Wells Fargo office. If a town or city only had one office, it could be depended upon to be near the transportation hub for the area.

As he walked in, Homer Withrow looked up and automatically said "You must be Pope. Glad you are here."

"I am Pope, Mr. Withrow. Whenever you are ready, I have a passel of questions to ask so I can get going on my investigation and catch up with Pack."

The manager pointed over to a vacant corner desk.

"Set your stuff down over there. That will be your home while you are here. Then, sit down with me and let's commence," Withrow said.

Pope placed his two bags and one shotgun under the desk and walked over to Withrow's desk and sat down. He opened his notebook and began asking questions about Pack. He asked about his description, residence, habitual haunts, financial situation, place of birth and similar questions to build a profile on the man.

"Mr. Withrow, is he married?" Pope asked.

"He is, but they do not live together. I never pressed him about the nature of the relationship, but I gather it is not convivial."

"Have you been in touch with her since he left?"

"Yes. She lives over in Kansas City. I rode over and talked with her. She has not seen hide nor hair of him for a month. I believe her. She's just mad enough to throw him under the cart's wheels if she could."

"Any female consorts in town?" Pope wondered aloud.

"Would not surprise me. We have some bawdy houses nearby. Several mornings, he came in smelling like lilacs in the springtime and had some makeup stains on his collar. I saved going there for you. My wife would not appreciate me going by, even for work," Withrow said.

"I understand. Please give me the addresses and I will check them out." Withrow did and Pope wrote them in his notebook, determining they would be his first stops.

"Other than horseback or shank's mare, what are the ways out of Independence?"

"Well, Pope, we are at the beginning of the West here. The California, Oregon and Santa Fe trails end or begin here, depending on which way you look at it. We have trains to every direction, if not from here, then from nearby Kansas City. You can take a river boat to St. Louis and connect on the Mississippi. There, you can go all the way to New Orleans and the Gulf of Mexico. I am afraid you have your work cut out for you unless someone tells you definitively where or how he was going," Withrow said.

"How about the letter he left. Might I examine it?"

Withrow took an envelope out of his desk and slid it across to Pope.

Pope examined the letter.

"Is it definitely his handwriting?" he asked.

"Seems to me to be, but I have some samples I watched him sign if you would like to see them, too," Withrow offered. Pope nodded.

One was a recent note to Withrow of about the same number of words as the final letter.

Pope positioned them in front of himself then reversed them so he was examining them upside down. He retrieved his magnifying glass from his investigative bag.

Withrow looked at him reading upside down as if he were crazy.

Pope caught the expression and looked up.

"It's a trick an old detective taught me when I first took the uniform off to become a San Francisco detective. If you try to compare handwriting facing the normal way, your eyes will automatically show you similarities. If you confuse your eyes by comparing upside down, you are much better able to see differences instead of similarities."

Withrow tilted his head in thought, accepted the premise and said nothing.

"My initial read is these were written by the same person. The note was scrawled quickly like someone might ordinarily do. The hostage letter seems to be written for a handwriting competition. It is neat and the letters are perfect. It looks too deliberate writing for a man at gunpoint getting ready to steal eight thousand dollars from his employer."

Withrow nodded.

"Good observation. I can't argue with it at all."

Pope put the letter back in the envelope and slid the papers back across to Withrow.

"Please hold these for evidence at the trial."

"You are thinking you will capture this miscreant and bring him in for trial, then?"

"I am thinking along those lines. I would like to look at the crime scene area before hitting the streets," Pope said.

On the way past his new temporary desk, he made sure to carry his magnifying glass.

Pope glassed the spin dial on the safe, looking for scratches. He found none.

He looked around the area carefully, spending more time scrutinizing one spot in particular. Pope took a fair-sized Barlow type pocket knife out of his vest and scraped something off the floor. He dropped the small flake in the palm of his hand and smelled it. Then, he smiled slightly and turned to Withrow.

"Let's look at the rear door." They went out and Pope studied the lock under magnification. No scratches suggesting the lock had been jimmied or even picked. They went back in to the safe. He picked up the flake scrapped from the floor.

"This is candle wax. Someone, Pack I presume, entered in the nighttime and used a candle for light to open up and raid the safe. The light would be suffi-cient, yet not be very visible to people walking by outside. *If* there even was somebody walking by. I doubt this was done at eight o'clock. More like midnight or two in the morning. So, folks walking by would be less probable anyway. This does not look like a robbery under duress and in haste. It looks to me like a planned, carefully executed operation. Maybe by one man, though I only assume one man did it, and cannot prove it from evidence I've seen today.

I will leave my gear here and go ask some questions. I feel like you think the brothel is the best bet, so unless you tell me I misinterpreted you, I will go there first."

Withrow winked and Pope got the message.

Notebook in hand with directions in it, Pope excused himself and walked out the door.

Ten more minutes of walking found him tapping on the front door of a frame house with flowers growing beside the porch.

A quite lovely young woman answered. Her immediate look said "police," without her uttering a word. Pope read it and showed her his Wells Fargo badge and credentials. Prostitution was not illegal there at the time, but getting rousted by the law was not an unheard of occurrence.

"Miss, I am here to ask a few questions about a potential client we need to find. He is a Wells Fargo employee who may have been kidnapped. His safety may depend on what we learn here." Pope knew it was a stretch, but dealt her the hand and played it.

"Who is the gentleman?" she asked, still not inviting him in.

"His name is Joseph Pack. He is the cashier of the office here in Independence," Pope answered truthfully.

"We are not in the habit of giving out names of our clients, detective. I will have to get Mrs. Belton to speak with you," she said with a purity and sweetness belying where she worked.

Pope stood at the closed door, hoping it would reopen soon without him rapping hard on it. It did.

A well-dressed, although overly made-up plump woman opened it. She had on an obvious wig and her décolleté showed more bosom than most women could proffer naked. Pope could have sworn there was even makeup there.

"I am Harriet Belton, the owner of this establishment, detective. I understand you have some questions Elva did not think she should address?" she said.

"Yes, Ma'am, I do. May I come in? First let me assure you my inquiries are solely about locating Mr. Pack safely and in no way related to your establishment."

"Well, then. Perhaps you should come in and sit down," she said.

They sat in a parlor with worn velvet chairs of the highly uncomfortable variety. The colors and overly sweet smells were not appealing to Pope in the least. Miss Elva might be a different matter altogether.

"This Mr. Pack….is he a medium height man, thinning dark hair. Neither ugly nor highly appealing?"

Pope gave her his best false smile.

"I have not met him, but your description seems to be accurate. He is missing from work and we have a note suggesting he has been kidnapped. Wells Fargo cares for its employees and my job is to recover him safely as soon as possible and detain his captors for prosecution," Pope said with misleading veracity.

"Well!" Mrs. Belton said. Pope decided it was a word she probably used frequently as a whole sentence, so he responded in kind.

"Indeed."

She liked the response, took a deep breath and called for the lovely Miss Elva.

Elva swished in, smiling sweetly.

"I am sure Detective Pope would like some liquid refreshment."

Pope looked at the dark hair and green eyes and gulped.

"Coffee, but only if you have it already brewed. It will be breakfast."

Hattie Belton shot an unsaid message to Elva, who smiled and departed as silently as she arrived. The woman must be part Sioux, Pope thought from her moves rather than looks.

"Well," Mrs. Belton began with again. "We do know Mr. Pack here. In fact, I believe he was here on Friday."

"Does he always visit the same lady?" Pope asked.

"Why, yes he does. Miss Hattie Jones. Always," she responded.

"Might I chat with her? In your presence, of course."

"That's not possible, she left me a note on Saturday about being called away to Kansas City where her mother was taken mighty poorly."

Pope smiled, but did not believe the story about Miss Jones for a minute. It sounded like he might be tracking two people. Which actually made it easier.

There was a loud clatter from what Pope guessed was the kitchen just as Elva appeared with a tray with a coffee service and a plate of small ham sandwiches.

A maid rushed in and whispered something in Miss Belton's ear and they both left together, leaving Pope alone with Elva.

"Miss Elva, thank you for this. It is far more than necessary. But, most appreciated. May I ask, what is your full name?"

"Elva Joiner. From Kentucky," she answered.

"How did you come to be here?" he asked.

"My parents died when I was fifteen."

"I'm sorry for your loss. How long ago was this?" he asked.

"Four years ago. I guess you are curious how a farm girl raised on Jesus ended up in a brothel?"

Pope was, but looked at her with a sad smile and said nothing.

"Harriett — Mrs. Belton — is my aunt. She took me in when I had nowhere else to go. I could have ended up doing in Kentucky what our girls do here. But, I chose this as a lesser evil."

"A good choice, given your immediate options, Miss Elva," Pope said as he bit into a very good little sandwich and wondered where the crust of the bread was. He sipped some coffee. It was good, too.

"Do you know if this Hattie really had a mother in Kansas City?" he asked.

"Hattie is a gold digger to my way of thinking, detective. I believe she would say anything to advance herself. She once said she was an orphan and had fallen into the trade in St. Louis near the docks. I never knew what to believe with her."

"What did she look like?" Pope asked.

"She was in her late twenties. I thought she looked older, but she had lived hard and looked it. Nice figure, not opposed to showing it to anyone she thought might be interested and return some sort of benefit to her. Mid-height, black hair, brown eyes."

"Thank you. I may have some more questions later. Might we discuss them over lunch or dinner?" he asked, knowing he was rushing things.

"We will see. That might be nice though I think I might have to do some talking to get Harriett to approve it."

"I am from San Francisco and will be going back after this case. I am afraid I have to grab enjoyable time when I can."

"I understand you are a good catch but with bad geography," she said, somewhat sadly.

They heard the "clop, clop" of a heavy person with hard heels coming down the hall.

As she came in, Pope said "Thank you for the coffee and sandwiches, Miss Elva. I am eternally in your debt."

She picked up the silver platter and walked to the door. From behind her aunt's back, she gave him a smile he felt he would cherish forever.

"Well! I am sorry for the interruption. A kitchen issue. Do you have any more questions, detective?"

"No, Ma'am. Not for now. Thank you and Miss Elva for the coffee and sandwiches. They were excellent and really appreciated. I have to find Mr. Pack as soon as possible for his safety. I may be on a riverboat or train or stage coach before lunch, depending on where my investigation leads me. So, your little meal may be my only one for a while."

He stood and she held out her hand, which he shook firmly. She walked him to the door and said "Do come back. I am sure we have ladies who would meet your taste, detective."

"Oh, thank you. But, I have never been with a lady of the evening. I have nothing against your business, but it's just not how my grandfather brought me up. One day, I'd like to marry. I would not want to have any experiences she would hold against me."

He expected a "Well!" but just got an almost quizzical look as he walked away.

Popes next visit was the rooming house where Pack lived. Since Pack had apparently moved out without any notice, the owner showed Pope his room. Nothing to be found there, nor did the owner have any knowledge of where Pack may have gone.

The train station was also a dead end. He hit a good clue at one of the livery stables. A man matching Pack's description had rented a horse and buggy on Saturday and abandoned it at the steamship landing. The manager there found the name of his livery on the inside front panel and sent a young boy to him with the information.

The liveryman described Pack closely. He could not remember the name. He said the last name started with a "C," but he could not remember more. Pope swung by the office, apprised Withrow of his findings, grabbed his bags and headed for the docks.

At the docks, he spoke with a ticket clerk who remembered a couple matching the description. He thought the woman was someone he had seen before.

Pope looked him in the eye and realized he just did not want to say where, though both knew exactly where he had seen Hattie Jones.

He pulled his ticket sales register. A Mr. and Mrs. Hosea Calkins was the name given. It was a connecting ticket from Independence to St. Louis, then south to New Orleans. They took a night boat from Independence on Saturday.

Pope knew steamboats were a good way to travel the Western Rivers, but not a fast way. They were not fast to begin with and made a lot of stops where people and freight were offloaded. He walked back over to the train depot and found a train connection which would get him to New Orleans a day sooner. He booked a ticket and checked his gear long enough to walk back and tell Withrow. He asked Withrow to send a cipher wire on his behalf to Hume to help Withrow arrange for a Missouri arrest warrant for Pack AKA Calkins in New Orleans. He knew Louisiana operated under Napoleonic law not the English Common Law of the other thirty-seven states. But, that was Hume's issue. There was a major regional Wells Fargo office in New Orleans, so there was likely a good connection with local attorneys.

Pope would send Hume a wire to get the status of the warrant from a stop along the way. He could always depend on train stations to have inside or nearby telegraph access.

He knew the warrant would not charge Pack with a crime, but would be something like "detain for extradition for suspicion of embezzlement." He was sure there was at least one, probably two, Wells Fargo detectives permanently assigned to the office in New Orleans. They would join him at the steamboat landing and make the arrest under the Taylor v. Taintor Supreme Court decision of 1872 for bounty hunters. It was a real stretch, but might work long enough to get him locked up. Even if they just said "You are under arrest!" and took him and the warrant to a police station, Pack could be held for extradition back to Missouri. The other detectives or some New Orleans officers might be helpful with the woman. Pope knew, as a former policeman, women could cause a scene and be hard to handle.

Publicly slapping one on the head with a black jack like he would with a man would not be a good for the image for Wells Fargo and would flat out just be wrong.

Pope settled back in his seat for a fairly fast and comfortable ride. He grew up riding horses, but knew for sure this would be a lot more comfortable than riding for eight hundred and fifty miles.

******

Pope arrived in New Orleans and got a room. He checked in at the docks and found he had, as told in Independence, arrived a full day ahead of the scheduled arrival of the Delta Damsel, carrying Mr. and Mrs. Hosea Calkins.

He went to the Wells Fargo office and telegraphed Withrow to find the status of a warrant or an extradition agreement. None had been signed during his inquiries during the train trip down.

The good news was he found an extradition order signed by the Attorney General of Louisiana waiting. The bad news was the single detective assigned to the office was investigating a stage robbery in Shreveport, almost three hundred miles away. He inquired about the cooperation with the New Orleans police with the office manager who rolled his eyes. He said there was no cooperation and his best bet would be to arrest the fugitive, legally or not and transport him back to Missouri on the strength of the extradition order alone.

Pope decided on a plan for the woman to keep her from starting a row when he approached them.

He ordered a bath at his hotel and got cleaned up. A shave and a haircut cost him two bits down the street.

Pope had never been this far south or east before and walked into the *Vieux Carré* for dinner. Despite the good restaurants, he could feel the danger emanating from the place. He was glad for the two .44's, one holstered under each arm.

Pope spoke pretty passable Spanish, but no French at all. He got help with the menu and settled on shrimp etoufee. It was unlike any stew he had ever had, but he became an immediate fan. The rich coffee with chicory and bread pudding with bourbon sauce was more sugar than he had ever had at one meal.

He was glad for the long walk back to the hotel and for the good bed in his room. The city did not appear to sleep and he heard frequent yelling and the occasional shot.

Pope slipped two shells into the breeches of the Greener shotgun and laid it on the floor beside the bed. That done, he fell asleep and slept until daylight. He had beignets and coffee *au lait* at the small diner downstairs at the hotel and prepared to greet the ten o'clock arrival of the Delta Damsel at Dock 11.

******

The tall detective in the charcoal gray suit and black derby stood at Dock 11 as the paddle wheeler pulled in. He watched as people got off, particularly couples. There were young ones, middle-aged, and older couples. What did not exit was a couple who met the description of the Calkins.

Pope went up the gangplank and showed his badge and credentials to the purser. He called the chief steward over and the three spoke.

The room steward found the Calkin's room abandoned the previous night after a stop at Natchez, Mississippi across the river from Vidalia, Louisiana.

The purser recommended a train west to Baton Rouge, get a horse and "ride like hell" to the Natchez Trace and take it into Natchez. He also said "carry two guns on the Trace, and be ready to use them."

Pope considered the last to be good advice, but it did not deter him in the least. He checked out of his room, stopped by the Wells Fargo office to advise them and have them send wires to Hume and Withrow and bought a train ticket.

Mid-afternoon found him on a horse galloping towards Natchez. He reckoned if Pack and his woman were coming to New Orleans, he would meet them on the way. If not, the trail led to Natchez anyway.

Pope stopped at a roadhouse on the southern end of the Trace. It fit the warning the purser had shared with him. The clientele was questionable. He found one room available without having to share with a stranger.

Pope took it at double the cost and slept with the uncocked ten-gauge on the bed with him. At least the breakfast was tasty the next morning.

His livery horse proved to be a good one and the rest and feed fueled him for a sustained canter at about twelve to fifteen miles per hour.

Pope did not encounter Pack along the Trace. When he arrived in Natchez, he stopped at the Wells Fargo office. It was a small one. He had them wire both Hume and Withrow of his location.

He then went to the police department and identified himself and his mission. They did not seem to know anything of value to him and did not express any interest in learning.

He checked hotels on the bluff above the river and seedier ones in Natchez-Under-the Hill, where the docks were.

Pope got the feeling at the third hotel the clerk knew more than he was saying. So, Pope resorted to a proven investigative technique. Money. A five dollar gold piece caused the man's Adam's apple to pop up above his dirty celluloid collar.

"They's some folk matching the description up to room 203. They should be down soon to go eat something. You set over there on the sofa and wait and you'll catch them."

Pope nodded and did just that.

After a while, he heard people talking as they walked down the stairs behind the hotel's desk.

The voices were a male and a female. The clerk, Pope's new best friend, looked towards the stairs and nodded. Pope stood up, his left lapel pushed away, showing the distinctive gold badge on his vest.

Pope did not have any doubt the man was Pack. He stepped forward as the now former Wells Fargo man recognized a Wells Fargo detective badge on a very big fit man approaching him.

He grabbed Hattie Jones and pulled her in front of him, as he pulled a small dollar fifty revolver with the other hand.

Popes hand was a blur as he drew the .44 Merwin & Hulbert revolvers in a cross-draw. Hattie screamed.

Pack pushed her hard towards Pope, blocking the detective's line of fire. She stumbled into Pope, grabbing him instinctively.

Pack did the unimaginable for a first-time white collar criminal.

He ducked his head and dove through the glass window in a shower of broken glass.

Pope shoved the prostitute aside and ran the few feet to the window.

Pack was getting up and turned to face him.

There was a "Pop" as Pack fired.

And, a "Bang" as Pope returned fire with Hattie now hanging onto his leg, trying to pull him down.

The sound of the two hundred grain lead bullet screamed off in ricochet. Pack rolled out of Popes view before the detective could get off a second shot with the screaming woman clawing at his pants leg.

He finally shook her loose and ran out of the front door of the hotel and turned the corner, skidding on broken glass. He kept his balance and sprinted in the only direction Pack could have run.

He squatted and peered around the corner of the hotel and ducked back, just avoiding a .32 rimfire bullet a foot over his head.

Pope, staying low, leaned head, shoulder and .44 aimed around the corner and saw Pack running. The detective sent a round after him, which sped the fugitive's run, but did not hit him.

He heard a horse whinny and then heard hoof beats as Pack stole a horse and rode away.

As a former policeman, Popes immediate impulse was to pursue the fleeing felon.

But, he was Wells Fargo first and foremost.

He returned to the hotel. The nervous clerk, perhaps no longer Popes best friend was standing. Hattie Jones was nowhere in sight.

Pope, more interested in recovering the money than the embezzler, bounded up the stairs, still leading his steps with one of the .44's.

Hattie Jones was shoving money and coins into her valise from a larger one, apparently Pack's.

He covered her.

"You know detective, we could go a long way on this money. You and me. I could make you so happy." She put a foot up on the bed and peeled her skirt back, exposing a length of leg.

"Right now, you are an accomplice to the theft of eight thousand dollars of money under the care of Wells Fargo and Company. You and the money will come back with me to the Wells Fargo office in New Orleans by the next stern wheeler southbound. In the meantime, I will count this money with the clerk downstairs as my signed witness. What happens to you in New Orleans is not my decision or interest. But, you *will* go back with me, handcuffed if necessary," Pope said in a way not giving her any interest in disputing.

"Aren't you going after Joseph?" she asked.

"Oh, I'll get him. But, my first obligation is to return our client's money. So, you gather your clothes while I put the money back in the big case. Then, we will go down stairs, count it and leave for the boat dock. You and I are going back to somewhere to get a train to Independence. I am not quite sure where the 'somewhere' is yet," Pope said.

"Am I under arrest?" she asked.

"No. I am taking you back as a material witness. You probably have information on Joseph Pack which will help me find him and will help the embezzlement case."

"You want me to testify against him?" she asked.

"I want you to give information material to the case. The testifying part is up to the prosecutor. So is the arrest part later. But, and this is a big 'but', helping us will help you. I can't promise, but help enough and maybe you walk free."

"Where will I go? I was a whore when I left and I will be an out of work whore when I return."

"I don't know, Hattie. Do you have family?"

"They are trash. I'd be better as a whore in a nice brothel."

"Isn't there some other line of work in a new town where nobody knows you?" Pope asked.

"Yes. That's what this was going to be."

"Maybe right idea, wrong man."

"I guess," she admitted showing a very human side,

which cracked the tough façade.

"Why don't you think of two sets of things: what you know which will help the case; and what legitimate thing you can do for your livelihood?"

"I'll try," she said and he believed her.

Pope knew men with a badge got callous after years of dealing with lies and violence. He did not think he had gotten there yet. He actually did not think he ever would. But, time would tell. God willing and a bullet does not get in the way, he was still early in his evolution as a detective.

They ended up buying a one-horse buggy, hitching the livery horse to it, saddle in the back, and driving up the Natchez Trace to Vicksburg.

They drove all the way with the shotgun between them on the seat due to highwaymen.

Once, they saw two men ahead in the road. Hattie took the reins and Pope manned the Greener. The men took one look at those two massive barrels and disappeared into the woods.

At Vicksburg, they left the rig at the Wells Fargo office to dispose of the buggy and work out the return or purchase of the horse.

Pope bought westbound tickets leading ultimately to Independence. He decided to carry the seven thousand eight hundred dollars remaining from the eight thousand himself.

Hume would be pleased to receive the treasure less

only two hundred. It would save going into operating capital to make good to the owner on a full eight thousand dollars. And, that was Wells Fargo's policy.

Pope got Hattie talking about the other girls at the brothel and eased into the subject of Elva.

Hattie did not like the fact Elva made a small salary and did not have to work the same way as the rest did. She confirmed Elva had never been a working girl and was like an assistant to Miss Harriett.

Pope kept his face and his questions about Elva as random and non-committal as about the others. If Hattie picked up on his interest, she did not pursue it.

By the end of the week, they were back in Independence. The reports were done and the money turned in. The prosecutor decided not to charge Hattie Jones as an accessory. Her only proviso was to stay in the Independence or Kansas City area until any subsequent trial for Pack was over.

Pope had to delay his lunch or dinner with Elva until he brought Pack in. He was confident of capturing him based on information from Hattie about where his family lived. He knew from experience fugitives with no money and no place to go generally gravitated towards home. So, that is where he was going to go.

Longview, Texas.

******

Again, Pope left by train, subsequently connecting with Southern Pacific into Longview. He stopped by the small Wells Fargo office then hired a worthy-looking horse and put his gear on it. He had his carbine scabbard rolled up in his bedroll and attached it to the saddle and put the Greener shotgun in it.

He dropped by the sheriff's office and introduced himself.

"I'm looking for a fugitive name of Joseph Pack. His family is from here. Any idea where I might find their place?" Pope asked the sheriff.

"Got a warrant?"

"I do," Pope said, presenting it and an extradition order for Texas.

"Everything looks to be in good order here. You head out Main to the left and go about five miles. It's a small ranch called the Poplar Grove. They are hard scrabble like a lot of folks around here, but not bad folks. Might get a little touchy for a fellow in a derby hat arresting their boy. You want a deputy to go with you?" the sheriff asked.

"That would be good if you can spare a man. I usually arrest fugitives alone, but a local officer sometimes keeps things from getting too frisky, if you know what I mean."

Pope watched as the sheriff stared at him, trying to size up the man in the Eastern dude clothes.

"Where you from, Pope?"

"I grew up on a small cattle ranch in Northern California. My grandpa was the only family I had. He was a mountain man. Still a tough piece of business!" Pope said.

"So, how'd a cowboy raised by a mountain man come to dress like you do?"

"Haha. Sheriff, it's a question I get a lot. Wells Fargo has some rules about how we are supposed to represent them. I have been thinking about a wider brim hat for travel though."

"Might keep the sun off your neck. The rain, too," the sheriff said.

"I will give it some further consideration. Maybe today. Any places around town sell Stetsons?"

"Brown's Men's Clothing down the street does. I got a man coming in with a prisoner in about an hour. Mebbe he could ride out to Poplar Grove with you."

"That would be appreciated, sheriff. How about I buy you some lunch first? On Wells Fargo."

"You got yourself a deal, detective. There's a good café four doors down."

"I'll check on Brown's after lunch. Before the deputy gets in."

Pope knew from his time wearing a San Francisco badge and from discussions with Hume, Wells Fargo knew and used every opportunity to maintain a good relationship with local officers. He had not seen any chance to work with the ones in New Orleans, but was not dissuaded by an occasional rut in the trail.

Their lunch was good. Pope learned the sheriff had been a Texas Ranger for five years before running for sheriff of Gregg County. He filed backgrounds away on folks he admired, still pondering what he wanted to do in his career. An obvious goal might be to replace Hume one day. But, he would be locked into an office in San Francisco if he did. Maybe being the sheriff of San Mateo County, California, since he will be inheriting a ranch there one day.

After lunch, they parted and Pope walked down to the men's store. He chose a black Boss of the Plains Stetson, more in keeping with a rider or a Western lawman. The owner recommended the proper way to shape it and Pope walked out wearing it and carrying his derby in a box.

He was surprised what a significant move this hat represented for him. But, as he passed a plate glass window in the general merchandise, he saw his reflection and thought it looked pretty darn good. A lot more serious and less like a dude.

He met Deputy Zeke Halley at the sheriff's office. They mounted and headed out of town towards the Pack ranch.

"Man, the next thing I'll be packing both revolvers on a gun belt," he thought to himself. But, he reasoned, he would be able to bring them into action much faster with his holsters on a wide belt.

The two rode through a log arch with the name of the ranch hand painted on a board nailed to the top.

"I already exchanged gunfire with Pack a week ago," he told the Deputy Halley. "He jumped through a glass window and when I went up to it, he took a potshot at me. I ducked and fired back. We both missed. But, the point is, he does not hesitate to shoot at a man with a badge if his freedom is on the line."

"I vaguely remember him. Kind of a squirrely fellow. One who'd lie to you while looking in your eye, but I don't remember him being violent," Halley said. "I am not sure how the boys went wrong. The folks are not too bad, hardworking, Bible thumping people. The older brother is the meaner one. Bigger, too."

"What does he look like?" Pope asked.

"Just like his brother Joe, but fifty pounds heavier."

"Great….somebody better shot than scuffled with?" Pope asked.

"Yes. Shot a couple of times, if it comes to it."

Pope rode on, wishing he had already bought and was wearing a two-gun rig instead of those shoulder holsters.

Halley rode around the side of the house while Pope went to the front door and knocked.

An old couple came to the door.

"Mr. and Mrs. Pack? I am Detective John Pope from Wells Fargo. I have an arrest warrant for your son Joseph for stealing eight thousand dollars from Wells Fargo. Is he here?"

Before they could answer, Pope heard shots and yelling from the rear of the house.

"Stay here, please." Pope went around the left side of the house, Merwin & Hulbert in his hand.

He saw Pack and a bigger version of him mount horses and ride off. Halley was on the ground, holding his revolver stretched out.

Pope saw the flash and smoke a millisecond before he heard the blast from Halley's .45 Colt. Joseph Pack flinched as he was hit, but kept his seat in the saddle and rode on, his speed unabated.

The brother turned in the saddle and aimed at Halley. Pope shot his arm straight out and fired the .44. The shot even amazed Pope as the older brother fell from the horse some seventy five yards away. The larger Pack hit the Texas soil hard and flopped. Pope thought for sure he was dead.

He holstered and ran to Halley.

"Damn, Pope! That was a shot!"

"Don't worry about it, I need to check you and see about stopping your bleeding."

He knelt and checked the wound. It was between the deputy's right lung and his collar bone. It would hurt and keep him from splitting firewood, but, sans infection, would not kill him.

He gave Halley a clean handkerchief.

"Here, Zeke. Press this real tight against the wound. It should stop the bleeding."

Out of the corner of his eye, Pope saw the old couple coming around the house towards him and the deputy. The old man had a long barrel shotgun.

Pope redrew and pointed the .44 at the man.

"Mr. Pack. Set the shotgun down. I need some help giving first aid to the deputy and your son. Don't make this worse, sir."

The man complied and the two proceeded.

Mrs. Pack assisted Halley while her husband went with Pope to check on his older son. Pope was fearful they would find him dead.

Pack had a wound in the side of his left thigh. He was still dizzy from the hard fall.

Pope grabbed the shoulder seam of Pack's shirt and ripped it downwards and the sleeve came off in his hand. He tied it tightly around Pack's leg above the wound.

"Mr. Pack? Do you have a wagon we could use to take the two men into town to the doctor? That's good. Why don't you ride your son's horse here back to the barn and harness up the wagon?"

The old man mounted stiffly but with the grace of one who had performed a mount many thousands of times.

He rode back, briefly reporting on their son's status to his wife.

Pope looked up at the tiny image of his fugitive disappearing in the distance. He got away. Again. The third time would not be a charm, however. Pope would bring Pack to justice on his saddle or over it. And, at this point, he did not care much which one it was.

The wagon appeared, pulled by a mule. Pope went over and helped Zeke Halley into the bed. They brought the wagon over to where the older Pack son was and put him in.

The Pack parents drove the wagon towards town and a doctor. Pope rode along behind, ready to take care of business should the wounded brother attempt to harm the wounded deputy. Luckily for the brother, either pain or common sense prevailed and he made it to the doctors with only one bullet hole in his body.

While the doctor was working on Halley, Pope went to the sheriff's office and notified him. He immediately called out a posse and went after Pack, now wanted for shooting a Texas law enforcement officer. Pope knew whether he or the posse caught Pack, he would stay in Texas for a long time before being extradited back to Missouri. It really did not make much difference to Pope. While he would prefer to snap the nippers on Pack's wrists, either way, the case would be solved and he could go on to another.

Pope went to the doctor's office and tried to question Pack's brother, who he found was named Thomas. The brother was angry about being shot and refused to talk. Pope advised him lack of cooperation would guarantee being charged as an accessory. That line of reasoning did not do any good, so he left him suggesting to the doctor he was dangerous and whatever pain relief had a sedative might be wise. The doctor nodded and the subject was closed.

Pope reckoned the posse would ride until dark, then come home for dinner. He saw them leave and nobody had overnight gear. They were better armed than posse's he had seen, but it was Texas, after all.

When the posse was heading home, Pope would be heading out. Doing what he did best. What nobody else did. Night trailing.

He had dinner and stocked his saddlebags with coffee, flour, salt, jerky, some bacon, and cornpones from the café where he ate dinner.

Pope put fresh water in his canteen, picked up some matches to go with his flint and steel kit and was ready to ride.

He left in time to get to the Pack ranch by dusk. Began looking for tracks where he had seen Joseph Pack riding.

Pope immediately picked up the trail and began riding across country. This was good. It would be unlikely to have other tracks contaminate his trail, like on a road.

He had not seen either a rifle or saddlebags on the horse Pack was using to escape. So, he would either have a hungry, thirsty and miserable camp, or seek somewhere he could eat and sleep. A friend. A hotel. A sanctuary of some sort. There did not seem to be such a place in the area where Pack's tracks still suggested he was still galloping from their distance apart. At some point, it looked like he was going to run his horse into the ground. Only a fool or a panicked man would do such a thing.

Pope saw the posse riding in his general direction, but a mile over. He almost missed them in the dusk due to the hilly terrain.

He did not think the posse had a very good tracker, if any at all. For them to be returning that far off the trail outbound suggested they were not actually tracking along Pack's real trail as he was. He was happy about this, because it meant they had not obliterated the hoofprints.

Pack grew up in this area. If there was a ranch here in the middle of nowhere, he would know it. He was either heading there or just killing his horse.

After an hour Pope was walking his horse and using the Dietz police lantern to see Pack's horse tracks. It was apparent to Pope the horse was slowing down, either by direction from its rider or sheer exhaustion and thirst. Pope had not seen any streams while trailing Pack and felt for the poor animal. Abusing his horse seemed a good enough reason to shoot Pack.

Pope thought, by now, Pack must think nobody was on his trail. It had to be near midnight. He was not going to risk holding the light up high enough to read his pocket watch and give Pack a target. Even for the cow dung revolver he was carrying when he and Pope had their little shooting match nobody won.

Pope caught a slight smell of horse ahead. He dismounted and tied the reins of his livery horse to a cottonwood branch.

He poured some canteen water into his new Stetson and let the horse drink out of the crown of the hat.

Pope slid the Greener shotgun from its scabbard and eased forward, literally following his nose.

The grass under his boots helped with stealth, but Pope was still careful to avoid branches above and the occasional stick below. A stick cracking this soundless night would sound like a rifle shot.

He heard a horse whinny, then saw the flicker of a small fire ahead. It was neither cold nor did Pack have anything to cook. The fire was a waste of time, in Pope's estimation.

He saw Pack huddled by the fire.

Pope aimed the shotgun and slowly cocked the right hammer.

The "click" sounded ominously in the night. There was no doubt what made the sound.

Pack froze.

"Pack. Detective Pope. I have a ten-gauge leveled on you. It will cut you in half at this range. Throw up your hands and prepare to be arrested."

Pack did so. He was flat out tired of running and looking over his shoulder.

Pope took the handcuffs from his jacket pocket. He cuffed Pack's hands together around a tree. Dipping his hand in the pocket of Pack's canvas coat, he removed the cheap revolver and emptied the cylinder.

He threw the cartridges into the woods and dropped the gun in his pocket.

"Pack, I'm arresting you for robbery of the Wells Fargo office in Independence, Missouri. The Texas authorities are going to arrest you for shooting a deputy sheriff. That arrest will occur when I deliver you back in Longview. You wait here and I will get my horse. Then, your horse will get some water, you will too and we will make supper. Act up and you get my .44 upside your head. Got it?" Pack nodded.

A few minutes later and Pope was watering Pack's horse with most of the remaining water in his canteen. The poor beast was dehydrated.

He gave Pack a swig, then put the rest in the coffee pot and brewed coffee to have with bacon he put on a grill to fry and cornpones.

He re-cuffed Pack in front and the two ate.

"How's Hattie?" Pack asked.

"She was alright last I saw her back in Independence. There were no charges levied against her, so she was pretty relieved."

"Did she ask about me?" he asked Pope.

"I remember she was more worried about herself when I saw her last." Pack said nothing and chewed a strip of bacon with great relish.

"I am a little surprised when you got the jump on me a little while ago you didn't blast me with your alley cleaner. What with me shooting at you and all," Pack observed.

"Don't worry, Pack. I would not hesitate to kill you if you force me. But, I am not a murderer. And, I do not get mad with people trying to kill me. Anger makes it hard to digest your food. Instead, I just take care of business and move on," Pope said.

Pack thought about it for a moment.

"You are either a fair, nice fellow, or the coldest bastard I ever saw. I just can't figure out which," he said.

Pope smiled.

"Just don't ever try me again. You do not really want to know the answer to your comment. I promise you this. By the time you find out, it will be 'way too late!'"

After the fire was extinguished and the camp gear repacked, Pope re-saddled both horses and bade Pack mount up. Pack was able to ride fine handcuffed in the front. Pope rode behind him. Ready to drop him if he spurred his horse.

It was night again by the time they rode into Longview.

The deputy on duty at the sheriff's office had the honor of charging Pack with attempted murder of a Texas officer. Pope got a receipt for the prisoner and left the extradition order with the deputy.

He knew Texas had first shot at Pack and would either hang him or put him away in Huntsville Prison for years. The chance of him making it back to Missouri was between slim and none. However, Pope had done his job for Wells Fargo. He solved the crime, recovered the vast majority of the treasure and arrested the culprit. Hume ought to be pretty happy.

Pope turned in his livery horse and carried his gear to the nearest hotel. He got a room and went straight to sleep.

He planned to make an interim stop at Independence to report to Withrow and visit Miss Elva before heading back to San Francisco.

Withrow was glad to see him and wanted to hear all about the case and its solution. The way both men moved around the country for Wells Fargo, it was pretty much destined they would meet again.

Miss Elva was less warm and encouraging when he visited her. Had her aunt put her rather large foot down? Or, was she just a flippant young woman? Pope did not have enough experience with women to know. Despite her not being what he considered his kind of woman, he'd had more open and comfortable conversations with soiled dove Hattie Jones.

Conniving, immoral or not, at least she was who she was and made no pretentions.

He wished them both the best silently, donned the black derby with his new navy suit and boarded the train.

CHAPTER 4

Even in 1882, there was some argument about the first train robbery. Some considered it Cincinnati in 1865. But, others claimed the Cincinnati robbery was a post-surrender military action by Confederate guerillas. Pope studied the robbery and determined it was just a robbery. Had it been a military action, the objective would be to severely damage the train and tracks. His investigation, well after the fact, was the greatest damage was loss of money by passengers. The Pinkerton's solved the next robbery. It was when the Reno gang robbed an Ohio & Mississippi train outside of Seymour, Indiana.

He found the James-Younger gang did not get into the business until they derailed a Rock Island train in 1873.

A spate of train robberies affecting other express companies prompted Hume to have Pope study and document the *modus operandi* of various train robberies around the country.

"Always try to stay ahead of history, detective!" Hume told Pope.

Pope prepared a thirty page report. It showed most train robberies to date had been crude and caused derailments, unnecessary injury and death and as much disruption of transportation and commerce as robbery loss.

Hume used it in his annual meeting of all detectives and had Pope deliver a brief talk with the high points. Hume's instincts proved providential a week after the meeting when the California Southern affiliate of the Atchison, Topeka, and Santa Fe was robbed between the stage station at Fallbrook and San Diego, California.

Pope, now academically the resident expert on train robberies, was immediately dispatched.

Since the area of from Fallbrook to National City, just below San Diego was the only north-south portion of the tracks completed for the California Southern, Pope took a Southern Pacific train to Los Angeles and a stage to the stage station that was the northern terminus of the completed tracks.

He learned the train was not yet a regular route, but train running intermittently from San Diego to wherever the tracks stopped to deliver building supplies, workers, surveyors and payrolls. The latter, he knew before arriving, had been the target.

It did not take a Wells Fargo insider to know paydays. Any worker or nearby trading post would know when workers were flush with cash. The people laying the tracks were largely immigrants. They were primarily Irish, Chinese, Mexican and a few Eastern Europeans.

Pope doubted if any of them were involved.

He wanted to interview storekeepers along the route and see if anyone seemed particularly interested in when the workers came in with money, where it was paid and how. Was it in currency? Coin?

Now wearing the Stetson, boots and a two-gun belt with his dark suits, he rode the same train several days after the robbery as it backed its way to San Diego station.

It gave him a good opportunity to question the engineer, conductor and express messenger from Wells Fargo.

"Where exactly did the robbery occur?" Pope asked the conductor, who was guiding the train from the rear as it backed at half speed.

"It was just south of here, detective."

"Is the train on a tight schedule? Or, can we stop long enough for me to look for clues?"

"Let me send a steward forward and ask the engineer."

A few minutes later, the steward returned at a run and said for the conductor to signal a stop when he spotted the robbery location. The train could wait ten minutes while Pope investigated the scene.

Pope nodded his approval and took his hatchet out of the saddlebags he carried with his gear.

He had already written the number and possible descriptions of the robbers, their weapons and the fact no horses were seen.

When the train approached the robbery site, the conductor leaned out and swung a red lens lantern back and forth. The train slowed and came to a halt. Once the conductor gave him the word, Pope stepped off.

The first thing he did was chop slash marks on the trees on both sides of the tracks to mark the place for when he returned. Then, he looked at boot prints. All were similar. Not worth noting. No abnormally large or small ones, nor any with distinctive heels or soles.

He saw the small tree trunks the robbers had dragged to the tracks and stacked to make a block-ade. They had been chopped, not sawn. He wrote this in his notebook. Most Western men knew how to split wood and chop in general. But, Pope studied the cuts. It seemed to him a professional lumberjack cut these trees. The cuts were accurate and perfect V's. No accidental hacks above the cut line. Efficient. He noted the details he observed. It might help in subsequent questioning.

Running out of time, he quickly searched in the trees to see where the horses had been hidden. He found six sets of prints, which tallied with the number of robbers reported

Two of the horseshoes had distinctive marks and he drew pictures of them in his notebook after examining them minutely with his magnifying glass.

It took him a while to get here and to draw pictures of the disparate horseshoe prints. They were in a protected area under trees.

Pope realized by the time he hired a livery horse in San Diego and returned, the tracks would be sufficiently age-obliterated as to be of little or no value. However, the description of the shoes on scene at the robbery would be good circumstantial evidence once arrests were made. The effort to document them would not be a waste of time by any means.

He never believed the first number reported in a gang robbery, since there was frequently a leader or a sniper who held back. However, six men in the gang did appear to be the case with this robbery.

Pope saw the conductor wave for him and rushed back to the train and climbed aboard.

"Any luck?" the conductor asked as the train began to steam off towards San Diego.

Pope showed him his notes.

"You can solve a case from so little?" the man asked.

"Often less. Then again, sometimes they just go unsolved. Sometimes it is good police work and sometimes, it is pure luck. Luck's that for you or against you!"

He got off the train at San Diego and stopped by the Wells Fargo office. The manager, George Dunstan, filled him in on all he knew about the robbery. Pope reciprocated.

Dunstan told him the railroad payroll amounted to two thousand dollars every two weeks, so two thousand was the loss on the robbery. The money was in small bills the entry level workers could use for food, drink and supplied. The Wells Fargo express messenger, who was the train equivalent of a stage shotgun messenger, was out but could be interviewed the next day. Pope put the day and the man's name in his diary.

He asked Dunstan for a hotel and livery recommendation and went to the former first. On the way, he stopped at the San Diego County sheriff's office. The chief deputy discussed known miscreants, but could not remember a logger or lumberjack criminal.

Pope went on to the hotel, which was in the area around Fifth and Island Streets. He reserved a horse for the next morning and sought dinner.

The area had more saloons than pure restaurants, so he sought a saloon with a good menu propped in its window.

Pope had switched back to his shoulder holsters for town, but retained the black Boss of the Plains hat.

He went into to a saloon and scanned the room, as he always did. A man in dealing cards looked up and their eyes met. There was not a challenge, but an acknowledgement between two men each recognized as dangerous.

It was recent San Diego resident and saloonkeeper Wyatt Earp.

Pope picked a table and was soon drinking a beer and waiting for beef and potatoes.

Presently, the game at Earp's table broke up and he ordered dinner. He sent the server over to Popes table and asked Pope, a stranger, to join him. Pope walked over and extended his hand.

"John Pope."

"Wyatt Berry Stapp Earp," the owner said.

"I recognized you. The man I work for speaks highly of you," Pope said.

"Who would that be?"

"Chief Detective James Hume."

"So, you're Wells Fargo like Jim?"

Pope let his left lapel come open. The gold badge and white bird's head butt of the .44 showed plainly.

"Looks like you had your grips trimmed down to be thinner in the front for a faster grip," Earp observed.

"I did. Seems to work well."

"Tilghman did, too."

"Back in Dodge?"

"Yes. Dodge."

"He's town marshal there now, isn't he?"

"Yes."

"What brings you to, town, Pope?"

"Train robbery up north of here. On the way to Temecula Canyon country."

"Get much?" Earp asked.

"Two thousand."

"Musta been a payroll for men laying tracks."

"Exactly. Six men did the robbery. I have a trail, though it's fading fast. Got some distinctive horse-shoe sketches. I'll get most or all of them. Might take a little time, but I'll get them."

Both dinners were served and the two dangerous men ate in silence.

Pope received his check. He guessed as owner, Earp ate for free. He was right.

"Good talking to you, Mr. Earp."

"Guess you are wondering why I invited you over."

"Mebbe a little," Pope admitted.

"People like us stand out to one another. Did you know this was my place when you entered?"

"Not a clue."

"But, you made me out as soon as you walked in the door. Before you recognized me. I did same. It's about who represents a threat, isn't it?"

"I 'spect it is."

Without standing and thereby dumping the Schofield revolver on his lap onto the floor, Earp extended his hand. Pope dropped a five on the table to cover dinner and shook with the former lawman.

Pope walked out the door with mixed feelings. He gave those feelings a lot of thought on the three block walk back to his hotel.

He concluded Earp would be a good man to have beside you when the bullets were flying. But, he did not particularly like the laconic gunfighter. Having concluded these two things, he walked on without giving it further thought. And, never thought about it again until reading many years later Earp had passed from old age.

He was relatively near the harbor and the town kept going most of the night. Pope did not feel it was dangerous, so he kept the Greener cased while he slept.

******

The next morning, he went to the Wells Fargo office and met with the messenger. The man gave a good description of weapons, apparel and demeanor of the robbers. Nobody seemed to stand out as the boss. That struck Pope odd. Every gang had a leader. He wrote the new information down in his notebook to study later. Another oddity was no rifles were present. Most robbers used rifles or shotguns instead of their revolvers.

Still turning this over in his head, Pope took his trail gear to the livery and chose a horse who looked as good as the liveryman claimed.

He put his equipment, including the shotgun and his investigative bag on the saddle and headed to the train depot. He followed the wagon road beside the track north. It was noon before he saw the first of his chop marks on a tree denoting the scene of the crime. There was nothing new to be learned there, so he tried to cut sign and identify a trail to follow. It was tough, so he went along the cut out timber where the new track was going to be laid. Eventually, he ran out of the cut path with its flurry of tracks. He tied the horse to a branch and did a full three hundred sixty degree circle around the spot where he stopped. The circle was a quarter of a mile. At the two o'clock position, had the circle been a clock face, he spotted six sets of hoof prints. They moved off to the northeast, bypassing Temecula Canyon and leading off into hilly country with small groves of trees interspersed throughout.

Pope knew they were definitely headed into wilderness country. He feared they might turn south into Mexico. He knew first-hand the political and lawless ramifications were greater in Mexico.

But, where this trail was leading him was almost as dangerous. He was going into the Pechanga Indian territory. It was expected, he learned from Dunstan, President Arthur would establish a Pechanga Reservation on this land any day. In the meantime, it was no man's land, claimed by the band, but not having a legal basis for the claim yet.

Pope wondered what laws governed it? It was possibly still San Diego County. Or, was it federal land? Or, had an executive order been issued and it was now tribal land. Whichever was the situation might affect his case if he arrested and brought to justice someone here.

The answer not being forthcoming and the crime not likely to solve itself, he pushed on.

"Life is full of chances, some big, some little," he thought to himself, "so sometimes, you just gotta spur your horse and go."

And, that is exactly what Pope did. He rode on, watching tracks and constantly scanning the horizon for threats, no matter who they might be.

The tracks led towards some smoke, spiraling upwards into blue California sky. Watching all around, he approached to within a quarter of a mile very carefully.

Whoever was in the cabin he saw in the distance was related to the robbery. He had tracked them directly here and knew his testimony would stand up in court.

Pope studied the cabin to determine the best tactical move. It was more like a plains dwelling, which might have spoken to the heritage of its builder.

Half was built into a hill, dug away for a room. The other half jutted out from the hill and was a more normal log structure.

Pope looked at the chimney, now emitting smoke, probably from a cook fire.

He tied his horse to a branch, not trusting him yet to think he would stay stationary with just his reins dropped. He made sure his pockets were loaded with both .44-40 and ten-gauge ammunition before leaving the horse.

Taking the ten-gauge Greener, he stalked circuitously to the hill behind the cabin.

A creosote bush was at the edge of the hill by the roof and chimney.

Pope pulled it up and shoved it into the opening of the tin pipe serving as a chimney. Then, he waited.

"What in hell are you cooking, Noah? Smells like its burning." Then, further words ensued, first an argument, then words bordering on panic.

"The cabin's on fire! Let's get out of here. Grab the money and the guns and all the ammo!"

Pope waited on top with both hammers eared back on the double-barreled shotgun.

The first man out dragged a canvas sack. It appeared heavy. Pope did not know whether it was the money from the robbery or their ammunition supply. He bet on the money as being the first thing they would grab.

A second man, then a third came out, looking at the cabin. They were trying to determine which part was on fire.

"Wells Fargo. You are under arrest! Drop your guns!"

The first two drew and looked up. Neither one saw the two loads of double-ought buckshot. They were cut down and crumpled dead.

The third drew also. But, Pope drew faster.

He also fell where he stood.

Pope waited five minutes. The cabin had to be full of smoke. Nobody could last five minutes without breathing fresh air.

He climbed down the hill and walked around to the front of the cabin. Nudging the three bodies with his boot, to confirm they were dead. He knew close range hits with ten-gauge buckshot was devastating enough not to require much confirmation. The man he shot with his Merwin & Hulbert was hit plumb center, but was barely alive.

Pope picked up all three men's weapons and moved them out of reach of the survivor.

He held his bandanna over his mouth and nose and went into the small dugout cabin long enough to verify it was empty. Pope could not chance being back shot by someone in the cabin.

He went over to the man moaning on the ground. He got his canteen and gave the man a couple sips of water.

Pope folded the smoky bandanna into a square and pressed it firmly to the man's wound.

"Partner, I hate to tell you, but you are shot through the heart. So I can notify next of kin, you need to tell me your name and those of the other two."

"I'm Noah Brown. The big one is Ben Lancaster. The little Mick is Rory O'Quinn. I ain't got no next of kin. Don't think they got any close kin either."

Pope wrote the information in his notebook.

"How about the other three, Noah? They left you to die. You don't owe them anything," Pope said.

Noah thought for a second. The time he took worried Pope, who knew he did not have much time left.

"I cain't spill the beans on my pards," Noah said.

"It's not spilling the beans. Confession is good for the soul. And, I'm afraid you are running out of time to fix your soul for meeting your Maker."

"I guess…the boss is Charlie Neely. His two buds are Bob Sawyer and Jacob Hite."

"Where do the live, Noah?"

"They all hang out up in Colton."

"Noah, you won't survive a ride back to a doctor. But, I'll stay here with you and give you water and make sure you and the others get buried properly."

Noah Brown looked up at him in something he thought was appreciation and died several seconds later. Pope reached over and closed the dead man's eyes.

He opened the sack and counted the money. It was a bit under a thousand dollars. Roughly half of the take. Neely, Sawyer and Hite had several days to spend some of the other thousand back in Colton. Colton was closer than San Diego, but he wanted to turn the bodies over to the San Diego County sheriff. And, not advertise to the rest of the gang their compatriots were dead. He saddled the three horses he saw in a makeshift corral and put the three bodies on and tied them securely.

He appreciated the term "dead weight" after struggling, particularly with Ben Lancaster who was over six feet and two hundred pounds.

Pope went into the cabin and found some .44 cartridges, which he confiscated for himself. There did not seem to be anything else for evidence. The bodies wore the bandannas they used as masks, so he removed them and put them in his evidence bag.

He did not want to camp with increasingly unpleasant dead bodies overnight, so he rode through the night, relying on his Dietz police lantern when the trail got too dark.

Pope attracted quite a crowd as the rode into San Diego mid-morning. He stopped at the sheriff's office and tied four horses in front and went in.

The sheriff inspected the bodies and wrote the names and descriptions before sending for the undertaker. There was no need for a coroner. The wounds and odor proved they were dead.

Once the bodies were removed and horses confiscated, Pope and the sheriff walked over to the district attorney's office and swore out robbery warrants for Neely, Sawyer, and Hite.

The sheriff sent a telegram to the sheriff in San Bernardino County telling him a Wells Fargo detective would be hand-delivering three arrest warrants the following day.

Pope sent Dunstan and Hume wires advising of

progress and the recovery of half the money, which he deposited in the San Diego office. As always, Pope got a receipt.

Having ridden through the night, Pope went back to his hotel and ordered a bath. After, he slept until dark, had dinner and went back to bed. The pursuit of the remaining three might be a tough one, so he may as well be ready for it.

******

The next morning, Pope boarded a stage for the ride up to Colton. Armed with the warrants, he would make the arrests and deliver the prisoners to the sheriff at the county seat, San Bernardino, only several miles away.

Pope rented a hotel room as a base of operations. He went to the post office and inquired about an address for Charles Neely. The postmaster was hesitant until Pope showed him the warrant and swore him to secrecy.

He said Neely had a small place about two miles southeast of town and gave Pope directions. He told Pope he thought Sawyer may have the same address, but had never heard of Hite.

Pope went back to the hotel and switched from his travel shoulder holster rig to this double holster belt rig. He rented a horse and rode to Neely's place. From a distance, he did not know whether to characterize it as a ranch or a farm. Either way, it was pretty hardscrabble.

He took up a position in some trees and watched for over an hour. Finally, a man in overalls and no gun came out and fed some chickens.

Pope walked towards him and the man spun around, alarmed.

"Howdy. My name is John Pope. I work for Wells Fargo and would like to ask you some questions. Are you Mr. Neely?"

"Naw, Charlie went down to National City. You don't look like Wells Fargo. You look like an officer."

"Well, I am Wells Fargo. You must be Mr. Sawyer, right?" Pope asked.

"How did you know who I am?" Sawyer asked, verifying his identity.

"I just knew. I have a warrant for your arrest for train robbery. So, don't do anything stupid and make me have to kill you."

Pope could see the man's glance flick back and forth between him and the ramshackle house. Neely could be there, despite what Sawyer claimed. But, there was only one horse in the corral. More likely, Sawyer's gun was there and he was figuring the prospects about getting it versus dying.

His considerations over, Sawyer chose the stupid option and sprinted towards the house, running barefoot through chicken droppings.

Pope drew and fired a shot a few yards in front of Sawyer's feet. The gunshot just sped him up.

"Aw, hell!" Pope said and took off running after the man.

Sawyer made it to the house with a margin of ten feet and spun and slammed the door.

Pope just kept coming and hit the door with his left shoulder at full speed. He rolled into the room on the floor and slammed into Sawyer. It was not exactly the approach he planned, but seemed to work as Sawyer went "Oof!" and toppled. Pope threw himself on top of him knee first. The knee, in Sawyer's groin, doubled him up and he went cross-eyed.

Pope determined the fight was over and rolled Sawyer, moaning pathetically, onto his stomach and cuffed him from behind.

"Where's the money from the train robbery, Sawyer?" Pope asked, roughly pulling the man up and sitting him in a ladder-back chair.

"I ain't saying!"

Pope kicked him in the chest knocking the chair over. Sawyer hit his head on a table edge and lay on the floor moaning more than ever.

"You sound like a little girl not a big, bad train robber. Jesse James would laugh at you right now," Pope said, leaving him on his butt in the floor.

"I asked you where the take from the train robbery is. I already recovered half from your dead partners. My patience is growing real thin, Sawyer."

"Dead? How did they die?" he asked.

"The three idiots tried to draw on me."

"You killed all three?"

"Yes. Just like I'm going to do you, unless you start talking."

Pope punctuated his threat by whipping out the right hand .44 in a blur.

Sawyer's eyes got appreciably larger with the action.

"It's in a leather sack under the bunk on the right," he said.

Pope retrieved the sack and counted the money, gun still out and wavering back and forth towards Sawyer.

"It's only six hundred. Four hundred is missing from your and Neely's cut." He let the large, short barreled revolver move back towards Sawyer and stay there.

"He gave Hite three hundred. And, he took a hundred to National City."

"Why is he going to National City?" Pope asked.

"He's going to rob today's train, too."

"How is he going to do rob it by himself?"

"By getting on posing as a worker and moving towards the express car and shooting the messenger."

"Then, he's coming back here somehow?"

"His horse is in the woods just north of San Diego. He'll ride back."

"Sawyer, where did Hite go?"

"He didn't fit in so the boss told him to hit the trail. He was from up near Lake Tahoe. He said he was going home. I liked him, but the boss didn't trust him."

"It sounds, from what you said, Neely was planning on robbing the train early in its route."

"He said he should be back here before dinner with another two thousand. Seventeen hundred for him for doing the work, three for me for just hanging with him."

Pope knew he had several hours before Neely returned. He took the money and Sawyer into San Bernardino to the sheriff, dropped the money at the local Wells Fargo office and rode hard back to the Neely place. He led Sawyer's horse back and put him in the corral.

He beat Neely. No additional horse in the corral and the door was still busted in.

Pope closed the door from the outside and stuck a sliver of wood in the jamb to hold it shut. From any distance, it looked normal. He hid his horse in the same clump of trees he had watched from, walked back to the house and awaited Neely.

Neely came in an hour later at a trot. He called for Sawyer as he went to the corral to unsaddle his horse.

Pope stepped around the corner of the house and aimed the ten-gauge at Neely's navel.

"I am a Wells Fargo detective and you are under arrest for train robbery. Maybe murder, depending on what happened today."

Neely got the twitchy, eyes darting look of a man getting ready to make a really bad decision. Then, he made it.

Pope shot Neely in the middle with the shotgun. Like the two at the cabin north of Temecula, there was no doubt about his status as he fell to the ground.

Pope went into the cabin and tore the blankets off both bunks. He doubled them and rolled them tightly around the man's midriff. He tied them as tightly as possible, then found a tarp in the stable and added that, also tied and knotted. "Hopefully," he thought, "the girding will keep Neely's insides pretty much inside for the trip to San Bernardino."

He got back in time to deposit the recovered money at the Wells Fargo office and the body and the two robbers' horses at the sheriff's. Not a timid man, Pope still skipped dinner. He was closer to Neely than to the two from the roof and the damage more devastating. By morning, he was ready for a big breakfast and to wire his results.

He had recovered the thousand from yesterday's robbery, solved the murder yesterday of the messenger, recovered one thousand six hundred from the cabin and another hundred from Neely's body.

The only amount outstanding was the three hundred dollars distributed to the sole unaccounted for train robber, Hite. Hite would be his quarry until caught. Hite's capture would close two train robberies and one murder.

*****

Pope boarded the Southern Pacific train to Los Angeles, then transferred north to San Francisco.

Chief Detective Hume was in the office and Pope scheduled a brief catchup meeting with him.

"Pope, what are you doing here? Have you already arrested this fellow Hite?" Hume greeted him, trying to hide a smile.

"Good as caught, boss," Pope responded, "but, I wanted to talk with you first."

Hume gestured for him to sit down.

"From a business standpoint, is it practical for me to go after Hite for a three hundred dollar recovery? By the time I catch him at the top end of California, a lot of it is likely to be spent."

"Pope, financially, you are correct. But, both Mr. Wells and Mr. Fargo have instructed me to bring in as many of the people who rob us and our passengers as we can, even if it costs more than we recover. Their ethics supersede profits. And, so does our reputation. So, young man, in response to your very intelligent question, chase him to hell and back if you have to. You can rest assured of my full support."

"Thank you, sir."

"Now, Pope. This one has been very violent. You have had to neutralize a number of people. Quite an accomplishment when three are trying to kill you at once. I bet they were surprised when you killed all of them first!" he said, tongue in cheek."

"It is said of Colt 'fear no man, no matter his size. Call on me and I'll equalize.' Well, a ten-gauge with buckshot multiplies the saying several times over," Pope responded.

"We call our men on stages 'shotgun' messengers for a reason. Not 'rifle messengers,' but *shotgun.*"

"How are you doing as your kill list grows? Need to visit with a priest or preacher or rabbi as the case may be?"

"No, sir. In every case, I fired at someone who was trying to kill me. Every shooting was righteous. I sleep well at night and have a good appetite."

"As you should. Changing the subject, what do you know about this Hite fellow?"

"I know his name is Jacob Hite and he is from and probably heading back to the Lake Tahoe area. My source expired before I could get a description. The first express messenger descriptions were pretty good. By eliminating the other five robbers I saw, I am left with one older one, maybe in his late forties, medium height, black hair and very strong build. He was described by the messenger as being built like a bare knuckles fighter."

"Sounds like a tough guy. Be careful, John. Don't take any chances. If you need to bring local deputies in or another of our detectives or two, do not hesitate. You are running a high case solution rate. I do not want to see it come to a crashing halt while you recover in some hospital."

"Nor do I sir. Very little of what I do is spontaneous. I will get him, but according to my plan."

"Do you know if he is on the California side or the Nevada side of the line?" Hume asked.

"I do not, sir. I will ask the officers and postal people on both sides. He sounds pretty distinctive. I am betting he also has a sheet of arrests and will be known to the local officers. I will keep you up-to-date."

"Do that, son. Good hunting!" As at the end of every meeting with his detectives, Hume stood and shook hands. It was a tradition of respect and caring.

******

Pope spent long enough at his desk to answer a couple of letters, including one from his grandfather, and do his travel and source expense reports.

It was late enough in the day for him to go to his room and air it out. He cleaned the shotgun and the right hand Merwin & Hulbert. He wiped the left one, though it had not been fired for a while.

His carbine still had its lever padlocked to an eye bolt he had installed in his wardrobe. He wiped the exterior with the oil gun rag.

Pope replenished his socks and underwear and bagged his dirty ones to drop at the Chinese laundry down the street from his rooming house on the way out in the morning.

He put more tooth powder in his travel container and salt and pepper. He also added coffee to his camping supplies.

Before going to bed, he practiced with his .44's. It was something he started a year ago.

He unloaded and reloaded with empty cases to protect the hammer mounted firing pins. He then drew and fired with both hands and singly for fifty times.

Once satisfied, he reloaded with hot rounds and put the guns beside his bed.

In the morning, he boarded a train to Sacramento, where he hired a horse and rode north towards the state line. He asked around in the Tahoe villages on both sides of the California-Nevada line. Nobody by the name of Jacob Hite or the description lived there.

The El Dorado County seat was in Placerville, so Pope rode there next. The undersheriff said he thought a man of Hite's description lived near the lake on the Nevada side near Glenbrook. He said the man had been a logger, though the mills were now closing down.

That struck a chord with Pope. The clean cuts on the trees used to stop the first train had suggested to him a lumberjack or logger. Not evidence for court. Probably would not stand up in court. But, good corroborative evidence for his file.

Pope got good directions on how to get to the area on the eastern side of Lake Tahoe. He reckoned he would have to camp, so he made it easier by picking up some food to take with him for the night.

He rode into the area, arriving before dusk.

As was his usual procedure, Pope tied his horse to a branch and, taking the shotgun, walked a quarter mile circle around his prospective campsite, looking for anything threatening. There was none, so he returned.

Pope unsaddled and hobbled the hired horse, which was a Morgan. He had chosen a site near a stream and under some trees. The horse had plenty of grass and water.

He took his trowel and dug a fire pit with an adjacent small hole. He carefully dug a tunnel connecting the two such that the smaller pit would suck in air and fuel the larger cooking fire. The larger one would burn more efficiently and with less smoke.

Pope strung part of his lariat between two trees and pegged the back of his small waxed tarp to the ground. He laid the tarp over the stretched rope and used guy ropes to attach the overhang to the ground, giving him an open shelter. He put the saddle and his bedroll inside, along with the Greener shotgun.

Once his fire burned down to coals, he began heating the coffee pot and made bacon to go with the biscuits he had brought with him. An apple was desert.

The lake was nearby. The sky was blue and what seemed to be a million stars sparkled. Not a bad night to be sleeping out.

The next morning, he substituted store bought corn pone for the biscuits and had more bacon and coffee. He washed in the frigid water of the stream and even shaved. Filled and refreshed, Pope broke camp dousing, then covering both fire holes. He walked the horse towards Glenbrook, eyes peeled for threats.

Glenbrook was primarily a scattering of cabins. There were very few people about.

There a small general store. He stopped and tied up at the hitching post and went in.

"Morning, officer," the man behind the counter said.

"Is it so obvious?" Pope asked.

"Yep. You wouldn't be a deputy. Your suit is too nice. Maybe a federal man."

Pope moved his lapel back to show his badge.

"How about a Wells Fargo man?" he asked.

"Fits with the suit. What can I do for you?"

"I'm looking for a man name of Jacob Hite. From around this way. May be a logger. Forties, strong build," Pope answered.

"A bad man to look for and a worse one to find, " the shopkeeper answered.

"Why?"

"He's crookeder than a Nevada rattler and a helluva lot meaner. You see him, just shoot him before he can get his hands or fists on you. If he does, you are most likely gonna be dead," the man said with gravity.

"Know where I could find him?" Pope asked.

"Not for sure. Heard he was on the run. Some sort of robbery. Other members of the gang had been killed. Rumor is someone heard him say he was going down to Arizona Territory."

"It's true he is the only train robbing gang member both free and breathing. Where can I find the person who said he was going to Arizona? I'd like to talk with him or her."

"I'm guessing from the low hang of those two revolvers, you might have had something to do with the dead part of the gang?"

"I might have. The person who heard him?"

"Bertie. She runs our only sporting house. Last cabin on the right. If there's a bandanna on the door latch, wait a few minutes. She'd be entertaining," the man warned Pope, who nodded his assent.

Pope walked down to the house on the end and there was not a bandanna on the door latch. He knocked and a surprisingly clean and presentable woman answered.

"Are you Miss Bertie?" he asked.

"I am, officer. How can I help you?"

"There goes the 'officer' thing again!" Pope thought. It had to be the gunbelt and Stetson.

"My name is John Pope. I am a detective with Wells Fargo and Company. I'm looking for a man named Jacob Hite. I understand you have had some contact with him?" Pope said.

"I did. Two days ago. Is the information worth money?" she asked.

"Well, there is not a reward for his arrest, if that is what you mean. Just answering a couple of questions may be worth some money though."

"Take a seat in one of the two rockers. I will get us some coffee. I could surely use it this morning."

"I could, too, Ma'am. Thank you."

Pope was struck. Despite less cloth on her body, she could be any pretty ranch or farm wife in the area.

She came back out the door and handed him a steaming mug of black coffee.

He took a sip. It was strong and rich, like he preferred and seldom got.

"How long was your conversation with Mr. Hite two days ago?" he asked.

"Not very long. He was drunk and in a hurry to get his business done. He is far from one who makes love."

"Please tell me as much as you remember about the conversation. Little things may not seem important to you, but may be the very thing which allows me to find and arrest him."

"You better find and kill him. Arrest is not in his mean constitution, Detective Pope. I tried to get him to talk a little. He's rough sober and rougher drunk. I asked where he had been because I've not seen him recently. He said down to San Diego, where he'd made some money and gotten in a scrape. What did he mean by 'scrape?'" she asked.

"He robbed a train as part of a gang."

"Oh. What happened to the rest of them?" she asked.

"Justice was served."

"Were you the 'justice'?"

"Pretty much. What else did he say?" Pope asked.

"He said he needed to get away from this part of the country permanently. I asked where he would go. He said he had a cousin down around Prescott, in Arizona Territory. He reckoned he would head down there and try it out."

"Did he mention the cousin's name, perchance?" Pope asked.

"Last name was Hite, like his. First was another 'J' name. Maybe Jethro or Jerimiah. I just cannot remember for sure. Said he worked on a ranch ten miles or so outside of town. Hite had never talked so much on visits before. I think he was worried in addition to being drunk."

"Worried about what, Miss Bertie?" Pope asked.

"I don't know. Being caught? Hanging?" she responded.

"He doesn't sound like a man easily shaken. Was this odd for him?"

"It was. I didn't think the devil himself would scare Jacob Hite. But who or whatever was on his trail did."

Pope could not help a small grin at the last statement and she caught it and returned it.

"Got time for some special treatment?" she asked.

"No Ma'am. Looks like I have to head to Prescott today. But, thanks for the information. And, the coffee and offer," he added as he set three five dollar pieces on the table next to the porch rocker.

"Next time you're through it is on the house," she told him. He smiled, got up and doffed the Stetson and walked back to his horse and rode out of town.

"There's a woman who would, or did, make someone a fine wife. And, she's running a one-woman brothel," he thought sadly. "But, then," he told himself, "she's seems healthy and happy with her lot in life, so who am I to judge?"

He turned in the horse and took the train past Sacramento all the way to Los Angeles. From there, he began the almost four hundred mile trek to Prescott by stage.

Most were red Concords from his company. All had hard seats and passengers could only tolerate the fast, dusty and under sprung ride because of the close spacing of stage stations with fresh teams for the whips or jehu's and fresh water for the passengers.

The stage stopped for a new team at Blythe, California on the Arizona border.

There was one drummer traveling and he seemed too talkative for Popes taste. He especially worked to maintain the interest of the lone female traveler. The drummer was presentable, though probably not as handsome as he thought he was. The woman was lovely. She did not have a wedding ring on, but did not offer a clue as to her status. She was not shy. Rather, she was not interested in sharing with anyone on the stage.

She was perfectly plump with a tiny waist and dark hair done up stylishly.

It was clear she was getting increasingly bored by the drummer's constant self-promoting chatter.

Pope was traveling in his derby and shoulder holsters after being identified as a lawman everywhere he wore the Stetson and two-gun belt rig. Each persona had its place, he thought.

He tipped the black derby down over his eyes and feigned sleeping. The other man on the stage was rough as a cob. He made no pretense of hiding the Colt cap n' ball conversion revolver in his waistband. The man scowled at the drummer and eyed the woman lasciviously. Pope noted this from the shade under his short brim.

He kept a sharp eye out in Blythe and the country east of it. There had been an Indian attack there two years ago and a stage would be considered a good target for a war party just as it would for an outlaw band.

He kept the innocuous leather bag with the short-barreled Greener in it close by in the coach with him. Nobody could tell the bag hid a ten-gauge shotgun and enough shells to hold off an invasion.

Pope knew the rough passenger represented the odd man out on this trip and he determined he had better watch him.

*****

About twenty miles into Arizona, He felt the hairs rise on the back of his neck.

He heard the crack of a whip and felt the fast-moving stage speed up even more. The jehu was pushing the six-horse team hard.

The messenger reached down and tapped three times on the door jamb. It was his signal that verified Popes intuition trouble was getting ready to happen.

The driver yelled "Whoa! And pulled the hand brake. The coach fishtailed back and forth in the dust covering the road, but the skill of the jehu kept it upright.

"Hold up there, Mr. Wells Fargo! This here is a robbery!"

The rough man in the stage slipped the conversion Colt out and was easing back the hammer.

The double action .44 Merwin & Hulbert magically appeared in Popes hand and was centered on his fellow passenger.

"Declare your side, partner or die right here before the dance starts," Pope growled at him.

The man eased the hammer down and handed the butt towards Pope.

Pope knew what was coming. A border roll, where the man would spin the gun around and fire at him from two feet away. As the man's hand started to roll, the stage was filled with a deafening noise as Popes

.44 spoke and a black half inch hole appeared between the man's eyes.

"Rufe, you fire the shot inside?"

Remembering the man's gruff voice as well as he could, Pope mimicked it with a "Yeah!"

Strange faces appeared on either side of the stage door and Pope fired left and right with the .44's, hitting both robbers. Three down! How many more?

Pope shouldered the door open, knocking the wounded right hand man to the ground, but scanning for another threat instead of him.

Pope looked to the front as the two original men tried to scurry away like rats in the night.

Their scurrying was interrupted by the double blast from the shotgun messenger's namesake weapon. Both hit the dirt and ceased to be a danger to anyone.

"Hey upstairs there! Just the four you and I shot plus the passenger, also dead?" Pope asked.

"Seems to be it. The whip and I don't like this portion of road. We vote to leave the bodies for the sheriff and high tail out of here. You good with doing it?"

"Let me push the passenger out and when you hear the thump, let's roll!"

Pope pushed him out the door and the coach took off as fast as six fresh horses could pull it.

Pope looked at the woman first.

"Ma'am, are you okay?" he asked.

"Other than scared out of ten years of life, I think

so. Who *are* you?" she asked.

"Wells Fargo detective John Pope at your service Ma'am," he responded.

"And, you, sir?"

"You could have warned me you were going to shoot past my nose," the salesman said.

"I could have. But, the man with the gun in the window was going to blow your brains all over me. This is a fairly new suit. I figured I'd better shoot him first. Why don't you sit back quietly and enjoy the ride, sir?" He looked at the woman.

"You want more conversation with this gentleman?" he asked her.

"I didn't want the conversation I already had," she said.

He turned to the man as the stage slid around a curve and bumped over a rut.

"Guess you need to take a nap or something between here and Prescott."

"And, if I don't?" the man asked.

"Ma'am, would you stick your fingers in your ears for a moment?"

"And, miss whatever you are going to say to him? I think not!"

Pope turned to the man and leaned in close to his ear."

"If you don't, I will throw your ass out the door at full speed. If you survive the fall, you have a long walk in Indian country. Especially without a canteen. Do you understand me?" Pope asked.

"You are a big man with those two guns. How about I knock your head off?"

Pope gave him a left jab in the jaw followed by a fist to the solar plexus. The man went "Oof!" and doubled over onto the floor unconscious.

Pope had put his weak gun hand at some risk hitting a hard jaw with his fist, but had protected his primary with a fist to the drummer's gut. Just like his grandpa taught him.

Though young and fit, he arrived in Prescott stiff and sore. He stopped in at the Wells Fargo office and advised them about both the robbery and his business in the Territory. A reporter took him aside for a brief interview.

Pope next went to the Yavapai County sheriff's office, reported the robbery and the location of the bodies. Then he inquired about Jacob Hite, wanted for train robbery. They were unaware of Hite's presence in the county and disinterested until paperwork was presented.

Chief Detective Hume had Wells Fargo lawyers working on an extradition agreement with the Territory.

The legal maneuvering was made simpler since Prescott was, for the second and last time, presently the capital of Arizona Territory.

Pope was able to go to the Attorney General's Office, make a sworn statement and pick up the agreement with assurances he could use it also to legally effect an arrest. At a time in the West when a man could defend himself in a gunfight, be arrested and held until he proved himself innocent, this was comforting to the detective.

Pope then took a duplicate of the extradition agreement between California and Arizona to the sheriff's office and presented it.

He inquired about a small ranch a few miles out of town owned by a family named Hite. It did not ring a bell with the sheriff or chief deputy.

He then began checking stage manifests for through-tickets like his own from California, at livery stables for horses hired or purchased.

He interviewed shop keepers in tack stores, as well as general merchandise and specialty stores selling trail gear, clothing and guns.

Pope hit a dead end. Could the soiled dove in Glenbrook have been wrong? Or, had he just beaten Hite to Prescott?

After a full day of interviewing, he decided he might have to spend the next day riding around looking for the ranch. Unfortunately, he did not have a name, either surname or ranch name. He only had "J. Hite" for the name of the cousin.

The next morning, he was out and about early.

He went to the property and tax office before mounting the livery horse.

An attractive lady, her dark hair stylishly in a bun, looked up and smiled as he came in.

Pope doffed his hat and gave her his best smile. It

seemed to work, as she lit right up.

"Ma'am, I wonder if you might be able to help me?"

"It's 'Miss,' and I'll sure try," she responded, her green eyes dancing.

"My name is John Pope and I am a detective with Wells Fargo." He flashed his badge beneath his left lapel. The green eyes widened at the ivory butt of the revolver.

"I am on the trail of a train robber. I have gotten the rest of the gang and just have this one man left."

"So, you came to me. Does he own property in Yavapai County?"

"His last known conversation before leaving the California-Nevada line was with a woman of pleasure. He drunkenly told her he had a cousin near Prescott and was going there to lay low for a while."

"What's his name, Detective Pope?" she asked. Pope found her so attractive he was having a difficult time focusing on Hite.

"Er...uh, his name is Hite. Nobody in the sheriff's office is aware of any Hite's around here. HIs cousin may be a J. Hite. The ranch is a small one, about ten miles out of Prescott."

"Detective, something is tickling the back of my mind on this. It may take an hour or so. Have you had lunch yet? There is a good place a block from here."

"I have not, but would surely be honored to take you to lunch there...so we could talk about the Hite place, of course," he said taking a long shot, he thought.

"That would be quite nice. Let me get my hat."

She turned and walked to the far corner of the room as Pope stood with his mouth open.

"I am Sarah Watson, by the way," she said.

Pope doffed his hat and said, "It is an honor to make your acquaintance, Miss Watson."

She stuck her hand in his right arm and they began to walk towards the café. Pope did not like having his gun hand encumbered, but ladies had to walk on the inside away from the street. So, she had to stay on his right side going there. Coming back, she could be on his left arm.

Pope was not overly worried. He practiced religiously with both hands and was only imperceptively faster with his right.

As always, he scanned for threats as he walked.

"Have you always been a detective?" she asked.

"No, I was a rancher with my grandfather, then an officer with the San Francisco Police. Finally, I made detective there and was lucky enough to get the eye of the head detective for Wells Fargo. He lured me away. It's a great company Miss Sarah."

"Tell me why it is good, detective," she asked as they walked.

"The two founders, Mr. Wells and Mr. Fargo still run the company. They hire good people and treat them well. They do good things for the community. There's a tradition if a customer loses something in our care, whether it is a strong box of gold or a passenger's watch, we replace it right away. The detective force costs more than we recover in stolen treasure. But the owners want the criminals to know we are serious about apprehending them."

"Are you supposed to bring them in dead or alive?" she asked casually.

"Management prefers we arrest them and they go before a judge and jury. But, they recognize train and stage robbers are dangerous, violent men and sometimes we have to protect others or ourselves and shoot in self-defense."

They arrived at the café and went in. They were seated near the front window. Pope was glad he could see the door and seated Miss Sarah in a way nobody was to his back. It had become a way of life for him and he expected it always would be. He watched as she watched him. She knew exactly what he was doing and why. How did she know these things? Just observant?

"I get the feeling you understand my precautions in how I walk, where I sit and all."

"Am I so obvious?" she asked.

"I just like to observe folks," he said.

"Have you ever heard of Kate Warne?"

"The famous head of female detectives for the Pinkerton's? That Kate Warne?"

"Yes. She died before my time, but I was one of the later female detectives. I rather miss it. But, like the silly woman I thought I was not, I followed a man to Prescott. I gave up my career for a rancher who really only wanted a passel of brats to work his land. Not the romantic life we discussed in Chicago when he wooed me away from my job with the Pinks."

They ordered and resumed the chat.

"Won't Pinkerton hire you back?" Pope asked.

"He is a very stubborn Scotsman. By the way, what should I call you?"

"How about John?" he said.

"John, he told me I was making a big mistake and once I left, there would be no return. He is a bull-headed little man. Brilliant and a bulldog in his tenacity. He is totally unyielding."

"Do you think you would like being a Wells Fargo detective?" Pope asked.

"Well....in the public eye, the two organizations are about equal in reputation and esteem. It would be back on the trains and stages again. And, packing my revolver."

"Or, two," Pope grinned.

"Yes, I noticed. Merwin & Hulbert's I believe," she said.

"They are. The new double actions."

"Do they work well for you?" she asked.

"They did yesterday."

"What happened yesterday? I have not seen the Journal Miner paper yet. It comes out today covering the last week."

"Just inside the Arizona line, one passenger and four outlaws attempted to rob the stage I was on," Pope said.

"How many did you kill, if I may ask?"

"Three. The shotgun messenger got the other two" Pope said.

"Your first kills?" He just shook his head and did not volunteer further on the subject.

"Does Wells Fargo have any female detectives?" Sarah asked.

"Not presently, as far as I know. We seem to be behind the Pinks on that score."

"Your chief is Hume, right?" He nodded.

"What do you think he would say to the prospect?" she asked.

"I don't know, but I will ask if you wish me to."

"Perhaps I should scribble out a job history for you to send him."

"Would it be short enough for a wire? He likes wires."

"I will make it short enough, John," she said.

Two bowls of beef stew came with freshly baked bread and they ate and chatted about Prescott and Sarah's life growing up near Chicago.

He walked back to her office with her and suggested she write out her detective experience with Pinkerton before looking in her records for the Hite's. He could go to the Wells Fargo office and send a telegram on her behalf to Hume while she researched. Pope knew his time in Prescott would be short and was strangely taken with this beautiful, strong woman.

Sarah prepared the short resume, he read it and asked a couple questions and left to send it.

By the time he returned, she had located a possibility. A man named Jethro Hite owned a property in Chino Valley, fifteen miles north of Prescott. It was only forty acres.

Apparently, Pope gathered from this information and the lack of knowledge by the sheriff's office, he farmed or ranched and kept a low profile with little contact with anyone. There was a small general merchandise there, according to Sarah. He probably obtained most of the supplies he needed there.

"Would you like for me to accompany you to the ranch tomorrow?" Sarah asked. "It is Saturday, so the tax office is closed."

"You know it might end up in gunfire?" he asked.

"I have thought of the possibility. While you were at Wells Fargo, the reporter who interviewed you yesterday dropped in. I'm afraid he has a bit of a crush on me. It appears you were quite the gunman at the stage robbery. He said a couple of deputies and people from the undertaker's are going out today to collect bodies."

"How do you feel about the reporter?" he asked.

"Are you throwing your hat in the ring after an hour of knowing me?" she asked. "I am probably a horrible person. Some modern woman who happily travels alone, packs her Colt Lightning revolver and solves crimes. Quite unusual, wouldn't you say?"

"Yes, quite unusual. Quite appealing also," he said and was rewarded with a smile unlike he had ever received.

"So, John, you aren't intimidated by strong women?" she asked.

"Sarah, if I may call you by your first name, I am not intimidated by anyone."

"I am beginning to see you aren't. It's very appealing. I bet you make women feel safe."

"I am afraid I have not been around enough women to make them feel any sort of way."

She considered his admission, then smiled. This man is handsome, deadly, and smart. The cases he spoke of while they were eating were complex ones. It is a shame, she thought, it was not a man like this she had chosen to chase halfway around the country instead of the walking mistake she picked.

"To answer your question, I would be honored to have you accompany me to Chino Valley tomorrow. I would encourage you to bring your .38 Colt. Should I hire a buggy?" he asked.

"No, I have a riding outfit and a horse will be fine. I will ride with a leg on each side of the horse, thank you. Side saddle is remarkably stupid."

"Yes, I always thought so, too." He said. "I need to check my gear and clean my revolvers. The problem with having finely tuned and fitted guns is powder fouling affects them more than loosely manufactured ones. But, as long as I am not in a protracted fight, I think I am better served with these."

"I live in a small house just four doors down from here. It's the only one with flowers in front. When will you pick me up?"

"How about nine? We can go to the same café for breakfast before riding up to Chino Valley."

"Sounds good. I look forward to getting back on the trail of a miscreant again!"

"And, I look forward to having you backing my play. I will see you in the morning."

Pope stopped by the office to advise the manager of his plans. It was always prudent to have a friendly source know where he was in case things went very bad very fast.

A telegram was there already from Hume.

It said "Stay Prescott Stop Will come talk Watson Stop."

"So, the boss was coming to interview Sarah. Interesting!" Pope thought. He would share it with her at breakfast.

Back at the hotel, Pope thoroughly cleaned the two Merwin & Hulbert revolvers, still marveling at their fitting and workmanship. They would be the finest revolvers ever built if powder was only cleaner.

He skipped dinner and turned in early. Though not wanting to admit it, he was excited about going on a search and maybe arrest with Sarah. His grandpa had told him about Indian female warriors, such as the Cheyenne Buffalo Calf Road, who allegedly knocked Custer from his horse, leading to his death at the Little Big Horn, and Dahteste, the Apache woman warrior who was still fighting with Geronimo. Why couldn't there be a white woman warrior? Maybe there was. And, maybe he would work with her tomorrow. He fell asleep with a smile on his face and awoke before the sun.

Pope hired a second horse. Not knowing Sarah's riding ability, he asked for a smaller horse who was gentle. He rode his horse and lead it, a pinto pony, to her house. He arrived just before nine on his pocket watch.

Sarah came out in a long skirt that was actually pantaloons which only appeared to be a skirt. She had on a blousy white top covered with a vest. It, in turn, covered a belt holster with the bird's head grip of a Colt double action .38 stuck out the top. The gun worried Pope. He might say something later, but it had a famously delicate action, prone to break at the worst times. Though only introduced five years ago, it was probably the least dependable gun Colt ever made. But, its double action, small grip and light caliber made it a comfortable hideaway and popular among women. And, to a young man who Sheriff Garrett just killed in New Mexico. His name was Bonney or Antrim. Pope was not sure of the correct name for Billy the Kid.

"Good morning! You sure do look lovely, Sarah."

"Thank you John. You are worth taking extra pains for," she responded with her smile which managed to wreak havoc on his demeanor.

They rode to the café and tied up at the hitching post.

Again, Pope wore his shoulder holsters and derby hat. He wanted them to look like an up-scale couple. They agreed during breakfast to portray a husband and wife seeking a small ranch to purchase. The only thing amiss in their portrayal was a buggy instead of riding, but they would explain it away if asked. Sarah was pleased and surprised Hume was coming to Prescott just to talk with her.

They headed north out of Prescott to Chino Valley. They stopped at the mercantile and Pope identified himself with his real identity.

The owner clearly did not like the Hite's. He said they were crude, rude and he did not trust the man or the wife. He said he particularly did not trust the thug cousin who had just shown up.

Pope and Sarah looked at one another and he secretly nodded at his fully-briefed partner.

"Will you describe the cousin, sir?"

"He's between forty and fifty, dark hair and strong build. Looks like someone who would rather break you in half with his hands than shoot you."

"Thank you. That sounds like our man," she said.

"Ma'am, are you a lady detective really and truly?"

"Yes. I was a Pinkerton for six years. Now, I am working with Wells Fargo on this case," she said truthfully.

"Do you think the cousin is at the ranch now?" Pope asked the man.

"I don't know for sure. But, I suspect he is there or out tending their cattle. I watched him ride in. He's a fella better suited for traveling shank's mare than on a horse. He don't sit a horse very well. I was hoping he'd fall off. We don't need his kind around here. Bad enough we are stuck with the original Hite's."

Remembering he brought the '73 Winchester, which used the same .44-40 cartridges as his revolvers, Pope repaid the man by buying a box of them. He put them in his saddlebag, grinned at his new pard and mounted.

"Ready to ride, pard?" he asked.

"I like the sound of that…..pard. Yes, pard! Let's ride!"

They followed the directions given by the shop-keeper and arrived at the ranch before noon.

Using their planned ploy, they knocked on the door and asked about the ranch.

"No, it ain't for sale. Git!" was the response by a sour-pussed man and his even more sour wife.

"I see. May we ask a quick bit of advice?" Pope asked.

"Cain't you see we are busy?" Pope could not see, looking around the dump, where they had ever been busy.

"It will just take a second," plowing on, he said "How many hands does it take to run a spread this size?"

"We do it with just us and my cousin"

"Perhaps we could bother him with one or two questions, since you are busy?" Sarah asked.

"No, you cain't! He's out in the west pasture tending cattle. He don't have no time for the likes of you."

"Thank you. We are sorry to bother you." Both turned and mounted their horses and rode out the way they came in.

"How big a circle do you want to make to come into the west pasture by the opposite direction?" Sarah asked.

"I'm thinking a half mile will be a good margin. After all, we are not in a rush. It sounds like it will just be our man and the two of us out here," Pope said.

"Sarah, have you used a Winchester carbine?"

"I grew up with one in Illinois, hunting for my family. Pa had been injured in the war, so I bagged the deer, squirrels and rabbits."

"Why don't you take my Winchester?"

"You worried about my ability to shoot a revolver?"

"Not at all. I am worried about the dependability of that particular model revolver."

"It's always gone 'bang' when I squeezed the trigger, John. But, if it would make you feel better, let's stop and switch the scabbard to my saddle. I can draw it fast enough if Allie quits on me."

" 'Allie'?" he asked.

"My revolver. I gave her a feminine version of my old boss's name. Allan J. Pinkerton."

"How about 'Pinkie'?" he asked.

"That would be a silly name for a gun," she said with a wry smile. "What do you call your revolvers?"

"My .44's or my Merwin & Hulbert's."

"You men have no sense of style. All you worry about is who is bigger, stronger or faster."

"Not me. All I worry about is who has the most beautiful pard. Which would be me."

"Let's go with your worry, then. I like it. Maybe you do have a sense of style," she said.

Once out of sight of the ranch house, they did a wide circle and approached what they thought was the west pasture from the back. They could see one man squatting by a campfire brewing coffee. His horse was standing, reins down.

About twenty scraggly cattle meandered about. The wind wafted in a blended odor of cattle and sweetgrass, not altogether unpleasant to the former California cowboy.

Pope tried not to think of himself as having been a cowboy. The gang operating around Tombstone ruined the term for most Westerners, though Earp and his men did a good job of decimating them. Or, murdering them, depending on which faction one followed.

"How do you think we should do this?" Sarah asked.

"We could keep the husband and wife looking for a ranch story, I guess," Pope proffered.

"Did Hite see you at the robbery?" she asked.

"No, I was not there. I don't think he saw me any-where. But, I cannot be sure."

"Well, keep your guns loose and we'll just ride in," Sarah said.

Hite looked up giving them a good look at him. It really seemed to be the fugitive they sought.

As they trotted towards him, the wind blew the tails back on both the man's and woman's coat. In the flash of a moment, Hite was able to see a badge and white handled gun on one and a gun belt on the woman. Something he had never seen in his forty-seven years.

Jacob Hite jumped on his horse and galloped off. Pope gave his horse spur-less heels and the chase was on. Sarah, forty pounds lighter, kept up with Pope's larger, faster horse.

Hite was a miserable excuse for a rider, as they had been told. Pope caught him quickly and yelled for him to stop. Hite did have spurs on his heels and used them, moving slightly ahead.

Pope urged every bit of speed available out of the livery horse and caught the fugitive.

He reached out with both hands to grab Hite and caused him to fall off. Hite was large and muscular, and as he fell, he pulled Pope with him. Both hit the Arizona sand hard.

Pope rolled when he fell, like a wrangler. Hite reacted like a fighter who had taken a hard punch.

Sarah pulled up her pinto in time to prevent running over both.

Hite head-butted Pope in the chest, knocking him over on his side.

Sarah pulled her Colt and squeezed the trigger to a resounding "click." She pulled it again and the trigger clicked, but the cylinder did not turn. The Lightning had died. At the worst possible time.

Pope hit Hite in the side of the head with as much energy as he could put behind his fist. This was becoming life and death, so he could not protect his gun hand. It had to protect him.

He slugged Hite on the other side of his head with his left fist. Hite just sat there looking at Pope like the Wells Fargo man was crazy.

He hit Pope with a left, then a right. The detective wavered in his similar seated position.

Sarah slid off the horse and used the useless revolver as a two pound hammer to the side of Hite's head.

Hite shook his head and slugged her in the stomach. She doubled up and vomited breakfast on him.

Pope stood up, shakily, with his iron handcuffs in his right hand like bigger, heavier brass knuckles. He swung his fist and connected with Hite's jaw, breaking it decisively. The next punch took out Hite's left collar bone. A boot in the kidneys finished Hite for the day, but it toppled the semiconscious Pope on top of Sarah.

Dazed still, he mumbled, "I've thought about this ever since I met you."

"What? Kissing a woman who just threw up?" She then started laughing at the situation and he joined in.

He controlled his mirth long enough to handcuff Hite in the front and tie Hite's lariat around his waist with a slip-knot to the rear where he could not untie it.

She poured water from his canteen into the palm of her hand and swished it in her mouth before spitting it on the ground. She wiped her mouth on her sleeve.

"Well, that was pretty ladylike wasn't it?" she asked.

"Does it mean I can kiss you now?" Pope asked.

"If you can kiss me after seeing me at my worst, you are either in love or an idiot. I never took you for an idiot, so kiss away."

He took her in his arms and kissed her long and hard. Kissed her in a way she had long dreamed someone would.

Hite interrupted by mumbling something.

They turned and he said it again through his broken jaw. It sounded like "doctor."

Pope told him to mount up. He did, as did the two detectives.

Pope took the loose end of the lariat tied around Hite's waist and gave it one wrap around his saddle horn.

"Hey, Hite?" Hite mumbled something else unintelligible.

"If you try to run with this rope on my saddle horn, it will pull you off backwards. And, if that happens and you live through it, I will keep you tied on and drag your ass through every sticky thing I can find on the way back to Prescott. You got that?"

Hite mumbled something sounding highly profane. In view of a lady being present, Pope did not ask him to repeat it. He did, however, give a resounding jerk on the lariat almost unseating his prisoner as a reminder.

They turned the prisoner in to the Yavapai County sheriff with the paperwork for his extradition.

"I have a galvanized bath tub," Sarah began.

"You can use it. But, since you are dirtier, you have to use it second."

"Will it be proper for us to bathe at the same time?"

"For one thing, I was not thinking of us sharing it… yet, at least. For another thing, there is no need in you trying to act modest. The entire seat of your trousers has been ripped out since the beginning of the fight."

Pope looked down and turned red. She was right. His trousers were as trashed as her revolver.

"Make you a deal!" he said.

"If it involves where you will sleep tonight, don't push it. The day is only part over."

"No, it involves me buying you a new revolver."

"You have a deal, cowboy!"

"They rode to her house, where she got off to heat water for the tub.

He led her horse and turned in both livery horses. Both his hands were swollen as he trudged back to her house, his saddlebags over one shoulder, his carbine and its scabbard over the other.

Pope knocked on the door and heard a faint "Come in," from the back of the small house.

He set the items down and walked to the rear.

Sarah was in the tub, submerged almost to her bare shoulders. Since she was so clean to begin with, the water was clear and Pope got to see how very perfect she really was.

"Stop goggling and please wash my back. I feel like I have bugs all over it from rolling around in the damn pasture."

She handed him a wash cloth and he washed her back. For far longer than its initial cleanliness required.

"Since you are behind me, why don't you get ready for the bath. When it's time for me to step out, you can hand me a towel. I only have one, so we will have to share."

"All right," he stuttered. She smiled broadly, her mouth out of sight.

"Are you ready, John?"

"I am. Here's your towel," he said as he handed her the wash cloth.

"Thank you," she said as she stood up and faced him, the six inch square of cotton dangled from two fingers in front of her hiding exactly nothing.

She looked down and smiled broader.

"Time for you to get in, cowboy."

He did and got his back washed. Having rolled around in the dirt with Hite, he did make the water much cloudier as he sat and washed.

Sarah left and returned with a cotton wrap, hiding details but displaying curves.

"Can I keep you as a pard?" he asked.

"At least for tonight," she responded. "beyond tonight is up to James Hume tomorrow."

"I suspect you are correct about your future," Pope agreed, the flirting aside for a while.

"Are you hungry?" she asked.

"Not really. The bath helped, but I'm more stiff, sore, and tired than anything."

"If you stayed here tonight, could you just hold me and nothing else?" she asked seriously.

"Not even a kiss?"

"Kisses are allowed. Just nothing more."

"I agree to your rules. You can trust my word over about anything in your life, Sarah."

"I believe I can. Let's go to bed and test your word."

She fell asleep on his shoulder, his arm around her. His arm began to tingle after half an hour, but he did not care. He was sore and tired, but wide awake. He did not care about his pain or fatigue either. Only one thing worried him. He may have found the perfect woman. And, probably tomorrow she will become an associate, traveling around the country in a dangerous job. He would rather have her running a Wells Fargo office in

San Francisco and coming home to him every night. Every night he was at home, he admitted. It never occurred to him she might want him to be at home awaiting her arrival from solving a case across the country.

The next morning, the two were still comfortable with each other. No first night regrets or nervousness. They went back to the sheriff's office and found Hite had been charged with train robbery per the agreement and the extradition order was moving forward. Once approved, a Wells Fargo detective would transport him back for trial. With any luck, it might be the two detectives who just learned how much they enjoyed working together.

The next stop was a gun shop. Sarah settled on a S&W First Model double action in the popular .44 Russian caliber. She got a nickel plated one with a four inch barrel. As a backup, she got the smaller frame one in .38 S&W caliber. The .44 fit in her existing holster. She selected a smaller holster for the backup. Sarah requested three boxes of each size cartridge. Pope made good on his offer and proudly paid for the purchases.

A visit to the Wells Fargo office updated them on Hume's anticipated arrival around dinner.

Pope rented a one-horse buggy and they drove north halfway to where they captured Hite and found a safe place to fire Sarah's new revolvers. She was inherently accurate. The trigger pull on the double actions were long and a bit stiff, but Pope promised they would soften after fifty or a hundred rounds each. He wore his

.44's on the belt holster and practice drawing and firing after Sarah had shot. She was impressed with his speed and accuracy, especially knowing it had kept him alive in the past. And, knowing the speed was hampered by swollen hands from hitting Hite.

On the way back, they discussed family lives. He told her about his mountain man grandfather with the small ranch in California. She asked about places to live in the Bay Area. He said he had a room, but it was getting too cramped. He planned to try to find a small house like hers to rent. She asked why he did not wish to buy.

"We are so far flung now, Hume is beginning to assign detectives to large offices outside San Francisco. So, I am not sure when I might be dispatched on a semi-permanent basis. The same may be true for you after a year in headquarters. I think we will both learn a bit tonight and tomorrow from the chief detective.

They spread a cloth in the rear bed of the buggy and cleaned all three revolvers and reloaded them.

On the way back, Sarah reached over and took his hand and held it for the remainder of the return. Luckily, Pope was able to control the buggy with one sore hand..

Her career options and their relationship as a result of the upcoming meeting was an unsaid source of worry to both. Things had happened quickly. But, in the West, this tended to be the norm. Neither worried about the speed of the evolving relationship, just the outcome. Something which would largely be beyond their control.

CHAPTER 5

Chief Detective James Hume stepped off the dusty stage, his black suit spotless and his derby hat at its usual jaunty angle. He was a handsome man in his middle years. He wore a perfectly groomed handlebar mustache.

"Sir," Pope greeted him as Hume presented his hand.

"May I present former Pinkerton detective Sarah Watson?"

"Miss Watson, it is an honor. Let me get my bag and we'll step into the office for a moment and perhaps all enjoy dinner together?"

"That would be delightful, sir," she agreed.

He took a carpet bag from the jehu and rejoined them. He greeted the office manager and found he did not have telegrams waiting.

Sarah recommended a hotel with both a saloon and attached dining room. She noted she would not be allowed in the former.

Hume checked into the hotel and took his bag up to his room.

Pope made reservations for three in the restaurant portion and they were soon seated.

"I would be glad to make myself scarce if you'd like to speak with Miss Watson privately," Pope said.

"Perhaps in a little while. In the meantime, let's get a report on your arrest of the final member of the California train robbers. You trailed this Hite person many a mile, John. I notice your hands are swollen and you have a couple of facial bruises. I take it he did not come willingly?"

"He was a bit hesitant. Miss Watson accompanied me and was able to help me at a crucial time by applying her revolver to the side of his head," Pope said.

"And, Miss Watson, did said application end the fisticuffs?"

"Hardly slowed him at all, sir. It gave John time to begin battering him. Hite was a lumberjack and apparent lifetime brawler. He was as tough a customer as I ever saw in my Pinkerton days. But, he met his match with Detective Pope."

"Indeed. I am curious. If it came to such an impasse, why not shoot him, since you had your revolver in hand?" Hume asked.

"My revolver picked that moment to die a silent death."

"And, what type was it?"

"A Colt .38 Lightning model, sir."

"Ahhh....well, I understand now. Have you re-placed it?" he asked.

She moved her jacket aside and he saw the S&W holstered on a belt beneath the right side of the jacket. He nodded, clearly in agreement with her choice.

"Being a curmudgeon as John will quickly attest, I have carried my 1862 Pocket Navy, converted to .38 rimfire, since I bought it as a new cap n' ball. I liked it so much I had it converted to cartridge. It may be small and underpowered, but it has never let me down," Hume noted.

Understanding a good nod beat chancing saying the wrong thing, Sarah nodded sagely.

Hume, one of the greatest people readers extant, knew exactly what she was doing and added a plus in her column in this preliminary interview.

"And, John, how goes the extradition?" Hume asked.

"Well enough, boss. I am told we should be able to transport Hite back to California within a week. Would you like me to bring him back?"

"Yes, you and one other. This man is apparently brut-ish. He may require two guards in the interest of safety."

"Miss Watson. At the risk of embarrassing you with praise, I would like to share two telegrams before I ask John to step into the saloon portion and enjoy a beer while we talk turkey. First, take a look at this one I sent a few days ago to your former mentor, Allan J. Pinkerton."

He passed her a telegram. Knowing how stubborn and mercurial the Scotsman could be, she had some apprehension.

The telegram from was from Hume to Pinkerton, and its wording suggested the two were on a fairly conversational basis.

"Allan Stop I will interview Sarah Watson for detective Stop What say you Stop J Hume"

"Nothing fascinating there, I am sure you both will agree. Here is his response," Hume said as he slid another telegram over to her.

"James Stop Excellent detective Stop Hire her Stop Allan"

Hume was not boastful when he made his next statement, rather he was as brutally honest as his reputation.

"There it is. Allan J. Pinkerton. Maybe the best detective in America. Or, maybe the second best. But, he endorses you. And knowing the little scoundrel, this is as lavish as he gets."

Sarah responded in perfect Scottish brogue, rolling her "R's."

"Aye, it is sir" Hume smiled and suggested Pope go enjoy a glass of beer for ten minutes.

He thoroughly enjoyed the beer. It was actually frigid, something not always found in the West. He thought about buying a bucket of the cold beer to soak his hands. Further, his only worry was not whether Hume would offer Sarah a job as detective, but whether the location and money would entice her to take it.

As was his wont, he positioned himself to watch the two. He had also become fairly adept at reading lips.

But, lip reading was not necessary eight minutes later when both smiled and shook hands. He looked down at his beer and raised his head as Hume motioned him back to the table.

"Well, John, I did not ask your opinion because I read your telegram and have been watching you carefully. I did not need to ask. It is obvious you hold the young lady in high esteem."

"Miss, or rather Detective Watson, will join our merry band. She has to give a week notice at her current position. The week tallies well with the extradition timing. She will be your second detective guard for transporting Hite back. I want him in leg irons in addition to nippers."

"Further, her years as a Pinkerton detective count for a lot with me. She is coming in as a full detective, not a trainee."

"Now, here's what I want of the two of you. I want you, John, to introduce her around. Any malarkey from anyone about a female, I want to know about it right away. I want you to show her the ropes. Sarah, I want you to share Pinkerton techniques with John. In instances where they are better approaches than ours,

I want the two of you to develop training on them. Show it to me, and I will approve you conducting the training. After a while and I am not sure how long the while will be, you will both go out into large offices as regional detectives. I may have to pull one or both of you back to headquarters at some point to be a senior detective just under me. Therefore, I do not recommend buying property, unless you can count on selling it in a bad market."

"I see a chemistry between you two. I can't fight nature. And, I've never understood cupid. Just keep it professional and hidden to the best of your abilities, alright?"

Both nodded. Neither protested.

"Now, I kinda figured I'd need this, so I thought ahead."

James Hume produced a gold Wells Fargo detective badge and handed it to Sarah.

"Normally, I'd pin it on a new detective. But, under the circumstance of you sporting a new S&W under your jacket, I will let you do the honors yourself," Hume said.

Taking a chance with impropriety, Sarah asked Pope to pin it on.

He did. Very carefully.

"Congratulations, Detective Watson. Welcome to Wells Fargo!" Hume said with genuine pride.

"I'll not let you down, sir," she said with more than a hint of emotion in her voice.

Perhaps the proudest one at the table was Pope.

"Now, Pope, I want a detailed report summarizing your interims. From a synopsis of the train robbery to each take down. You may collaborate on the portion here in Arizona Territory up to the point where the two of you depart to deliver the prisoner back to California for trial. I don't need to remind you again, this man will take any opportunity to use his strength and guile against you. Do whatever you have to do to protect yourselves."

"Yessir. We will," Pope assured him.

The waiter came with coffee and Hume ordered fresh cherry pie for all in celebration of a case closed and a new detective on board.

"Well, now, detectives. I have business back in California and must be getting to it. My longtime friend, Detective Morse of the Morse Detective Agency and our Detective Thacker have been working with me on this stage robber who has left several poems for us to enjoy. Pope, I believe you have read reports about him. He is called Black Bart and robs frequently along the Siskiyou Trail, anywhere from north of San Francisco up to Oregon.

He's getting to be quite a nuisance and the owners have been on my case over his continued successes. The two of you may have a shot at him if my two most senior detectives fail to arrest him."

Hume paid the bill and they walked with him to the Wells Fargo office, where the two detectives bade farewell to the chief detective.

Pope noted on the way back, Sarah's smile, always beautiful, was constant today.

"You look pretty darn happy to be back in the saddle again," he noted.

"I am. And, I will always be in your debt for the contribution you've made for this."

"I will always endeavor to keep you happy," he said and won an even brighter smile.

The train robbery and ensuing pursuit up to the California-Nevada border and back to Arizona Territory had been a protracted case. It took a day to write the report and post it to Hume in San Francisco.

After, they awaited final approval of Hite's extradition. The Attorney General for the Territory, since it was a federal territory, called upon the US Marshal to deputize Pope for the trip back. He did so, however refusing to deputize a woman. The deputation came in the form of a signed warrant making it effective only for the delivery of the prisoner, who had fled across a state line to avoid prosecution. It expired upon Popes delivery of Hite to the US Marshal in San Diego.

Pope knew Sarah was furious over the refusal to deputize her, but she held her thoughts to herself. Instead, she worked her week of notice at the property and tax office. At her urging, Pope moved out of his hotel room and to her cottage.

Pope went to the Wells Fargo office and secured two medium padlocks each with two keys. He took these to a blacksmith and ordered ankle irons connected by a foot and a half chain. These with his handcuffs, or "nippers," should restrict Hite's movements during the trip to San Diego by stage. They would take the stage to Blythe again, but then transfer to a southbound stage to San Diego.

He held off on getting tickets until the Attorney General's office gave him a specific date for the extradition to become effective.

Pope took the trashed suit from the fight with Hite to a cleaners and they agreed to clean it and try to repair the split trousers.

He stopped by and picked up the person he now regularly introduced as his partner for lunch.

"Not too long until Friday," he observed.

"I know. I am ready to get started. On our instructing, I guess I need to learn Wells Fargo's investigative methods so I will know what would be new to introduce from the Pinkerton Agency," she said.

"Makes sense. We use sketches and photographs of suspects, measurements of foot prints, comparison of bullets to rifled barrels on revolvers and rifles and a book with pictures of the people we think or know have committed crimes against us. We do studies of robberies of a type over time. For instance, I did a paper on train robberies since the war. Each of us carries an investigative kit. The contents differ by detective, but notebook and pencil, sketch pad, magnifying glass, tweezers, pocket knife and evidence sacks are common items," Pope said.

"Our work was so diverse, we really did not carry investigative kits much.

I guess the big difference is Pinkerton is hired to investigate anything. Theft, murder, kidnapping, union issues, plus the robberies and embezzlements Wells Fargo investigates. Wells Fargo only investigates crimes against its interests."

"That's true, Sarah. So, we are pretty much looking at stage, train, messenger and office robberies and maybe the odd embezzlement. Sometimes, they spill over into cases with sworn agencies. We focus on our specialties and occasionally have to go undercover. I would think a Pinkerton detective would spend a lot of time undercover."

"We did, John. A lot. It was exciting at first, but both boring and dangerous as time went on. I won't miss the undercover work at all," Sarah said.

"Allan Pinkerton wrote some good books on detecting. I have read most if not all," Pope said.

"Haha and I have not read any of them. But, I trust he and his sons used the texts for the training we received in Chicago as rookie detectives."

"Do you have any of the training materials you could use in developing a plan with me to train our folks?"

"No, they rather scrupulously picked them up after each class. But, I remember most of the content."

"Perhaps writing it down will give it order for our training," Pope suggested. Sarah nodded.

"Will you be my boss, John?" she asked hesitatingly.

"No. Not at all. I may be one of the detectives you shadow for orientation purposes. We all report to James Hume. He keeps his hand in everything. Detective Thacker is most senior below Hume. There are a very few others who are deeply undercover. Most of them are long-timers. I may have quickly risen to the number three level. But, who knows? If Hume is not available, Hume's assistant parcels assignments to Thacker or sometimes me to make," Pope said.

"I am glad you are close to the top. You are awfully young for it. Are the others older? Forties or fifties?"

"They are. I am only twenty-seven. I reckon my rising up the ladder has been a trial by fire."

"As in gunfire?" She asked, receiving a nod. She took his hand again. It was something he enjoyed and she seemed to do it more every day.

Pope looked at his vest pocket watch with his free hand, not wanting to give up Sarah holding the other.

"I guess it is time to walk you back to your office," he said.

Late in the afternoon, the assistant to the Attorney General of Arizona Territory advised him he could have Jacob Hite on Saturday.

Pope went to the Wells Fargo office and purchased stage tickets for the three of them to go to San Diego. Once there and they turned Hite over to the US Marshal in San Diego, he would get two stage tickets to where the current track was completed, then they could take a train all the way through Los Angeles and on to San Francisco.

In discussing the move after dinner, he found Sarah did not have much more than he did in the way of household goods or clothes. They got a travel trunk, filled it and expressed it to his attention at the rooming house in San Francisco the following morning. For the next two days, even coffee would have to be purchased out and Sarah would be limited on costume changes.

Sarah gave up her deposit on the small house in Prescott, without any concern and the two picked up Hite from the Yavapai sheriff on Saturday morning. The US Marshal was there to observe the transfer of his prisoner.

Normally, Pope would sit by the door and have the shackled prisoner towards the middle of the four person seat. He always chose the rear seat so he could shoot forward, should a robbery or break-out attempt occur. But, he did not want the felon to sit pressed against Sarah. Even with leg irons and handcuffs, he could quickly injure her.

As a precaution, due to the close seating, Pope got the black jack or sap out of his investigation bag and slipped it into his right jacket pocket. He was wear-ing the newly cleaned and repaired suit from his last interaction with Hite. This time, he would kill the bastard instead of fighting with him. But, he did not want to fire shots in the coach. Especially with Sarah next to the prisoner. She wore her revolver on the opposite side from where Hite was sitting, which made it difficult for him to grab it.

Pope suggested she not wear the backup .38, but carry it in her purse and keep it also on the opposite side from the prisoner.

They discussed escape attempts often occurred during privy breaks during team changes at way stations. Sarah would have to be the backup from a distance.

Pope checked the manifest for the stage from Prescott to the California line. Three other passengers. They were a woman, her husband and another unrelated man. He would seat them on the opposite side for their safety. Sarah would speak with them privately before the stage departed from Prescott.

Hite's cousins were present at his transfer. Sarah took them aside and asked, for the prisoner's safety, if they knew of anyone who might try to spring him during the delivery to San Diego.

They were crude taciturn people. The woman's comment was so unladylike Sarah had to restrain herself from slapping her silly. But, she considered the source and reported back to Pope she learned had nothing new. In their private talks, Pope told her his investigation of Hite convinced him the man was a loner with a personality disorder not endearing him to much of anybody. He doubted Hite would have friends who cared enough about him to try to set him free. Nonetheless, the two Wells Fargo detectives organized the escort just as if they expected a gang to try to free him with violence.

******

Most of the Concords had two places to carry the green "treasure" boxes. One was under the driver's or jehu's seat. The other was bolted under the rear passenger seat where Hite would be sitting. Pope borrowed another set of handcuffs from the US Marshal and put one wrist cuff on the eye-bolt where a lock box would be bolted and the other on the chain beneath the big bruiser's ankles.

Hite started the trip loud and profane. Pope warned him there were ladies present and he told Pope something that even embarrassed the hardened lawman. After several warnings were ignored, Pope slammed the blackjack against his neck just below the base of Hite's skull. His head drooped onto his chest and he remained unconscious for a half hour.

Hite was recalcitrant but quiet for the next several hours, only complaining he could not rub his sore neck with the cuffs on. Pope told him if he did not shut up, he would be assisted with another forced nap.

Pope and Sarah had spoken with the jehu and shotgun messenger about the prisoner and one more topic of great concern. The army had shared with the US Marshal and the Yavapai sheriff about a Chiricahua chief named Juh leading Apache war parties throughout the region. While a stage had not been attacked by hostile war parties for seven years, it appeared to be a serious risk now.

Sarah positioned Pope's cased Greener shotgun and his Winchester 1873 on her right side, near the door. The floor chain on Hite would prevent him from getting to them.

They made it through six stage stations and team changes until the stage's passengers heard the jehu yelling to his team and cracking his whip loudly. Something as surely afoot as the two Wells Fargo detectives looked at one another.

Pope stuck his head out of the door window and peered backwards. Indians! There were approximately twelve. They were on ponies and closing in fast, rifles held high.

"We are under attack by an Indian war party! Probably Chiricahua Apaches. Gentlemen, are you armed?" Neither was. Pope told the woman and two men to crouch in the floor between the seats.

Sarah passed him the rifle and a box of cartridges. She took the shotgun out and slid two massive buckshot shells into the twin bores.

Pope looked over at her and grinned. She looked back, but with a serious expression. He did not think she was scared, just concerned. "This could get very messy," he thought.

"But, you have fought Indians before, right?"

"I have. But, remember I was only ten and had my grandfather coaching me."

"Well, now you have me, cowboy, so let's get on with it."

"If I get an arrow through the head, I love you," he said.

"Stop it! The arrow part. The other part you can continue."

"Would you two shut the hell up? I could get killed here," Hite added.

"You shut up, or one of the Indian bullets may come from my gun," Sarah told him.

Pope leaned out of the door window. He could see the buckshot from the shotgun messenger knocking up dust in the road well ahead of the war party. He stuck the Winchester out and fired.

Regrettably, his first round hit a pony. The animal went down in front of several others, tripping one, but dumping three braves in the dirt. One was struck by a horse behind him and rolled over without moving.

Pope levered and fired, hitting another brave on a pony and two of the ones on the ground. Nine left.

Instead of backing off, the braves sped up and closed the gap. They began to fire and bullets went

"Thwack" against the back and body of the stage. None penetrated. Yet.

The braves got within fifty feet. Pope passed the Winchester to Sarah and Hite grabbed for it.

Pope slammed the forearm of the Winchester into his throat and Hite slumped gagging and gasping for air.

Sarah took the carbine and box of ammunition and began to reload it.

Pope leaned out again, this time with a .44 and squeezed off several shots. One more fell. Eight threats remained.

One brave rode to the right, away from Pope. He grabbed the door beside Sarah. She unclasped it and pushed it open. The brave swung outwards and she shot him with her bigger revolver. He let go and rolled under the stage which bumped over him. The stage almost rolled, but the jehu keep the dusty side down with great skill.

Another brave took the right side, but was greeted with a face full of buckshot from the shotgun messenger and fell backwards off his pony. Six remained.

A remaining brave shot the left rear team horse and he stumbled in his harness. The stage went out of control despite the jehu's best efforts. The shotgun messenger dropped his namesake weapon to hold on for dear life as the stage swerved from side-to-side in a cloud of dust.

The stage rolled. The jehu let go the ribbons and jumped as far clear as he could. He was on the right and it rolled to the right, but missed rolling over him. The messenger cleared the wheels coming over towards him and landed in the center of the road.

Five of the six people inside the stage tumbled together, but they and their limbs all stayed inside. The stage came to rest on its right side in the grass beside the road, terrified horses screaming.

The stage lay on the right door. The left door was facing skyward.

The male passenger, who was traveling alone, pushed the door open. He leveraged his body up into the door and was shot by a brave.

He fell back in on top of the wife.

Pope quickly jumped up and fired a reloaded Merwin & Hulbert at the brave, killing him.

Pope felt a hand on his leg. It was Sarah who was climbing up his body to get to the opening. Her nose was bleeding, but he did not see any further wounds.

She made it to the door opening and turned right. He had the left.

Sarah shot a brave on her side and he died on the spot. Four remained.

She got the husband below to hand her the rifle and box of cartridges.

Seeing the availability of the Winchester Model 1873 carbine, Pope tossed the Merwin & Hulbert to the jehu, who had lost his revolver in the melee.

He used Pope's gun to kill the third remaining

Indian as the two last braves jumped him.

Pope rolled over the side of the stage and landed on the ground. He dived into the wrestling men on the dirt. He swung the blackjack with all the strength he had and soon the threats were neutralized.

"Are you okay?" he asked the jehu.

"I am. Just a trifle sore from the hard bounce. The shotgun messenger came limping around the stage with his recovered scattergun, injured but ready for action.

"I gotta take care of these horses!" the jehu said. The messenger helped him begin to unhook them from the coach and cut the harness off the one dead and one wounded horse. The jehu used Pope's revolver to put the poor animal out of misery.

Pope helped Sarah to the ground. She was unhurt except for bumping her nose against him in the roll.

"How about the others?" he asked.

"The man traveling alone is dead. The couple are too shaken up to climb out right now. I am not sure about Hite. Nothing out of his big mouth."

"We better check on the Indians first. I don't want to be killed by one who was playing possum on us," Pope said.

All were dead. The ponies had run off. Pope disarmed them and piled the weapons. In his estimation, none were worth saving for anything except evidence. He found some .44-40 cartridges and confiscated those to replenish the ones he had used.

The Wells Fargo men had the horses settled. The stage, if not damaged would be fine for the remainder with a four-horse team. The harness and hitch were salvageable, though the dead horse had to be cut out. They took a line from the gear in the back and climbed up.

"Y'all inside want to try to get out before I use part of the team to right the stage? Or, you can stay inside. Your call," the jehu asked.

"Ask them about the prisoner," Pope requested.

"Oh, and how's the man in chains?"

"He hasn't moved since the rollover," the husband said. "We will stay in here while you dump her back onto the wheels," he added.

The jehu tied the rope around the door and door jamb and climbed back down. With Pope and the shotgun messenger helping push from the other side, he used a two-horse team to pull the Concord stage right side up. He checked the wheels, large in back and smaller in front. They seemed all right to him.

The couple climbed down from the righted stage and Pope got in to check on his prisoner.

Hite had a pulse, but was unconscious. Pope slapped him on the face a couple of times. He was only mildly responsive. The detective dismounted from the stage and shrugged at Sarah and the two other employees.

"I don't know if he's in a coma, or what. We will just have to watch him. He may have broken his neck in the rollover. I just don't know what to think…" he said to them.

"I see the shogun. Did you find all your weapons?" Pope asked. They had. "Any treasure aboard?" he followed up.

"No, an odd run without it. But, we didn't have a cent. If you look, there ain't no green box under my seat. I know you know about nothing under the passenger seat inside, 'cause you hooked that fella up to the hasp in there," the jehu said. Pope nodded and helped the two reconnect the now four-horse team.

"I have spoken with the couple. They are shaken up, but not injured. They said they never saw people shoot so well as us!"

"That brave swinging on your door was a moving target and you sure plugged Ma'am," the shotgun messenger commented.

"To paraphrase a Greek philosopher named Plato, 'necessity is the mother of accuracy,'" Sarah replied. Pope had never heard either iteration of the proverb before, but he decided to remember it for further use.

"For the record, we are leaving twelve bodies on the ground here," Pope said.

Within about an hour, Hite recovered consciousness. He still was having a difficult time focusing and did not make much sense when he tried to talk.

It took them until the third team change station to find one with telegraph capability. Pope wired to headquarters to advise the army about the attack and its location, as close as he could determine.

Hite still needed to be steadied when walking to the next stage. He remained the same when turned over to the US Marshal in San Diego.

The two detectives compiled a report for the Marshal and Hume about the attack, the stage rollover and Hite's apparent injury. When the stage rolled, the passengers were thrown about, except for the chained prisoner. Hite slammed back and forth against the hard wooden rear of the coach. Pope was pretty sure it was those hits causing his current issues and wrote it into his report.

The marshal accepted the report and read through it.

"Hite was injured when the stage rolled over and has been a bit off, since?" he asked.

"Yes, sir. He's a cagey one. It may be well to have a regular or a head doctor take a look at him before the trial. He might be trying to pull something. Or, he may have actually gotten injured. I am not qualified to say. He was not bleeding, so there was nothing we could do. And, we had a war party coming down on us at the time. You are welcome to their weapons. They are in the rear of the stage for evidence in case anybody wanted proof Indians attacked us," Pope explained.

"No issue as far as I am concerned, detective. The red stage is full of bullet holes. It's pretty plain somebody attacked you. And, you have a dead passenger. No powder burns on his face where the bullet hit. So, it was fired from a distance. When I got the telegram, I spoke with the office manager here in town. He also told me you were not carrying any express money on this trip.

If there is a shame about anything, it is this man is going to carry the sentence for the whole robbery," the US Marshal noted.

"At least he will be doing it alive. The gang is, as far as we know, too dead for prosecution other than him," Sarah said.

"That's true, detective. Hard to prosecute a dead man. Deputies, get this man over to the doctor we use before taking him to the lockup. Let's see what his story really is.

Detectives, I hope your next escort is less exciting. But, it sounds like some real good shooting was done," the US Marshal said.

They shook hands and Hite was taken to the doctor. Pope expected to be called back to San Diego for the trial. Possibly Sarah too, now she was a Wells Fargo detective.

"I reckon the whole case file cannot be closed until Hite is sentenced for train robbery and goes to jail. But, for practical purposes, we solved it and can move on to other things until we have to return to testify," Pope said. "The tracks north don't get us to Los Angeles, much less San Francisco. So, it is another stage for us to Los Angeles, then a train to our headquarters city," he said.

The green-eyed beauty leaned over and whispered "I look forward to the train. I think the stage, even before it rolled over, bruised my bottom parts something fierce. I wonder if there is a place nearby with liniment I could buy?"

Pope slipped out while Sarah was at the Wells Fargo office and made sure there was liniment available to rub on her after dinner. First, he wanted to eat a decent meal. Arm in arm, they went to Earp's saloon. Women were not allowed in the saloon, but could go to the restaurant portion where Pope had eaten before. While they did not eat at the table with the proprietor, he came over and welcomed them.

Though both were charming at the brief meeting, Sarah confided something about the sometimes lawman bothered her. Pope agreed. They also agreed the food was excellent.

Having just carried saddlebags and two long gun scabbards, Pope did not have much to take to the hotel. With her carpet bag in hand and her trunk sent ahead, Sarah had less.

They got two adjacent rooms. There was no connecting door.

Sarah let her glossy black hair down and brushed her teeth before tapping on Popes door. He greeted her with a big grin and a bottle of liniment held high in one hand.

She walked to the bed and discarded her dress and tossed the night gown she carried on top of it. Sarah lay unadorned on the bed on her stomach. Her bottom was actually bruised, so Pope rubbed liniment into it and her back. She was asleep in the middle of the bed within minutes, arms akimbo and snoring lightly.

He smiled at her and watched his probably next fifty or so years as she slept. He found another blanket in the wardrobe and curled up on the floor beside the bed and went to sleep.

Somewhere around midnight, she tapped him on the shoulder and motioned for him to join her up in the small bed. Sarah pressed her warm length against him and was asleep instantly. Pope was awake longer, happy over this unexpected addition in his life. Grandpa would love her.

*****

They made it back to San Francisco the next day. On the way, they discussed living arrangements. It would be ideal to have one small house, but the address conflict would be apparent at the office. They decided to try to find adjoining rooms or small apartments with a connecting door. Hume would cover her expenses for a hotel until she could get settled, so they found one once they arrived in San Francisco. Sarah decided to leave her trunk at the headquarters building until she really needed the contents. While she was settling into the hotel, Pope went home and checked availability at his rooming house. There was none. He checked the neighborhood and found a possible for her to review. A two-story building with outside entrance to a second floor had a small apartment with a kitchen, living room and bedroom. It had an adjoining bedroom available with a connecting door. The price was about the same as two rooming house rooms.

Pope put a refundable deposit down to hold it several days until he could bring Sarah to see it and pass judgement.

On Monday, they arrived at Wells Fargo from different directions.

Pope went to his desk and started going through mail and message notes from the clerk for the headquarters detectives.

CHAPTER 6

Sarah planned on reporting to James Hume.

But, he waylaid her outside the building and motioned her to follow him. He went to a small restaurant where he had a table in the rear. He already had a pot of coffee and tray of pastries waiting.

"I realize this is a bit irregular, but I need to see you before you enter the building and become a known Wells Fargo detective," he said as he poured two cups of coffee.

"I am afraid I am going to have to send you on an undercover assignment before you have a chance to meet everyone or become acclimated to our operation. But, I have to ask you a question first."

"Go ahead sir," she responded.

"Would you be uncomfortable going undercover with John, portraying man and wife? Before you answer, I believe him to be a man of high moral responsibility."

"Sir, at the risk of getting fired before I ever start, John and I have feelings for each other. We don't know where they will go. Our careers here may help determine what happens with us.

But, to answer your question, there is nobody in the world I would rather portray a wife to than John Pope. And, I would and have trusted him with my life. You should have seen him fighting a brawler and then shooting during the Indian attack. He is one terribly dangerous but wonderful man."

"Sarah, I am glad to hear you being so candid with me. I hope you are equally candid throughout a long career. This is a good company and is loyal to its employees. If you and Pope get married at some point, one of you might have to run an office while the other is a detective in the same town. I don't think I can offer the flexibility of sending both out on cases in opposite directions.

But, I wanted to ask you about the undercover job separately. Since you concur, I will keep your detective status secret even here in the office. You will see why when I brief you both on the case later in the morning. For now, do not move into a desk. I will meet with you at a restaurant where I interviewed and hired John. He will know where it is. Go to your hotel. He will pick you up there at eleven o'clock and you two will proceed to the meeting place."

Hume went on to his office and settled in behind his desk. After a while, he stepped to the door and asked his secretary to come in

"Get Detective Pope to come in, please," he said.

"John, I want you to go to the hotel and get Sarah and the two of you meet me secretly at the Tadich Grill just after eleven today. This is an irregular case and I want you to hold it close to the vest. Do not share with a soul. I will fill you both in at the Grill."

Pope picked up Sarah and they walked down to California Street to the Tadich Grill. Sarah said it might be prudent to not speak of the reason they were meeting their boss in public.

The manager sat them at a reserved table. Hume had not arrived yet.

"We are going undercover and will be briefed as soon as he gets here. No one is to know I am Wells Fargo yet," Sarah said.

"What do you know about the case?" Pope asked.

"That we will be undercover as husband and wife. Hume got my permission first."

"It must be some sort of inside job. I have never seen him keep anything like a new detective from the rest of the men. This sounds very serious to me," Pope said.

"I got the same impression. We will find out shortly. I skipped breakfast. I hope the food is good at this place."

"It is particularly good when the boss picks up the bill there," Pope said. Sarah picked up a menu and saw why. It was more costly than a mere detective would usually choose.

Hume arrived and sat down.

"Thank you for meeting me here. You will see why I have chosen an irregular way to brief you once I begin speaking."

He poured himself a cup of coffee and passed the pot to Sarah.

"When I tell you about this case, only you, Mr. Wells, Mr. Fargo, the victim and I will know about it. And, of course the perpetrators."

Both detectives leaned forward unconsciously.

"Joseph Lane is the Deputy Superintendent. That means number four in the company. He is liked and highly respected both within the company and in the community. I have known Joe for some years and consider him a friend.

His sixteen year old daughter has been kidnapped. The letter says snipers are positioned near his house and if they see police arrive any time of the day, Joe and his wife and other children will be shot as well as his daughter Mattie. Joe was ordered to stay at home except for whatever trip he needs to make outside to arrange for the ransom. The letter demands twenty-five thousand dollars be readied in bearer bonds. Three days from now, Wednesday, further instructions will arrive regarding the delivery. I am assuming Wednesday will also be the delivery date.

We have to presume the people know me, so I cannot go there. Either the extortionists are outstandingly good, or it's an inside job. That is why I don't want Sarah identified as one of us yet.

John, you have developed a high profile within the company and SFPD as a good detective. We are going to have to disguise you. We will have theater makeup artists do the work on both of you. As soon as the note arrived and Joe called me, I thought of you two. I want you to portray a cousin and his wife who dropped in for an unannounced visit. Apparently such visits happen all too frequently in the Lane household," Hume said.

"So, we have two goals," Sarah began. "One is to locate and free the girl and two is to identify and bring down the extortionists, who may be insiders at the company, right?"

"Those are the overriding goals. You have some others. I want you there, armed and ready to protect the Lane's. I need someone inside the house to keep me apprised of what is going on. Particularly the next communication of when and how to pay the ransom. They have a large house with several live-in employees. Joe says they are trustworthy. I say nobody is trustworthy in this matter until you prove they are by your observation and questioning."

"Boss, how will we communicate with you?" Pope asked.

"So far, John, we have used notes picked up and delivered by the milkman, the egg man and the mailman."

"Sir, since the house may be watched, could we

string telegraph wires from a next door neighbor's house to communicate with the office?"

"Let me consider it a bit. We may not have enough time," Hume said thinking aloud.

"We will have to come and go without raising suspicions. I may be the best for that. Who would think a woman may be a detective, unfortunately?" Sarah said.

"Yes. You could go shopping for groceries daily with the cook. As a handyman cousin, I could go and pick up boards, tools, paint and the like. I could also do some gardening and try to detect any snipers. Mr. Lane could help with information about neighbors. You know….it could be a neighbor instead of an insider with the company," Pope said.

"That is possible. When I spoke with Joe, he said it was impossible, but who knows?" Hume said.

"If there was a sniper, boss, he would probably know where the girl, Mattie, was being kept. I could make him tell me what communication schedule he was on with the person holding her, then make him tell me where she was," Pope said.

"Yes, John, but we are getting ahead of ourselves here. If you had to kill him in self-defense, it could get the girl killed if the sniper does not make a check-in," Hume noted.

"Yes, it would have to be perfectly executed," Pope agreed. Jumping ahead to another topic, Pope asked "Boss, can you share who may be the insider?"

"Yes. There is a fellow in the Comptroller's office. He handles bonds for the company and is our resident expert on bearer bonds. I have looked at his salary compared with his lifestyle and they are 'way off. He is in debt over his head. His family has some unsavory characters. I have taken Thacker off Black Bart to watch him."

"Are we going from here to the makeup artists?" Pope asked.

"You are. I do not need to be there. Your personas will be a couple who is slightly older than your current ages and somewhat affluent. You should arrange to arrive by a hack as soon as possible. They know you are coming and will greet you as Cousin John Lane and wife, Sarah Lane."

"I will need a favor, boss," Pope asked.

"What is it?"

"An unarmed messenger to hand deliver a note."

"Alright, John. I trust your judgement sufficiently to not ask further. A messenger with identification will meet you outside of the theater where you will be made up. Make sure he sees you *before* you are made up." He handed Pope an envelope. In it was a note with the theater address and one hundred dollars in small bills for expenses.

"Sarah, since nobody in town knows you, use your discretion on whether or how much make up you need."

"Yessir. I will decide there."

"Good hunting, detectives. Keep my friend and his family safe and let us solve this one a soon as humanly possible."

Hume dropped a five on the table. It was more than enough to cover the coffee and pastries and left ahead of them.

Pope asked the maîtres'd for a pen and some note-paper and wrote for several minutes, filling two full sheets. Sarah, who had been taught to read upside down in the Pinkertons, watched as he addressed the envelope for the note to Israel Pope and wrote a ranch name and California town on it.

"Your grandfather?" she asked.

He grinned at her.

"Yes. Time to pull out the big gun. Until you, he's the only one I had when I needed help. This one may require my whole team!"

They left and went to the theater by foot. A messenger was already there and presented identification. Pope gave him the letter and more than sufficient cash for transportation to the ranch and back. He urged the man to deliver it as soon as possible today.

They walked around the block to a main street with him and once he was out of sight, returned to the theater.

Inside, the makeup artist and a costumer were waiting.

Sarah spoke with the latter and while Pope was getting his mustache and short hair dusted with a gray powder to age him, she walked out pregnant.

He did a double-take and she beamed.

"See, I told you sharing a malt with two straws was not a smart idea!"

"The benefit to the pillow pocket on the front of the dress is my ability to carry two guns where nobody will possibly see them. Smart, huh?"

"Brilliant, mother!" Pope exclaimed.

"Don't you look distinguished! If you are going to look that good in a decade or so, I will surely latch onto you now."

"I thought we were already latched."

She said nothing beyond her smile, which always communicated her intents to him.

Pope and Sarah flagged down a hack and had it wait outside both her hotel and his room while bags were hastily packed, then on to the Lane residence.

The neighborhood was very nice and all the houses were large and well-maintained. The cab stopped at a two-story home with a circular drive, a wraparound porch and dormered windows across the front. San Francisco Bay was several blocks away and they could smell the salt air.

They had the driver bring their bags to the front door, then paid him. Sarah rang the bell.

A maid came to the door and looked down quizzically at the bags.

"Hello, I am Joe's cousin John Lane from San Diego, here for a visit with my wife, Sarah."

"Please wait in the foyer. I will get Mr. Lane."

They could hear her speak to Joseph Lane in the parlor beyond the foyer.

"Mr. Lane, there is a John Lane who says he is your cousin here. His wife Sarah is with him. Are you expecting him?"

"Oh, yes, Millie. But, in a week. One of us got confused. No matter. Bring them in here and take any bags to one of the guest rooms."

As they came in, Lane, a stocky man in his late forties, feigned joy and hugged John and took Sarah's hand with a slight bow.

"My dear cousin, it's so good to see you. I thought you were coming next week! My mistake, surely."

"Well, here we are anyway! Joe, it is so good to see you. I don't believe you have met Sarah formally. She is the former Sarah Watson of Chicago. Worked with a friend of your man Hume's up there," Pope said.

The maid had left the room, but in an abundance of care, Lane just mouthed the word "Pinkerton?"

"Indeed! I am so happy to have her with me now. And, as you see, soon we'll have a baby for your little ones to play with. Speaking of the girls, how are they? Anything new?" Pope asked.

"No, Mattie, who is sixteen is away with friends for a while. We have not heard from her for a couple of days. Martha is here, she's eighteen now and quite the young lady. Oh! Here's Harriett. Sarah, this is my wife Harriett. Sarah is Cousin John's wife. You, of course know John from Martha's baptism years ago."

Pope was impressed how well Lane was playing his part, but could see stress painted all over his face.

He leaned forward and whispered "Is there a place we can meet with you, Harriett and Martha behind closed doors where the staff cannot hear?" Lane nodded.

"Harriett, could you have Millie put together a lunch for all of us? In the meantime, I'll get Martha and we will have an impromptu family visit."

Harriett left and returned shortly, as did Lane with a very pretty young lady. He introduced her to his temporary cousins and they adjourned to the library. He closed the door and all sat around a table. He turned to Pope to conduct the meeting.

"I am Detective John Pope with Wells Fargo. Before, I was a detective with the San Francisco Police. My partner is Sarah Watson. She is also a Wells Fargo detective. Before, she was an agent for the Pinkerton National Detective Agency. By the way, the tummy is a pillow which hides two guns. She is not with child. Our function is to both protect and investigate. We might have to ask questions you have been asked before. Nobody at Wells Fargo except the two owners and Chief Detective Hume knows we are here. We have to keep it confidential to be able to assist you the most. Sarah?"

"Thank you, John. We will portray husband and wife and are comfortable doing it. The pillow? Not so much! I would ask you to stay away from windows, especially at night. If you need to go out, take one of us with you. Joe and I have to get used to calling you Joe instead of Mr. Lane, what guns do you have in the house?" Sarah asked.

"A hunting rifle from before the war. It belonged to my father. A shotgun and a revolver I carry when I know I will have to work late."

"Plenty of ammunition?"

"A box or partial box for each."

"Please keep them loaded and close at hand. Have you been coming and going, other than Joe, who was told to hang around here?"

"No," Harriet spoke, "we have all stayed here."

"How was Mattie taken?" Sarah asked.

"From her bedroom in the night," Lane said.

"No sign of entry. Broken lock, scratch marks for jimmying?" Pope asked.

"None broken. I did not look further. And, Jim Hume knew not to come here, so you will be the first to examine them," Lane said.

"I will get my kit and look at them as soon as we finish here. I want to be careful around the help, in case the 'inside' part is here not at work," Pope said.

"Oh, I am sure our staff is not involved," Harriett said.

"We have to treat everyone like a suspect until

Mattie is safely back at home," Pope told them. "And, Harriett, please drop it to Millie I am owner of a lock shop in San Diego. It will provide cover for us when we are looking at the front and rear door locks.

Joe, was her window open or closed the night she was taken?"

"It was open."

"Perhaps after we look at the locks, you can pretend to give us the garden tour and we can see if there are places to reach the roof without a ladder and can get a young woman down the same way?" Pope asked.

"I do not think there are, but I guess we have to eliminate all possibilities, don't we?"

There was a light tapping on the door. It was Millie announcing lunch.

They ate then Pope looked at the doors with Lane while Sarah asked the two women about their neighbors and about Mattie's friends. Especially her friends' families.

Pope examined the locks with Lane looking on. There were slight scratch marks on the lock for the rear door. To further confirm the rear door was used to gain entry and egress, they walked around the house and looked for ways to get onto the roof without a ladder. There were no trees with branches close enough to use to climb over to the roof. An examination of the upstairs windows showed no scratch marks.

"Joe, this strongly suggests a professional lock

picker, probably with a picklock set. When, exactly, did you realize Mattie was not in her bedroom?"

"About eight the next morning. Girls her age tend to sleep a lot. I guess going through growth spurts tires them out."

"Do you remember what time she went to bed?

"Yes, she was up late for a sixteen year old. She went to bed at midnight."

Pope wrote "kidnap time between midnight and eight in the morning" in his case notes.

"What was she wearing?" he asked.

"A white summer nightgown."

"Was a robe or coat taken?"

"I don't know. We will have to go ask Harriett."

They found Sarah wrapping up her questions.

Harriett confirmed her youngest daughter was wearing a thin, white nightgown when she went to bed. No robe or coat was missing.

Pope looked at his watch. An hour until the mailman came for note exchanges between him and Hume. He excused himself and Sarah and adjourned to their room to compare notes and write a condensed report to the chief detective.

"What did you learn?" Pope asked.

"I learned the victim is precocious, had a suitor from a less-than-popular family named Howard. They live at this address." She handed Pope an address only two blocks away. He added the Howard possibility, his findings about lock pick scratches on the back door and what she was wearing. They went back downstairs and gave the folded note to Martha, who was the go-between for them and Hume.

Later, the mailman came and picked up their note and dropped off another to the detective. It said Walter McKee was out sick, something not normal for him. Hume said senior detective Thacker was tracking him down.

Harriett took the two detectives aside for a private talk.

"I guess you are not married. It is uncomfortable for me with young daughters to have you sharing a bedroom. I would like to move one of you to the other spare," Harriett said.

"I understand, Harriett. But, if we as a wife and husband take different bedrooms and one of your staff is involved, it will cause suspicions, don't you think?" Sarah responded.

"Well, I just do not like it."

"Alright. How about you tell Millie, Sarah is having a hard time sleeping with her delicate condition and my snoring is ruining what sleep she has?" Pope suggested.

"Thank you," Harriett said and rushed off to have her maid make up the other guest bedroom.

"So much for snuggles, cowboy."

"Afraid so. But, it is the cost of keeping peace in our dear Lane family. I am still not convinced the financial man, McKee is our prime suspect on this."

"If he is," Sarah said, "he has a friend or two help-ing. I cannot imagine he knows how to pick locks."

"Let's go for a walk just before dusk. There may be someone I want you to meet."

They did and circled the long block twice before encountering a tall gentleman with a beard turning from gray to white. He was dressed in a nice suit and wore a black Stetson. The man was walking a blue tick coon hound on a leash.

The dog started yipping with glee as soon as he saw them and pulled the older gentleman along faster than he had planned to go.

Pope squatted and the dog jumped on him, licking his face. He patted the dog's head and scratched his ears, when the dog would hold still long enough.

"Miss Sarah, I thought I raised this boy well enough to introduce his grandpa to a pretty lady before going all crazy over his dog!"

"You are Israel Pope? I have heard so much about you!" she said as she embraced Popes grandfather.

"You two look so much alike. I am blessed the ap-ple did not roll far from the tree, Mr. Pope!" she said."

"Johnny, I like this one already. Now git up here and greet your grandpa properly."

Pope stood and hugged his only family member for over seventeen years.

"Guess old Scout missed you. This old scout did, too."

"Thanks for coming grandpa. And, Sarah is in

disguise. That's a pillow and two guns in the front of her dress."

"Well, alright. I like her even more yet."

They walked around a block farther from the Lane house and both briefed the former mountain man on everything salient about the case. Particularly, the victim's former suitor's home address several blocks away.

"I will keep a real close look on the house and its comings and goings. As tight as when we watched the war party what killed my son, his wife and my granddaughter."

"John said he had fought Indians before the recent attack we were in. But, he never gave any details," Sarah said hoping to learn more about Popes past.

The senior Pope turned to his grandson.

"You mind if I tell her about them fellas?"

"Maybe we should keep this meeting short and hold the stories until a celebratory dinner after we get Mattie Lane back safe and sound," Pope said. His grandfather gave a nod Sarah recognized right off.

"I will be asking more questions along the way, so get ready," Sarah said.

"You sizing him up for a purchase, pretty lady?"

"No sir, he's already in my remuda. I'm just interested in his traits."

"I am standing right here, you know. You are talking about me like I'm off in a field somewhere."

Sarah gave him the smile and he was satisfied. Israel Pope saw it and said, "Whew, boy! You don't have a chance. Just grab this one before she gets away." Pope nodded and Sarah beamed.

"Well, no way this looked like a policeman's ball, but we better break up and see each other on walks in the morning and evening to exchange findings," older man said.

"Thanks for coming at no notice, grandpa."

"Wouldn't miss this buffalo shoot for the world. We'll get the little missy back and give hell to the ones what took her. Mark my word on it, sonny."

"Never a doubt, sir. See you later." Israel Pope handed him an address and room number. He had rented a room in a hotel several blocks away. When questioned about the hound, one look from the deadly man changed any concerns the hotelier had.

Pope patted his dog again and they parted until the morning.

"He is really something! I like him. A lot," Sarah said as they walked back.

"Does Hume know he's here?" she asked.

"No, he may never know. Grandpa is my or perhaps now I should say our, secret weapon. What crook would suspect an old man with the worlds' handsomest dog to be investigating him?"

"You just wanted to have him pass judgement on me, really though, didn't you?"

"His approval on anything means the world to me. But, no. I don't need anyone, even Israel Pope, to convince me about you. I am convinced as much as any former cowboy turned detective can be."

"You can be pretty romantic for such a stone cold killer, you know?" Again, the nod.

CHAPTER 7

Mattie Lane was scared and infuriated. Mature mentally and physically for her age, she thought she was ten feet tall and bullet proof. The past few days had proven she was neither.

Her dignity had been stripped away when she was kidnapped in a light summer nightgown and any vestiges of dignity disappeared when she was tied to a bed spread-eagled with each wrist and ankle tied to a bedpost. She was allowed to use the ceramic thunder mug to relieve herself a couple times a day. One of her two male captors watched.

Her meals were store bought cornbread and water. Once, a store bought biscuit was substituted. The menu held for breakfast, lunch and dinner. James Hume had bounced her on his knee when she was a giggling toddler. He would come and get her. And, she hoped, have his men kill her captors.

Mattie did not know any of the three. One weaselly young one seemed like someone she had seen before. But, she did not know where.

She had read about kidnappings. Sometimes, the kidnappers got the ransom and still killed the captive. In the case of an attractive young woman, which she knew she was, it was the before death part she worried the most about.

******

Walter McKee was at his rooming house. This was the first day he had taken a sick day in the several years he worked for Wells Fargo. He was more scared and nervous than really sick, though he had thrown up several times. He should not have done what he did. And, now it was too late. He would get caught and go to prison. He knew what happened to slender young men in San Quentin. The thought made him vomit in his porcelain chamber pot again.

He wondered how long it would be until they caught up with him. McKee knew Hume's men were good. Maybe he should take the money and run. Go to Oregon. No, Canada. A different country.

He did not realize Detective Thacker was conducting surveillance outside his building. Watching the single window in his room. Thacker was one of the best detectives in America. He always got his man.

Upstairs, McKee shivered and rolled up in the wool blanket on his bed though it was summer.

They would get him. He knew it.

******

Sarah and Pope went back to the older sister after dinner. Hume had sent a sketch of Walter McKee via the mailman today. They showed it to her. She did not recognize the man.

Pope left Sarah speaking with Martha about what it was like to be a lady detective.

"It's really Mattie who would be the best detective," she said. "She has worshiped Mr. Hume since she was a little girl. She has told him she wants to work for him as long as I can remember."

"Well, maybe now she can. I am the first, but, hopefully not the last."

Sarah went back to her room. Luckily, it was adjacent to Popes. As she cleared the top of the staircase, she saw him come out, his suit coat and black derby hat on.

"Where are we going?"

"I am going down to the docks and spread some money around. I will get my old snitches to find out about this Howard bunch. They live in a really nice house. 'Way too nice for the bunch of low-lifes we have been led to believe they are. And, I would like you to ride shotgun on the homestead here. Speaking of which, let me get the Greener so you can have it in your room," Pope said.

It took Pope half an hour to walk to the dock area and find some of his old sources. He told them what he wanted and he paid generously up front and promised a lot more if given information he could use for an arrest. He included part about a girl being kidnapped and promised one hundred dollars for her current location. He told them to leave word for him at the dock Wells Fargo office, which had been hastily been rebuilt after being destroyed in his last SFPD case.

The next morning, on the milkman run, Pope sent Hume a message. He said to wire the dock office and if they get a message for him from any source to wire Hume. He asked Hume to send a messenger to get it and deliver it to him. He said with just one day to go, they had to risk the cover to get information which could save Mattie. The mailman brought back an acknowledgement in the afternoon.

This time, Sarah took the morning walk. There was a small community park with a bench. She shared it with Israel Pope and they watched Scout frolic in the grass.

"There are three fellas who come and go. I have not seen a woman yet. Odd, because it just looks like some businessman's home," Israel Pope said.

She took out the sketch of Walter McKee and showed it to him.

"Does this look like any of them?"

"It favors a little skinny young one. I can't be completely sure. But, it's not far off," he said.

"That's important. I need to get possible identification back to Wells Fargo as soon as possible."

They parted and Sarah rushed back to the Lane house.

"Your grandpa says there is a possibility McKee has been at the Howard house."

"The mailman just left. I have to get this information to Hume. I will wash out the gray powder and go into the office as myself or, if I can find a kid, send him a message to meet me."

He left immediately and found a hack. They made it to Wells Fargo in good time. He had written a quick note to Hume and had it in hand when they rolled to a stop.

Pope saw a young worker getting ready to go into the building. He called him over to the cab and flashed his badge.

"Here's two-bits, I need you to rush this note up to Chief Detective Hume as soon as possible and come back and tell me he has it."

The man rushed into the building and came out the door several minutes later.

"I gave it to him. He says he will meet you."

Pope held the cab there. Hume exited presently and Pope had the driver motion him over. Hume got in.

"What do you have John?"

"A possibility, sir. Remember I mentioned a former suitor of Mattie's who came from a questionable family? I have a source who thinks he has seen McKee at the house in the past couple of days."

"This is the difficulty with no good communications. Thacker has been sitting on McKee while he is sick at home for a day. Do you know if he was at the house yesterday?" Hume asked.

"I don't. My information was for the past couple of days.'"

"We only have today. Tomorrow is money day. I have McKee's address in my book. Let's take this cab over and meet with Thacker. We'll hit the house and see what McKee has to say for himself."

They took off and arrived shortly. Thacker was sitting on a curb across the street under a tree.

"What's up, boss? Hey, Pope."

"McKee may have been seen at a house of interest. It's time to go talk to him," Hume said.

All three pulled their guns and rushed up the stairs to the third floor.

"McKee! It's Detective Thacker from work. Open the door. Open it now!"

They heard scurrying about inside and Hume nodded. Pope crashed the door and Thacker went in low.

The financial clerk pulled a gun on three experienced detectives. He and Thacker fired at the same time and McKee hit him in the shoulder. He fired a couple more shots and disappeared out the window.

Pope went to the window, expecting to see a dead

man three stories below. Instead, he found a landing for an outside staircase like on his rooming house. There was no blood on the steps.

Pope turned to Hume.

"Go, John! I will get Thacker to a hospital in the cab out front."

Pope climbed out of the window and ran down the three flights of steps. From the top, he saw McKee disappearing around a corner. At the bottom step, Pope broke into a sprint in the direction McKee had taken.

The small financial man was carrying a carpet bag. It clearly impeded his running because Pope caught him in two hundred yards and tackled him.

Pope ended up astride McKee in a perfect position to handcuff him. He dragged McKee to his feet.

"Walter, what the hell are you doing shooting Thacker? He has a family with four children. There was no call for you shooting him!"

"I was scared."

"We aren't old time San Francisco vigilantes, Walter. We are professional. Now, I'm going to lift your gun out of your vest pocket. If you resist me, I will be real unprofessional. You understand what I'm saying? McKee nodded up and down and Pope disarmed him.

"Now before we get to the police department and they start beating things out of you, an innocent young girl's life is in the balance. Where is Mattie Lane?"

"Who?"

Pope backhanded him across the mouth and he went down. Pope dragged him back up.

"Don't play coy with me McKee. I used to work the docks for SFPD. I remember how to make people talk."

"The only Lane I know is my boss, Joseph Lane."

"Right. So where in hell is his daughter?"

"How on earth should I know?"

"If you don't know about where she is, why did you shoot at us?"

"It's in the bag," he said nodding to the suitcase laying on the grass. "I have not endorsed and cashed it in. You will see it right there!"

"See what?"

"The five thousand dollar bearer bond I filched from Wells Fargo," he said.

"You don't know anything about the whereabouts of Mattie Lane?"

"No, why should I?" And, disappointing to Pope, he believed McKee.

"Okay, let's go to the iron bar hotel and check you in."

An officer was sent to the hospital to verify Detective Thacker, almost a legend himself, had been shot. McKee was charged with attempted murder and theft of a bearer bond. Pope refused to leave the bond as evidence, telling the desk sergeant to copy the descriptive information on the bond and Pope would give them a receipt for it. He knew it was a document anyone could endorse and be paid five thousand dollars for on demand at any bank.

Pope went to the hospital. Thacker was in surgery, but the wound was not deemed life threatening. Hume was still there.

"Get him? Where is the girl?"

"I got him. He's been arrested for shooting Thacker and stealing this," and handed the bond to Hume.

"Well, I'll be damned! We solved the wrong crime. Oh, well. Good job, John. Now get back to Joe's house and solve the important one."

Pope rode back in the same hack he had left waiting once again and paid a steep fare upon arrival at the Lane residence.

"What's been going on, John?"

"We thought we were on to something with the kidnapping, Joe. But, it was something else.

We have been watching the house of one of your daughter's former suitors because he was nearby and has a questionable family."

"Who?"

"Josh Howard," Pope said.

"Oh, that little jerk. I never liked him. Not at all."

"You think he's involved?"

"He's just one possibility we are following. Anyway, a person matching the description of another possibility was seen at the house. I'm sorry to advise you he was one of your employees."

"Who?"

"Walter McKee. As it turns out, he was not involved. We sure thought he was. Detective Thacker is in surgery from McKee shooting him. I apprehended him after a chase and he's in jail. I recovered the reason he's been acting strange and shot at our detective. He had brought a five thousand dollar bearer bond home and was going to run with it. I recovered it and Hume has it now."

"That little snake! But, nothing new on Mattie?" he asked.

"No, but I am hopeful. I have put out feelers among my former snitches down at the dock area. I spread a lot of money around and promised even more. We are still watching the Howard residence. Just because it was not McKee does not rule them out of anything."

"What else are you doing?" Lane asked.

"I have a deep cover man working the neighborhood here real hard. I have a gut feeling she is close by."

"You know, John, I have been feeling the same thing. Maybe it's because I want my baby to be near. I don't know."

"What you and Harriett and Martha are going through has to be horrible. Just know finding Mattie and bringing her home safely is the number one priority in Hume's, Sarah's and my lives right now. And, we have other people, some good ones on our side, others who are criminals, who have been good sources to me for years. These folks are working for money. But, it doesn't matter if we get the key lead from a piece of pond slime as long as Mattie gets back safely."

"I wonder what tomorrow will be like?" Lane asked.

"Hard to tell, Joe. A person not directly involved will probably deliver the instructional note. I think it will repeat the type and amount of money, the threat about police and not paying, and directions on where to drop it. I hope it will also have directions on where to find Mattie. Sometimes they do, sometimes they want to get and count the money first, then release the hostage."

"Do the hostages always come back alive?"

"Let's don't even discuss such a possibility. Let's focus on getting her back safe and sound and what you will do to celebrate. I'm sure Hume asked you, but do you have any enemies? Even someone you may have passed over for promotion, or fired?"

"He did, John. I have wracked my brain thinking about it. I fired a person who was threatening years ago, but I heard he moved to Chicago or Cincinnati or somewhere."

"You look like you are considering something, Joe. If you are, please spit it out."

"You detectives are mind readers. Yeah, I was. Last year, I got in a bidding war on some beach property down near Seal Rocks and Cliff House. I won and turned around and sold the property for development. The other fellow, Eldon Canfield, lost his deposit and a lot of money on architects, zoning and lawyers."

"How much do you think he lost?"

"Oh, at least twenty-five grand." Lane froze when he said the number.

"That's what the kidnaper's want! I'm sure it is a coincidence."

"It is worth pursuing. In my experience, there is virtually no such thing as a coincidence in a case. Please write out as much as you can with names and a time line and anything said between the two of you. We will jump on it right away."

"Joe, before you start, do you think this is something Canfield is capable of pulling off by himself? You know, at least breaking in and kidnaping her. Or, would he have to hire thugs?"

"He certainly would not do it himself. He thinks he is too high and mighty to get his hands dirty. But, he would not have to hire anyone. He has a whole gang of thugs on his various construction crews."

"Construction crews? You think he has anybody with lock experience?"

"Sure. He builds post offices, banks and even rebuilt the Wells Fargo office in the docks area that blew up not long ago."

"I am going to slip out and pass this around to my snitches. I have to go tell Sarah first. I will see you in the morning," Pope said.

He tapped on Sarah's door to relate the new information to her. Martha was sitting on her bed, both women cross-legged in their thin gowns. Both looked up and smiled. Neither were concerned about their outfits.

"I hate to interrupt, but I am going out for a while."

"John, do you want me to leave so you two can speak privately?" Martha asked.

"No, not at all. There is a person Joe had a business deal with in the past year. It got pretty confrontational. The man, an Eldon Canfield, lost an amount about equal to the ransom demanded. I am going down to the docks and put his name out to a couple of my old sources. Canfield builds banks, post offices and Wells Fargo offices. He built the one Dave Neel blew up. Solving that case led to me joining Wells Fargo. My point is he has at least one lock specialist working for him. Joe says a lot of his construction men are thugs. It's worth following up."

"Just remember, you need to sleep sometime. And, you have not had any recently I can recall."

He looked at her trim belly, hardly concealed by the gown and said, "You know, I kind of like you with the little pillow belly, Mom."

Sarah responded by throwing a bed pillow at him. He ducked but Martha's got him in the head as he went out the door and closed it.

This whole woman thing was pretty new to him. But, he liked it. It merited further investigation.

With two .44 Merwin & Hulberts, a pair of handcuffs and a Bowie knife, the well-dressed man in the dark suit and derby pushed his way confidently through people who would murder their priest for five dollars. If they had a priest.

He found the particular source he wanted. The man was well aware of Eldon Canfield. He said Canfield had a man who "fixed" things for him. His name was Jack Powell and the locksmith was a slender man named Kelton. The source did not know Kelton's first name.

Pope took out the sketch of McKee.

"Does Kelton look anything like this?" he asked.

"Yeah. A lot like him. Could be him, as a matter of fact."

"Sam, do you know where these two hang out?"

"They are kinda Cliff House men. But, I heard they had some work in town. Shifted base of operations to somewhere a half hour or forty-five minutes from here."

"What does Jack Powell look like?" Pope asked.

"Forty. Almost your height. A lot heavier, but not fat. He's a brawler and knee-capper. Don't get in close with him. He'll gouge your eyes or stick a pig sticker in your gut."

"Does he carry a gun?"

"Yeah, but with him, a gun is an afterthought."

"Sam, how about his hair color, facial hair type, general dress?" Pope asked.

"He's got black hair, kinda long. Drooping mustache. Makes him look like a Mexican, but he ain't one. Wears a wool coat and jeans. And, always boots." Pope gave him a couple of bucks and headed back to the Lane house.

He got back after midnight. It was now the day of the payment. Wells Fargo was going to bring it to the house by messenger. Pope was tired. He tried to make connections with what he already knew and what he had learned tonight. If it was Canfield and his thugs, how did they get to the Howard house? Or, was the man who looked like McKee there not the locksmith, but an unrelated person? And, where were the parents at the Howard house? He drifted off, his last thoughts on the raven-haired, green-eyed beauty sleeping twenty feet and one wall away.

*****

Both detectives awoke with apprehensions. Today was the big day. The day they would hopefully recover Mattie Lane safe and sound. Or, recover her body. They had to be correct with every move. Any shot had to be deadly accurate. There may not be time for another.

Pope quickly wrote the information about Canfield in a brief note to Hume for the now-regular milkman morning visits.

He gave the note to Martha to pass off as she had each day.

"What can we expect?" Joseph Lane asked again.

"We can expect the note to arrive and the delivery to be demanded immediately thereafter," Sarah answered.

"So we will not have time to react with someone to follow you. But, we will plan ahead and have you followed discreetly."

"By whom, John?"

"By my secret weapon. The best tracker who ever lived and one who nobody now would suspect," Pope responded.

"Are you going to tell me who it is?" Lane asked.

"Only if you demand I do. Even Hume is unaware of this man's participation."

"In view of it being my daughter, I do demand to know. I will, however, protect your and his confidence to the greatest extent possible."

"Fair enough. Have you ever heard of the mountain man, Israel Pope?"

"Last of the real mountain men? If he's who you are speaking about, my answer is yes."

"He is my secret weapon."

"I notice the similarity of last names…."

"My grandfather."

"Isn't he kind of old for this sort of endeavor?"

"Joe, I wish I could, at under thirty, keep up with him on foot. And, I wish I could shoot half as well as he does right now. If age has slowed him down, I cannot detect it."

"What will you have him do?"

"He will be hidden in your back garden any moment now. I will share the directions you get in the ransom note. He will leave before you and position himself to follow you."

There was a knock at the door. A buggy was out front and a uniformed Wells Fargo messenger stood holding a briefcase. Another holding a shotgun, remained at high alert by the buggy.

"Joe, take the case and invite him in to check the bonds. Have him tell the guard what he's doing."

The man came in and opened the case on a table. While Lane verified the contents met the requirements of the ransom note, Pope talked with the messenger.

"Hello, Seant," he said to a fellow detective.

"John. The man at the curb with the ten-gauge is Clint Fuller. He's about the deadliest shotgun messenger we have."

"Perfect! You have another jacket and hat or cap?" Pope asked.

"I do. Just like you requested in the note to the chief. He said you would have further instructions for us."

"I will wait here for the delivery directions. I'd like you two to pull around the corner," he pointed which one, "and change out of the uniform. Once the note comes, I will come to you. Mr. Lane will wait ten minutes before he leaves. With three of us, we can switch off if need be to follow Mr. Lane. Getting Mattie back safely is our primary goal. Recovery of the bearer bonds and arrests are a distant second. Real damn distant." Pope said.

"Seant, thank you and Mr. Fuller," Lane said as the pseudo messenger left.

"Bonds all good?" Pope asked.

"Yes, twenty-five bearer bonds in one-thousand dollar denomination. Probably better than cash."

"And, now, we wait," Joseph Lane said with a sigh. Pope nodded and turned to meet with his secret weapon.

"Good morning, grandpa. Hey, Scout" The hound rolled over for a belly rub and was accommodated.

"All ready? If I were them, I would deliver and demand both after dark. Or, they may think daylight is better to spot one of us following Joe Lane."

"Is it just us on the trail, boy?" Israel Pope asked.

"No sir. The messenger who just delivered the ransom is really a fellow detective. The guard is Clint Fuller, a top shotgun messenger. They will position in civilian clothes two blocks down and one block east. Once we get the directions, I will come out this way and tell you. You start following Joe. I will go to the buggy and follow from a distance, ready to rush in fast, if needed."

"Sounds doable."

"I will get a dish of water set out here for Scout and meals for both of you, depending on when the note is delivered and how."

He went into the kitchen were Millie was cleaning up breakfast dishes and Harriett was supervising unnecessarily.

"Ladies, I have a man and a tracking dog hidden outside. Please don't go out there or speak to him above a whisper until this matter is resolved. I need a pan of water for the dog. And, we should feed them as meal times come around. Thank you."

He was given a pan of water for Scout and delivered it with a couple ham biscuits and cup of coffee for his grandfather.

Pope thought a few seconds about Harriett Lane. She was a rigid, stern looking woman to have at least one pretty daughter. The lovely Martha said she was the ugly one and her baby sister was as beautiful as Lillie Langtry. Pope was not sure where this streak of beauty came from. He did give the mother credit for running a good household, though her maid and cook Millie did all the work.

Pope knew holding out on Hume would be a career ender. So, he wrote a note for the afternoon run saying his grandfather was visiting and an old gray bearded gent walking his dog would be a great non-police looking surveillance asset. Just a statement, not a request. He hoped it would fly through.

Nothing had happened by lunch. Millie prepared a plate for Israel Pope and some meat scraps for Scout. Sarah insisted on carrying them out to them. She sat with the old scout and the canine one in the shadow of the rear steps, out of sight to virtually anyone watching the rear yard.

Sarah used her interrogation skills to find out as much as possible about the family, John and Israel's experiences as a mountain man, then scout. She learned about the ranch in Alameda County.

Well after the food was gone and they sat chatting, John came to the door.

"It's here. Joe is instructed to leave right away and walk south down this street for six blocks, turn right and go three blocks. There will be a vacated four story yellowish building. He is to leave the bonds just inside the door and proceed home. He will be advised of Mattie's location once the ransom has been verified.

I don't like leaving the money without the girl.

But, we have to work with what we have got.

Grandpa, do you have a clear picture of the path to take?"

"I do, sonny. Scout and I will leave now and lead Lane. I will veer off before the yellow house." He got up and put the leash on Scout and started walking.

"Good hunting!" Pope said just loud enough for his grandfather to hear.

"We don't know if there will be another note there, the girl will be brought back and dropped off or what. Please keep your guns close and guard the family, Sarah. I know you want to be on the chase, but your job may be the most important one."

"Right on all counts. Be careful!" she kissed him as he left through the back, heading to the buggy several blocks over.

Ten minutes later, Joseph Lane left, twenty five thousand dollars' worth of bearer bonds in a briefcase, and began the nine and a half block walk to the yellow house. The streets were hilly and blocks were long and the man used to sitting in an office all day was breathing hard by the end of the third block and had to slow down.

******

"Well, little dolly. This is your big day. Daddy better cough up the ransom, or you are going to not make it to your next birthday. But, don't you worry. You will have some real fun before you die. Hell, you might have some fun even if daddy pays up and we let you go!" the dark haired man advised her as he looked at her bare legs and more.

Mattie was smart enough to know antagonizing her captors might cause the "fun" to start. Or, a disfiguring beating. Or, worse. So, she bit her lip and said nothing.

He dropped her plate and cup on the bed, untied one wrist and gave her an unwelcome caress before leaving.

She sipped the tepid water from the dirty cup, then began to nibble on the stale biscuit. She missed Millie's cooking. The pretty woman in her late forties was her best friend, next to Martha. She wished her mother was more like Millie, who smiled all the time.

The dark-haired man walked down the steps and to the kitchen.

Nobody else was there. The kid who told him about Mattie Lane was running point, watching to see if anyone was following the father. School was out and so was his job until September.

The man's brother, the only one he really trusted, was working the ransom pickup. He should be back in less than an hour.

******

James Hume was angry and had his friend Morse push the buggy hard across town and out toward Cliff House and the Pacific Ocean.

They arrived by nine thirty in the morning.

The two detectives stormed in to see a man Hume had worked with on construction a number of times. His name had come to Hume this time on a note from Pope. Eldon Canfield.

The receptionist at the Canfield building looked like a high grade prostitute and probably had been.

"I'm James Hume from Wells Fargo. I want to see Canfield right now!"

"Do you have an appointment?" she asked.

The stare her question engendered did not leave further room for discussion. She got up and tapped on Canfield's office door.

He was interrupted while having a breakfast slug of Tennessee whiskey and looked up angrily.

"There's a Mr. Hume from Wells Fargo demanding to see you, sir."

Hume was a primary contact with a company whose custom meant a lot to his bottom line. He stood and waved for her to usher him in.

"Mr. Hume. This is a bit of a surprise," was his bourbon-breath greeting.

"You have had private dealings with one of our senior executives, Joseph Lane," Hume began, not mincing words.

"Yes. I assure you, though they did not end well for me, they were according to the letter of the law."

"I understand you lost around twenty-five thousand in the deal."

Shocked Hume knew about any of this, he nodded.

"Lane's youngest daughter has been kidnapped. The kidnapper has locksmith skills. The ransom amount happens to equal your losses. Is there anything you want to tell me about this?" Hume said.

Canfield's face turned red. Hume knew it was anger not embarrassment.

"Are you intimating I am a suspect in this kidnapping?"

"No, Canfield. I am telling you straight out. You would be a person of interest to the police. Now, I have known and worked with you on construction of highly secure buildings for a number of years. You have always been straightforward with me. Which is why we are sitting here talking like men. If you know anything about this kidnapping or have access to anyone you employ who could help us, now is the time to step forward."

"Are the police involved?" Canfield asked.

"No. Not yet anyway. We want to get Mattie back safe and sound. I would care about any child of one of our employees. But, Eldon, this one has called me "Uncle Jim," all her life. She means the world to me. I want to get her back safely. If we can get the ransom back, that would be a good thing, but it's 'way down low on my list right now," Hume said.

"So, you came to get my help, not accuse me. I need to know which."

"I came to get your help. The relationship with her father and the coincidence of amounts would make the police knock on your door. I wanted to talk with you first. I do not plan to involve the police if we get her back, unless there are arrests to be made."

Canfield thought about the several implications of the statement for a minute.

"Stella, find Hayes for me. Tell him to get in here like his tailfeathers are on fire."

"You know who Robert Hayes is, don't you?" he asked Hume.

"I do. A very competent fixer. I first met him as sheriff of El Dorado County. He does not think very highly of me, nor I of him," Hume said.

They sat and chatted for some minutes until a rough-looking man who looked like he had won too many bar brawls walked in.

He saw Hume and balled a fist. Harry Morse quickly reached into his coat under his left arm. Canfield stood and spread his arms placatingly.

"This is a meeting of businessmen on a serious subject. It's my office and I expect professionalism.

Robert, the two detectives have come to us for help and we are going to give it. Jim Hume and I have worked together for years. We have not always agreed, but we have been straight with each other. Jim, Robert led the crew on the rebuild of the office down at the docks after the explosion.

Why don't you tell Robert what happened with Lane's girl and what we may be able to do."

"One of our executives has had his sixteen year old daughter kidnapped a few days ago. The ransom is being paid today. As far as I know, she has not been returned. I have asked Detective Harry Morse of the Morse Detective Agency to consult with us on this matter.

You have a lot of contacts in the area. If you have heard any rumors about a big job going down, I'd be interested in hearing it. Otherwise, it would help if you put out the word and see what people know. The only thing I know for sure is they are smart enough to demand bearer bonds instead of other money and one has some lock picking skills. The lock picking is a place you might be able to help."

"There's been a little buzz about three planning something outside of their abilities. Two brothers and a younger fellow who works for a girl's school. I don't know any names, but I'll put some feelers out. I ain't doing this for you Hume. I wouldn't do a damn thing for you. But, I got no war on kids and don't take well to folks who hurt them. I grew up with a pa what beat me silly every time he got ahold of a bottle. Hurting kids is a sore point."

"Well, after all these years, Hayes, we have found something we agree wholeheartedly on. Let me know what you find out. We are out of time. You hear something, the time of day or day of the week does not matter," Hume said.

Hume thanked the two and he and Morse got into the buggy and drove hard towards the city center, Morse on the ribbons, if two reins could be called ribbons.

"What did you take away from those fellows, Jim?"

"The big thing I got was one of the three worked for a girl's school. Is the school where Mattie was chosen to target? If so what did this person do at the school? I doubt he was a teacher. Janitor most likely. Or, long shot he might be a handyman. Steer this thing to the San Francisco Girl's High School. Mattie goes there."

"It's closed for the summer," Morse reminded him.

"I know. But, maybe some staff is there. We are out of time. And, we have no idea if the note has been delivered, what Pope is doing, if he has shot anyone else. Anything," Hume said.

"Yeah, Jim. That boy does surely burn some powder. When I was waiting for you in the bull pen, some of us were trying to come up with a kill count for him. We couldn't, but it has to be a lot."

"Certainly more than Earp or Masterson. Maybe not as many as Hickok. But, a lot of those numbers are from dime novels. Who knows what the real truth is," Hume said offhand, preoccupied with the case. The long-time detective knew it was right, but was concentrating on rolling down Geary Boulevard to the Girl's High School at Bush and Hyde Streets.

He had hardly pulled the brake on before Hume jumped out and bounded up the steps to hammer on the locked door. A man came. He was a janitor and said the Principal was in working. He got her and she sat in her office with the two detectives.

"Mrs. Smith, I have to speak with you in the strictest of confidence, alright?"

"Why, yes Detective Hume. I remember when you came to see Mattie Lane in a little play we put on a few years ago. I will be glad to help however I can," she said.

"Mattie is why we are here, Mrs. Smith. She has been kidnaped. We have a small lead regarding a crime to be committed by someone who works for a school. Since this is where she goes to school, I want to ask you about your staff. Probably service staff, though if you have any worries about teachers, I'd like to hear them."

"No. No worries about my teaching staff. All old hands with me. Our janitor met you at the door. He was a slave in the south somewhere and migrated here after the war. Probably the most dependable employee I have. Now, the handyman is a different matter. I gave him a chance. He was something of a street urchin from down by the docks. I suspect he had been in trouble with the police out there.

He does good work here, but does not take any upon himself. If he sees something that needs to be done, he waits for me to order him to do it."

"Any problems with him, Ma'am?" Morse asked.

"Not problems I can prove," she said.

"But, you have your suspicions?" Hume asked.

"Since he has been here, small things have disappeared from the girls' lockers. I cannot prove it was him, but someone worked the locks without breaking them."

"You mean, picked the locks?"

"Yes, I guess you could call it that. I know he can do it. One naughty girl locked another in a locker and she was screaming to beat the band.

I got Henry—that's his name, Henry Brown—to open the lock. He used a little tool of some sort and it popped right open. He's a little weird, but I am sure he is harmless."

"Yes, lady. And, you are a naïve idiot!" Hume and Morse both thought soundlessly.

"Do you have his home address in your files?" Hume asked.

She got up and went to a wooden file cabinet and fingered through some 3x5 cards.

"Aha! Henry Brown. Lives in a rooming house at this address" and wrote it down on a small notepad for the detectives.

"Does he ever come in during the summer?" Morse asked.

"Oh, heavens no. I guess he would if I sent for him. I may just before we start the fall term. There are some pipes I want tightened."

"You said a little weird. What did you mean?" Hume asked.

"He is not the sharpest pencil in the drawer, Detective Hume. He kind of stares at some of the girls as they walk by. I would guess he did not have sisters."

Both detectives were lost on her reasoning about the sisters, but did not pursue it.

"Did he ever seem particularly interested in Mattie?" Hume asked.

"He probably was. She was one of the prettiest and nicest girls in the school. Everyone loves her, so why wouldn't he?"

"Thank you, Mrs. Smith. Remember, nobody knows about this. We are handling it for now. Not the police."

They left for Henry Brown's rooming house.

"Damn it, Harry! We should have come to the school first!" Hume said, slapping the dash of the buggy.

"School has been out for over a month, boss. We didn't have the lead on a school employee, but we did have other leads to follow. I don't think we should beat ourselves up over not checking here first," Harry Morse said.

Hume nodded, but was not convinced. Sometimes, he held himself to an impossibly high standard.

They arrived at the rooming house. It was clearly a place they would stand out and not be welcome.

"I'll be bad cop. You be worse cop," Hume said. It was a role either former sheriff could play without batting an eye.

They went through the door hard and fast, yelling for Henry Brown in voices both honed as county sheriffs.

Doors flew open and angry, unshaven and unwashed men came out. One started to block them and Morse felled him with a right jab. He stayed down, which attracted the attention of the next several.

"Where is Henry Brown's room?" Hume demanded to know. He got stares, so he pulled out a silver dollar and held it up by the edge. A man nodded as if to say 'this way," and started up the stairs. He stopped at a room in the middle of the second floor corridor and nodded again.

Morse kicked and the door flew open, its lock shattered beyond repair.

He entered, gun drawn. The place was a smelly dump and was empty.

"When was the last time you saw Brown?" Hume asked.

"Three, four days ago. Just for a minute. He grabbed some clothes in his hands and ran out," the man said before disappearing as quickly as he could.

Hume and Morse searched the room and found nothing remotely evidential. They questioned several men still in the halls.

One said he hung out with two brothers . He did not know their names, but thought they slept in a deserted house near Lafayette Park. Hume flipped him a silver dollar and they got in the buggy and took off again.

******

Pope left with his grandfather. The latter took up a position on the route where he could watch for another watcher until Joe Lane showed up on his route to the drop-off point.

Pope walked ahead and met with the fake messenger, really Detective Sean Murphy. Murphy had shed the messenger jacket and cap and now wore a navy suit coat over the messenger trousers. Pope greeted Murphy and famed shotgun messenger Clint Fuller warmly.

"The dance has started, boys," he said. "Now, we have to see what girls came to the party."

"I am ready for close dancing and distant," Fuller grinned pointing at the shotgun and a long range Remington rolling block .45-70 under a tarp in the back seat. To help camouflage their presence, Murphy pulled up the canvas convertible top and buckled it down.

"Sean, head down Webster Street and stop at about Jackson. I will get out there. Go past the park and give Clint the ribbons. Clint, you drop the top again and serve as the cavalry. If we get a runner, you can ride him down. Or," he said pointing to the two long guns in the back, "stop him some other way," Pope said.

The buggy hardly stopped at Webster and Jackson Streets before Pope rolled out and slipped behind a big elm in someone's front yard.

Ten minutes later, he saw Israel Pope and Scout walking by. The dog caught his scent, but the old mountain man urged him on.

"No time to chase squirrels now, boy!" he said to the hound.

Pope grinned from behind his tree. He knew the old man had not actually seen him. Equally, he knew man and beast sensed his presence.

Almost fifteen minutes later, Pope saw Joe Lane walking along, obviously nervous and winded. He carried the briefcase in his left hand. Lane kept patting his right jacket pocket with his right hand. A sure tell he had a revolver stashed in there. Damn! "Why wouldn't he just let the professionals do the gun work?" Pope thought as Lane passed by, not having a clue the detective was mere feet away.

Pope looked down the block in the direction from which his grandfather and Scout had come. He did not see anyone and ducked in several hundred yards behind Lane. As he passed an untrimmed hedge on a street going to pot, he heard a familiar bird whistle and answered it. He knew he had just passed his grandfather's hide.

Pope crossed a street. He saw Fuller positioned in the buggy a block down. He knew Murphy would be a block in the other direction, but did not see him. The net was laid. Hopefully, it would enable the safe release of Mattie Lane.

He saw the father approach the yellow house. Lane paused and looked in both directions, then went in the foyer. He returned without the briefcase and walked back towards Pope.

Pope did not trust the financial executive to not acknowledge his presence verbally or physically, so he hid behind a tree and squatted down.

Lane walked by still looking furtively from side to side and patting the revolver obviously in his right jacket pocket.

Pope continued to watch the house. Presently, a large man, whose general appearance reminded Pope of Hite, appeared and went into the house's foyer. He appeared immediately and stood in the doorway for several seconds looking up and down the street.

Seeing no threats, he walked briskly down the street towards where Pope was hiding.

Pope assumed the house where Mattie was being kept would be in close proximity to the drop house. Walking brazenly down the street in broad daylight with twenty-five thousand dollars in ransom was too risky to do for very long.

Pope resumed his place squatting behind the tree and the man walked by. Staying in the yards, all of which had hedges or trees, Pope followed him close enough to never lose sight. When Pope got to the cross street, he waved for Fuller and Murphy to follow.

*****

While the man was picking up the ransom briefcase, Henry Brown was doing a bad job of making sure his cohort was not being followed.

He had fallen too far behind the man and missed Pope completely. Now, he was adjacent to Israel Pope. The old mountain man stepped in behind him and said, "Sonny, stop for a minute."

Without looking back, Brown turned into a yard and took off at his highest speed. Israel ran behind him and said "Git him, Scout!"

The large coon hound sped up and lunged towards the thin young man. Two paws of a sixty pound body hit Brown at terminal velocity and he went face down in somebody's side yard. Israel was standing there, all of them well out of sight from the street the whole cast was using.

He drew a Bowie knife with a ten-inch blade and sliced Brown's suspenders off his trousers.

"Git up, boy.

A few seconds later, Israel was behind the scared young man and tying him securely to a tree. He grabbed Brown's soiled shirt sleeve and ripped it off and over his wrist and hand. The sleeve made an effective gag, tied very tightly behind Brown's head.

"Now, boy. In my Indian-fighting days, I'd have done you up like this, skinned you alive and taken your greasy scalp. I don't have time today. Maybe, I'll just scalp you. Or, geld you."

Brown was rightfully terrified. The old man looked deranged to him. The next thing Israel heard was a stream of uncontrolled water hitting the grass. He stepped aside quickly.

"You stay right here. Mebbe your pants will dry out before the officers get here. The police will want to discuss charges for kidnapping with you. God knows what will happen to you, if little missy is harmed in any way. Who else is involved?"

Brown mumbled and Israel loosened the gag for a second.

"I ain't saying nothing to you, you old fool!"

"So, you got brave after watering the lawn did you?" He touched the point of the massive knife to Brown's navel and started moving it south. It stopped between his legs and the point slightly penetrated wet cloth.

Brown broke down sobbing with fear before the blade moved deeper and told him his compatriots were the Lang brothers. George and Augie.

"Why, thank you, son! Have a good nap!" and Israel slugged him in the jaw, and he fell into a long state of unconsciousness.

Israel looked at the street and saw a burly thug coming with what looked like Lane's briefcase. He silently melted behind the trees out of sight. Scout remained equally silent.

Israel Pope assumed it was either George or Augie Lang.

Before he could begin shadowing the Lang brother, he saw another person moving his way through the yards, out of sight from the street.

"Good tracking! Hell, I musta trained that one," he thought, enjoying the tradecraft as his grandson slipped silently into sight beside him.

He pointed to the man left tied to the tree and said "He is one of three kidnappers. He was making sure Lane was not being followed. Missed you completely."

Staying in the shade of trees in front yards, they followed the burly man and he turned the corner and within half a block, went into a big house. It was obviously abandoned, with a shutter hanging awry and a yard with grass almost knee high.

He turned and looked at the door, as he had at the yellow pick up house, then went in.

"I guess this is it, grandpa. I have one man in a buggy and one detective on foot. Where they are right now beats me. But, we cannot wait for reinforcements. I saw the Bowie back there. Are you packing your .45 with the long barrel?" he asked.

"Don't be silly, boy. Of course I am!"

"How about this? I will go to the front door and try to surprise them. You wait with Scout around back and take down whoever sneaks out?"

"It ain't a great plan, but I think she'll work," Israel Pope agreed.

Pope waited for his grandfather and Scout to ease their way around to the backyard, then walked to the front of the house. As lightly as he could, he climbed three steps to the door. He tested it. It was locked. Reaching in his vest pocket, he removed a small leather case and removed a medium feeler pick and his tension wrench. Within five seconds, he heard the lock click open. He replaced the tools and filled his right hand with two pounds of .44 as he slipped into the house.

Pope could hear men talking upstairs. They got louder as they began to argue.

"I say we enjoy the girl then kill her!" one said.

"No, I did not agree to murder. We can enjoy her, leave her tied here and she will figure out how to get loose. We will be long gone before she can get anybody's attention."

"Alright, dammit! I will take my turn with her. You go down and wait for Henry to show up. Leave the bonds up here. I will check them afterwards and make sure we got what we asked for."

Pope heard cloth rip and a woman scream. He could not wait a second longer and went up the steps gun first.

Augie Lang, who was the less burly brother, came around the corner and stopped, shocked, at the head of the stairs. He pulled a revolver.

Pope squeezed twice and took out the third button on Augie's shirt with two .44 rounds that touched. Pope threw himself against the wall as Augie tumbled end over end down the steps.

Pope thought he heard the man's neck crack, but did not give it a thought. It was irrelevant.

He bounded up the steps towards Mattie, only to see the burly one climbing out the window.

Pope fired a shot, being careful because he had to shoot past the girl.

He saw Lang disappear. Pope did not know whether or not his shot had scored. But, grandpa and Scout were down there.

Pope saw Scout attack Lang and grab the hem of his jacket. Lang slipped out of the coat and ran. Israel Pope fired a shot from a hundred yards, but missed and Lang entered the woods behind a house and disappeared.

Pope turned to the young woman on the bed.

"You are from Uncle Jim?" she asked. He nodded and took off his jacket. He cut her bindings and she sat up. He wrapped the jacket around her. One look at the destroyed gown told him it was a lost cause. She threw her legs over the edge of the bed and fell right onto the floor.

"I guess I haven't walked much. I am really tipsy. Who are you?"

"Call me Pope," he said as he picked her up in his arms and carried her down the stairs.

The first thing they saw was an empty buggy out front. Fuller had pulled up and bailed out, carrying the big rolling block rifle. Murphy was running from a bit down the street, gun in hand. Both had heard the shots.

"Men, I have a top man with a tracking dog around back. Listen to him, he rode this kind of trail before any of us were born. I'm going to take this young lady home, so I'm stealing your buggy."

Without waiting for an answer, he lifted Mattie up onto the seat, rearranged the coat around her bare form, hopped in and slapped the ribbons. He turned the buggy on one wheel and took off towards the Lane residence.

As he drew out of sight, a second buggy was pulling up in front. They heard the shots, also, on an otherwise silent afternoon from the yellow house described to them by Henry Brown.

They saw the door hanging open and heard voices and a dog yipping to get on the trail in the rear of the house.

As they went around the side, they saw the two Wells Fargo men, rifle and revolver drawn, starting into the woods behind a tall man with white hair and a short white beard. He had a hound on a leash.

As Hume ran ahead, the man and dog disappeared into a wooded area. He did not hear his senior detective swear.

"Damn! There goes a ghost from my days as Sheriff of Alameda County. What's that old mountain man doing here?"

He ran behind his friend.

CHAPTER 8

Pope slapped the reins on the horse lightly enough to keep him at a good safe pace.

He looked down at the girl snuggled up against him and transferred the right rein to his left hand and pulled his coat around her where it slipped off. She looked up and beamed at him.

"You warm enough Miss Mattie?" he asked.

"I'm fine. Did you kill the one they call Augie?"

"I did. It was him or me," Pope said.

"I heard more shots in the yard. You must have only winged George. He was going to have his way with me until you saved me."

"So it appeared."

"Thank you, Pope."

"Sure, but it was a big effort led by Jim Hume and a lot of people."

"But you killed Augie and saved me. That's what

counts to me."

Pope did not know how to respond to this, so he nodded and drove on.

They pulled up to the Lane house.

"Miss Mattie, you stay here wrapped in my coat. I will tell them you are here but need a blanket or something."

"Alright, Pope."

He knocked on the door and for the first time, saw Harriett Lane smile as she saw her daughter in the buggy. So did the raven-haired detective with the green eyes and the ten-gauge shotgun at the door.

"Is she all right, Pope?" she asked silently. But, he was learning to read her mind. He nodded and she knew all was well.

Harriett, Martha and Joe Lane ran out to the buggy and Millie followed with a blanket to give at least a modicum of propriety.

As Sarah and Pope walked out, they heard Mattie say "And, Pope killed him. Dead. I heard him thud and thud as he fell down the stairs."

"Miss Mattie. We need to take the buggy and get back to the scene. We have a fugitive at large. Joe, will you take the shotgun here and guard everybody until we catch the ringleader? I have a good hound on his trail," Pope said.

Sarah reached under her dress and pulled a pillow and a two-gun rig out.

"I guess I should name the twins Smith and Wesson, she said sheepishly. Both daughters eyes got wide as Sarah strapped on both guns and climbed into the buggy. Pope shook the ribbons and they took off.

It did not take them long to return to the area of the house where Mattie was held captive.

They did not see Murphy or Fuller. They did see the buggy with Hume and Morse go by, searching several streets over. They were just a brief glimpse and gone before either detective could flag them down and move them to where they knew the culprit was being tracked.

They knew the area because the dog barking was just a dog to everyone else listening. To Pope, it was a hunting hound he had raised from a puppy and he would have known Scout on the trail anywhere.

They got as close as they could and tied the reins to a hitching post in front of another vacated house.

"Ready?" he asked Sarah, who smiled broadly. She was obviously ready for some adventure after being cooped up for several days.

They cut through the yard and some trees beyond. Scout's yips signaled he was both close to them and his excitement indicated he was close to his quarry. They came up behind Israel Pope from a distance and Pope warned his grandfather with the same bird whistle they had used for years.

The old mountain man did not need to look back. He just waved his arm and went on at a pace about twice as fast as a normal man's walk. Pope knew his grandfather could still maintain this pace for hours.

The two detectives had to speed up to a run to catch him and even running, it took them several minutes.

"Scout's close, boy. We are on him. He better not shoot the dog. If he does, I will skin him alive, scalp him and leave him hanging from a tree for the whole damn world to see."

Pope knew his grandfather was dead serious. He couldn't help but grin at the old man, who returned the same grin. Sarah watched this and began to grasp the depth of the bond these two shared.

They came upon a house which had been vacant so long it had moved into the ramshackle category.

Scout was out front making his "I treed him. The raccoon is up this tree" howling barks.

"He's in there, boy. Let me go flush him out," Israel Pope said.

"No, sir. It's my paid job. How about you take the back and shoot him if I chase him out. Sarah, stay here and watch my back."

Without waiting for an answer, he moved towards the front door. The bolt had been thrown.

Once again, he retrieved the small leather case and picked the lock, losing precious minutes to a man who knew they had arrived.

Pope stepped back to the hinge side of the door and pushed it open as gently as he could but still getting it all the way open.

It was darker inside than a graveyard at midnight. He wished he had his Dietz lantern.

He drew the right-hand .44 and entered, staying close to the door going in and then immediately flattening against the front wall.

Even after his eyes acclimated to the darkness, he could not see where George Lang was hidden.

It became a waiting game. The first man to move or make a sound would be dead.

The house was moldy and dusty inside. Pope had to pinch his nose to keep from sneezing.

Lang was not smart enough to pinch is nose, and sneezed loudly. To avoid becoming a target, he moved to the side as Pope put a bullet in the wall at the spot from which he had just moved.

Lang fired at Pope's flash and hit him in the shoulder. Pope felt a horrible flash of nauseating pain and fell back against the wall. He must have groaned because he heard Sarah yell "John, are you alright?"

The front door was Lang's closest exit. He knew a woman was outside, but in the heat of the moment, did not consider a woman to be a threat.

He rushed the door.

Pope saw the shadow coming in his direction and instinctively fired. He heard a sound like a fist hitting a side of beef. Pope heard a simultaneous grunt, but Lang kept moving.

Wounded badly, Pope rushed him in the dark.

Their bodies collided.

The two clinched in a silent life or death struggle, choking, gouging and punching in the doorway.

Lang grabbed the detective in a bear hug from the front. Lang was still holding Pope's weight in the bear hug. Pope wrenched Lang;s gun out of his hand and it flew away in the dark.

He released Pope who felt a second wave of intense pain, a dizzying flash of pinprick stars and then fell to his knees, then face down on the dirty floor.

Lang grabbed Popes gun from where Pope had just dropped it.

He was unfamiliar with the double action Merwin & Hulbert, so he aimed at Popes head from point blank range and manually cocked the .44.

A loud "Pop! Pop!" sounded as a .44 sounded and shot flame four feet through the darkness and Lang stood stunned and surprised as the bullets from Sarah's Smith & Wesson plowed into his chest.

Dying, he raised his arm and aimed at her from several feet away.

There was another "Pop!" and he fell. Pope collapsed and his smoking number two gun hit the floor, its work done.

Sarah, her gun raised but unable to get the next shot off fast enough, saw Lang's head move as Popes bullet hit the back of his head dead on, killing him instantly. He died, not with the usual look of surprise, but so quickly he had the concentration of aiming at her on his face.

She saw the damage to the back of his head as she stepped over him.

Israel Pope moved behind her and she saw it was him and dropped her gun to her side as she rushed to his grandson, sure he was dead.

Sarah holstered and turned Pope over with nauseating fear at what she would find.

She saw him smile at her and her world changed that instant for the better. She gave him her famous smile and he closed his eyes as he grimaced in pain.

The tall, old mountain man entered, seven and a half inch barrel Cavalry Model first. He looked down at the floor. He quickly holstered.

They both took the big detective by his uninjured right shoulder and dragged him out to the front stoop where there was more light.

He was still unconscious, but they could see and hear the excruciating pain moving him caused.

Hume and Morse had heard the shots and driven the buggy over. They were bailing out and approaching, guns at the ready.

"It's over boss! Lang is dead. The ransom should be inside.

John is hit in the thigh and has a nasty wound through his collar bone. We need to get help for him," Sarah said.

"Here. Take this handkerchief and hold it like a pad

against that upper wound. Israel was already tying a bandanna around Pope's leg above the thigh wound.

We'll get him to San Francisco City and County Hospital. Men, help load him into the buggy. Sarah, you get in first to hold him," Hume ordered.

Once in, Sarah pressed the padded handkerchief firmly against the shoulder wound.

Hume slapped the reins and the horse began the fast run to the hospital on Potrero Street.

Pope was still unconscious when Hume pulled up in front of the two-story wooden building. He ran in to get assistance while a very worried female detective held Pope.

A doctor, two nurses and a couple of orderlies came out with a gurney and loaded Pope onto it. All seven rushed into the hospital with the injured detective. Pope was transferred to an examination table and they started cutting his coat and shirt off at the top, while another nurse worked on the trousers to get to the thigh wound. At the same time, others were taking his vital signs.

"How long has he been bleeding?" the doctor asked.

"About fifteen minutes at this rate….maybe twenty," Sarah answered.

"Alright. We can assume he's lot a fair amount of blood. We need to address blood loss right away. Family or associates, or whoever you are, you need to leave and go to our waiting area. Let us do our thing and save this man," the doctor ordered.

******

At the vacant house, Israel Pope and Scout paced impatiently as Detectives Morse and Murphy checked Lang and recovered the ransom. Morse verified the bearer bonds were all there.

"Men, we need to finally bring the SFPD in on this. We have one recovered kidnap victim, one ransom recovered in full, one kidnaper in custody and a dead kidnaper in each of two abandoned houses several blocks apart. It should be a pretty easy case for them.

Israel, my old friend, I know you are itching to get to the hospital and check on John. Here's my plan. Fuller, stay here and await the police. Israel, his dog and I will take the buggy. I will drop them off at the hospital and circle around to the police department and speak with the chief detective or whoever's the most senior one there and he will send their representatives to you. Sean, you ride with us to where Israel tied this Henry Brown person to a tree. Hop out and cuff him and frog-walk his butt back here for the SFPD. I know Jim Hume would ask you to do those things if he was here. Israel and I will head on to the hospital."

All but Fuller got into the buggy for the short run to Brown, where Detective Sean Murphy climbed out, handcuffs in his fist.

They pulled up to the hospital in a bit more time than Hume's trip, but not by much. Several nurses and orderlies tried to prevent Scout's entry, but Israel's expression left no room for argument.

"How's my boy, Miss Sarah?" were the first words out of the mountain man's mouth.

"He's still in surgery for the two bullet wounds, Mr. Pope. I'm very worried about him. I did all I could to staunch it, but...."

"Don't you worry about John Pope. He's tough as a cob. He'll pull through this. You just watch!" he said.

After holding back for an hour, she finally broke and rushed to the tall old man, clasped him and began sobbing into his chest. With some initial hesitation, he put his arms around the young woman. Then, he realized she had quickly become family.

Two hours later, the doctor came out. He was smiling.

"Any next of kin here?"

"I am!" Sarah and Israel Pope answered simultaneously.

"He's resting fine. I gave him a little morphine. He took two medium caliber slugs, which I removed. The one in the right thigh was just in muscle. It will heal up fine.

The one in the upper chest broke his left clavicle or collar bone and luckily, the bullet angled up and exited through the back of his shoulder. I say 'luckily' because it just missed the sub clavicle artery. I cleaned it out, stitched the two holes and set the collar bone. He will be wearing a sling for a while to keep his left arm immobile. We are trying to load him with liquids to help with the blood loss. There's a thing some doctors do where they pump someone else's blood in intravenously. Sometimes, the blood doesn't react well in someone else's body. I decided to not risk it. He's young and very fit. I have every belief he will pull through this fine.

He came out of his concussive unconsciousness for a few minutes before I gave him the morphine. Regaining consciousness was something I was looking for and pleased to see.

You can see him now, but he is out like an empty oil lamp at midnight, and will be for hours."

Hume stepped aside as the older man and young woman hurriedly entered the recovery room, curtained off from the surgery.

Sarah dropped to the chair on his right side and rested her cheek on his hand laying on the bed. His grandfather went to the left. He could not touch the shoulder area because of the wounds and recently set bone, so he rested his hand on Popes head, as he had done many times to comfort him as a little boy, when he awoke with nightmares over the attack where his family died.

Jim Hume stuck his head in the door and watched. He had known the name Israel Pope since coming to California. After briefly meeting the legendary character, he understood more about his detective's stamina, determination and will to survive. Hume knew he would survive this and go on to excel as a detective. And, for a while, until she settled down, as was sure to happen, so would the beautiful woman who sat beside Pope. People came and went. He attracted the best and wanted to get the most benefit out of them until they moved on.

"As they always did," Hume thought with regret. He planned to die at his desk or in the field as an old man.

******

Harry Morse walked into the detective bureau at SFPD, looking for the head. He was not there, but his old friend Detective Sergeant Howell was.

"Got a big one for you, Bud. All nice and solved. One prisoner is downstairs locked up, two are ready for the morgue. Both righteous shootings. A kidnaping where the victim and ransom were returned. Think you want a bow tied around this one?" he asked grinning. He knew a really big case solved and nobody hurt but the bad actors was a virtual gift to a detective.

"Forget the bow, Harry. But, gimme the facts. This sounds almost too good to be true," Howell said.

"First off, it was your boy, Pope's case."

"Haha. I see where the bodies come in!"

"Not so fast! Pope smoked one and I hear a female Pink just hired by Hume did the other. Granted, Pope softened him up some first at the very least. He died real convincingly either way. The woman adds a lot of interest by the news hounds, I promise you."

"Damn, Harry. You are enjoying the telling of this story 'way too much, aren't you?" Howell asked.

"I am. It's a good one. It may be solved, but the bigger part of the gift is I will show you how to release it to the newspapers and look like the big expert. The chief detective is getting old. We have got to start grooming you as the obvious choice to replace him."

Howell liked the idea and started taking prolific notes to back up his new-found expertise in a kidnaping and solution about which he had known nothing two minutes ago.

Within minutes, he had the gist of the crime and rounded up two detectives, a team from the coroner's office and a black police patrol wagon and patrolman driver. Morse led them to the two residential scenes.

By the end of the following day, the SFPD had their case wrapped up. Henry Brown's statement was taken, though it did not add much they did not already know. The detectives were looking into any associates of the Lang brothers, but nothing new was gleaned from those inquiries either. Since his boss was out of town, Sergeant Howell handled press interviews out of the detective bureau, with a little help from his friend Morse.

******

Pope's morphine kept him asleep all night the first night. The hospital provided another chair and Sarah and Israel stayed beside him. Scout sat with his head laid next to Pope, touching him.

The next day, Joe Lane brought both his daughters to visit and extend thanks on part of the family. Pope was conscious, but drugged to prevent movement while the bone was setting and the wounds were beginning to heal.

He smiled and whispered at both girls who clearly adored him and Sarah. Both were gleeful watching the hound protect his master.

The sisters could tell how tired Sarah was and asked if they could sit with Pope tonight and give Sarah some rest.

Their father worried about the danger of two young women being alone in a hospital all night long. The mountain man also saw how stressed and tired the woman was who he expected to produce the heirs he so desperately but silently wanted.

"Mr. Lane. I've protected wagon trains and whole villages, I will be downstairs guarding the door and listening for anything going on up here. If the girls want to stay, don't worry about them. It would be kind on their part. Miss Sarah is about done in. She needs some rest back at her hotel."

The father relented, as he was wont to do with his daughters and promised to have them back after dinner time for the night. Mattie winked at Martha, unseen by anyone except the mountain man, who missed very little.

The effects of the narcotic wore off by midday and Pope realized what pain he was in for the first time. He said nothing, but the two people sitting with him saw it in his involuntary grimaces as he moved even slightly.

"Boy, the good Lord was looking over your shoulder on both those bullets you stopped. The one at the shoulder almost got an artery. The one in the leg could have, too. But, you had a fine nurse looking after you all the way to these saw bones. So, I guess I ought to say you had the good Lord and a good woman on your side. How could you lose with such a combination."

"Grandpa, I never heard you wax so religious before," Pope said.

"Well, sonny, when you get old and start thinking about how many times you cheated death and how one day it could be you. Then, you get a little more religion. And, when you come close to losing the one person in the world you care about, you surely get religion. I have to say though, I am beginning to think of missy here as family," he said, patting her on the hand.

The statement and pat earned him the famous smile.

Pope watched the interaction with more emotion than he wanted to show. He might be stone cold facing off a bad man before pulling leather, but not so much when it came to these two people.

"Sarah, you actually killed Lang. My shot was just insurance to make sure he died quickly enough to not do any more harm," he told her, the mountain man nodding in agreement. Pope had killed enough men in his recent past. He did not need another credit.

"Grandpa, where are my Merwin & Hulberts?" Pope asked.

"Missy has them in her purse," he answered, using the name he often called her with affection. She, of course, loved it. She had never had a nickname before. Especially one bestowed by someone she was finding more every day to be a legend in the West.

"John, the fact Lang could not figure out the double action trigger and manually cocked it bought me enough time to shoot him."

"And, shoot him you did, my love!" he said, causing her eyes to widen. This type of expression was new.

Israel Popes face set in a pleased knowing expression he had often shown when the boy he was teaching exceeded even his tough standards.

"So, Sarah, did we solve it?"

"By the number of objectives we met, retrieving Mattie safe, getting the money and neutralizing the three criminals, it would appear we did."

"I hear hesitation. Talk to me some more."

"Allan Pinkerton always told us 'you are not finished until you are positive there's nothing more left to learn.' Something is nagging at me. These three did not seem to be smart enough to come up with all of this and pull it off. Bearer bonds are not something I would think they could even spell, much less understand the negotiability aspects of them."

"The handsome gentleman across the bed from you always taught his grandson, 'go with your gut, it's seldom ever wrong." His grandfather nodded.

"It's up to you and Mr. Hume, honey. I think I will be the proverbial one-armed paper hanger for a while."

"Wal, you are welcome to come home to recuperate. I'll even cut up your steak. I sure as hell won't feed it to you though," his grandfather said.

The two shared a look of enjoyment Sarah knew immediately was not new to them. Their chemistry fascinated her. Over strong protest, Sarah fed a light dinner to her patient while his grandfather laughed aloud at the younger Popes protestations.

At dusk, they heard a carriage arrive outside the open window. It was, from the voices, Joe Lane dropping off his daughters to sit with Pope.

Sarah leaned over and whispered in his ear while Israel went down to greet them.

"The pretty older one is almost obsessed with the whole detective profession. My woman's intuition, which is always dead on, says the beautiful younger one is simply obsessed with you. You have a woman and don't need a girl. Don't you forget it, you hear?"

Pope realized it was not a suggestion. It was an order. An order he agreed with. Why want a girl when you had this woman? There was no reason of which he could think.

The girls came in, bringing a paper box with fruit tarts Millie made for them.

The mountain man perked up and asked about Millie. They had enjoyed chatting when she brought him food and Scout scraps.

The girls told Millie about Scout being there protecting Pope. There was a bag of neatly cut scraps of roast beef in a bag for him.

Sarah, before leaving, gave Pope a long, passionate kiss on the lips. She did it every night, but tonight made it longer to impress the two lovely young women to "forget it. He's spoken for so don't think about trying to compete." As Israel Pope escorted her downstairs and summoned a hack for her ride back to the hotel, she was surprised at herself. She was not the jealous type. Or, was she?

The two bade goodnight and the senior Pope sat on the wide steps and fished the bag of beef scraps out of his jacket pocket for Scout.

While the hound chewed with great vigor and enjoyment, he removed his tobacco bag and pipe and used some tinder and his flint and steel to produce a glowing spark to light the tobacco in the bowl.

He sat and smoked, contented with life, knowing

his grandson would recover and listening to the light snoring of his other best friend beside him.

Upstairs, the nurse tried to shoo the girls out so she could readjust his hospital gown to check his wounds and replace dressings.

The Lane sisters claimed to be family and demanded to stay and observe. The nurse continued.

Pope did not bother to voice an opinion. He was in sufficient pain to be sweating during a cool San Francisco night. The nurse checked the chart and gave him a mild sedative to allow him to rest and particularly to stop moving and potentially damaging the newly set collar bone and double stitched holes.

He fell asleep and the girls resumed their chairs on either side, each lost in their own thoughts. And, Mattie holding his hand as Sarah had. Not having a hand due to the sling on his left arm, Martha settled for a leg.

Pope slept and occasionally groaned, but less so as the sedative took its effect. Martha moved her chair and stroked his hair, getting a look of reproval from her younger sister.

By ten o'clock, both were asleep. Mattie with her cheek resting on the hand she was holding and Martha with her head on the edge of his pillow.

Israel Pope came in and looked askance at them, but did not move anyone. He figured it was a young girl thing and harmless. Even if they thought they were, there was no way either of these children could push the striking woman with the raven hair aside.

He had never bothered to tell Pope about White Feather, his second wife. She had raven hair, too. Some days, he would hear an eagle call in the distance. She always said an eagle was her spirit animal. Who was to say otherwise?

Perhaps it was time to tell him about his step grandmother. Israel Pope had outlived two wives and had raised one son and one grandson alone and at different times. The son died the same way his mother had. And, like the stepmother he was never to know. By arrows. And, for now, the grandson only knew one case of retribution. But, there had been another. A longer trail and even more violent than John Pope's. Israel had presented the scalps to White Feather's father, both men still grieving. Each man understanding the other's loss. Israel never knew what his friend did with the twenty scalps. He did not care. He only cared his beloved White Feather could now sleep in peace.

John Pope moaned lightly. Mattie stirred and kissed the hand her face laid on. Israel Pope, unseen, watched with no opinion. He did not presume to understand women in their teen years. He never had a chance with his granddaughter. John's sister. An arrow or bullet, he never knew which for sure, had taken her before he could even meet her. But, he believed she could sleep in peace also. And, she owed at least part of the peace to her ten year old brother, levering his rifle with accuracy and vengeance as her grandpa did the same.

******

Sarah had never reported in to the Wells Fargo office. She reckoned enough people knew her as a detective now, the need for being undercover had passed. She left a message early at the front desk for James Hume. Pope had said he got in before the roosters crowed.

He sent his secretary down to escort her up.

"How's Pope?" was his immediate question. She told him. Before she could express her concerns and desire to follow up on the case she feared prematurely closed, he did it for her.

"Henry Brown is going to be transferred to county jail tomorrow to await trial. I want someone from here to take his statement and ask some good questions. Both Thacker and I are tied up. Morse is heading out of town on one of his own agency's cases and I cannot contract for him to do it. Do you think you could?" he asked.

"I would be glad to, sir. I have this nagging feeling we don't know everything yet. The case is not really closed to me."

"Look after our boy, but run with the case as you see fit. Keep me informed about your progress. When you think it is time to close it, please do so."

"Would you clear up one thing I am confused about?" she asked.

"Fire away, detective."

"Does Harry Morse work for Wells Fargo?"

"Good question! Yes, he works *for* Wells Fargo. But not *at* Wells Fargo. He may be the best single detective in America and is a close friend I hire frequently because of his talent and his contracts. And, yes I said the best. Including your old boss Allan J. Pinkerton," he added.

"That's quite a statement, especially coming from a man who I thought was equal to Allan."

"Maybe I am. It's not for me to say. But, I repeat, I think Harry's the best of all of us. When you work with him, observe and remember. You will become an even better detective for the experience, Sarah."

"Thank you, sir. I will be in touch," she said as she breezed out of the door on a mission. Actually, two missions. One was to arrange the Henry Brown interview with the SFPD and two to check on her beloved John Pope and see if the two panther cubs had made off with him in the night.

Sarah hit the usual lack of respect at the police department until she finally got Detective Sergeant Howell. He knew she had been a Pinkerton and was Popes partner. Somewhat wrongly, he felt he was the reason Pope was such a good detective. His ego did not extend to the shooting part, however. He realized he could not hit the broad side of a barn with a shotgun at twenty paces.

He arranged for her to meet with Brown in his cell that afternoon before the transfer. The interview was with the proviso he sat in to "protect her." She said nothing. And, she realized he had probably been a pretty tough street cop in the day. He could take her in a brawl. But, she could shoot the damn mole off without otherwise damaging his proboscis he called his nose.

She hailed a hack for the short ride across town to the hospital.

The Lane girls were leaving as she arrived. Martha greeted her with her usual enthusiasm. Mattie's greeting was more like a competitor.

"Ha! In her little teenaged mind," Sarah thought to herself, convincing herself she really was not worried about the lovely young lady's obvious crush on Pope.

"How's my patient today, girls?" she asked.

"He had a good night and is eating breakfast now. He will be real glad to see you, Sarah," Martha beamed.

"Thank you both for spelling me last night."

They got into their father's carriage and it pulled off.

She did not see Israel and assumed he had ducked out for breakfast or a nap. She did not know where he was staying.

Pope was finishing his breakfast, which consisted of coffee and a piece of toast.

He lit up when she walked in.

"How was your night with Martha and the rescued baby shark?"

He looked at her for a second, then broke out in laughter. He had to curb his humor because it was painful.

"Yes, John Pope. Hilarious," she said.

"Are you jealous about Lillie Langtry, Junior?"

"I am confident and not jealous of anyone!"

"That's good, because you have every reason to be confident and no reason to ever be jealous. You are breathtaking, my raven haired beauty. And, I have to admit, far more than I deserve."

"Well said. And, true on all counts. But, I love you and you are stuck with me."

"Thank, heavens, Missy," he said using his grandfather's pet name for her.

He was rewarded with what he had been waiting for. Her beautiful smile.

"Have you seen the doctor yet, John?"

"I have. He examined my two bullet holes and repaired collar bone, which he calls a clavicle. He said all are progressing well. I will be here another couple days, then home for a week of bed rest. Then, light duty for a month. He won't tell me how long I will have to wear this consarned sling. It appears for at least a month, maybe more."

"Good thing your primary gun hand is okay," she said. "I have something for you."

"The kiss you obviously forgot?"

"No. Here's the kiss," which she gave him, "and here are your .44's."

He took them and inspected both. Both cylinders were filled and he smelled gun oil.

"You cleaned them! I definitely will keep you. This clinches it."

"You better. I never cleaned anybody's guns for them before. But, then, nobody else's gun ever saved my life before."

He nodded, knowing there was nothing to add.

Sarah told him she was going to question Henry Brown in a couple of hours and his old boss, Howell, would be present.

"He's already been interviewed by the police, but I wanted to do one for Wells Fargo. John, something bothers me about this case. My gut says the Langs and Brown weren't savvy enough to think of this kidnapping and the odd choice of ransom on their own."

"I don't disagree. I have been drugged and was groaning so much, I have not had a chance to think it through. I trust your instinct completely," he said.

"So, did Jim Hume," she added.

They visited several hours until both his grandfather and his lunch arrived.

She kissed him and hugged Israel, then walked down the street to a small restaurant for a light lunch before going on to the police department to meet Howell.

Sarah passed Howell her .44 Russian S&W revolver and he put it in his desk with his own before going to the cells. She conveniently forgot the smaller .38

version stashed totally out of sight.

They had a jailer bring Henry Brown to an anteroom.

The detectives introduced themselves. Brown looked like something the dog dragged in. He was dirty and disheveled.

"Mr. Brown, I am here to round out the kidnapping case for Wells Fargo, whose executive's daughter was taken and who put up the bearer bonds for the ransom. I just have a few questions for you. Detective Sergeant Howell is running the case for the San Francisco Police and will agree with me any help you give us will be shared with the prosecutor and help your situation." He nodded and she continued.

"How did the three of you arrive at asking for bearer bonds?"

"I don't know. George said that was what he was writing in the demand letter. I never heard of bearer bonds. I'd have asked for gold or silver coins. It was a little surprising he knew about that kind of stuff."

"How about Augie?" she asked.

"I ain't no genius. But, that Augie….He was as dumb as a brick, that one was."

"What was the plan about the captive Mattie?"

"I was not told ahead of time. All I know is Augie wanted to have his way with her then kill her. George told him he didn't agree to murder anybody. He said they could both have at her, but she had to be left alive in the house."

"It sounds like there was a leader other than George," she prompted.

"Mebbe so. I don't know. They looked me up. I didn't know either."

"Why did they choose you, Henry?" she asked as Howell took notes for himself.

"I dunno. Maybe 'cause I could identify her from school. Maybe 'cause I knew about picking locks and could help with taking her to begin with."

"Who actually kidnapped her?"

"Me and George. Augie had a rented buggy. He waited around the corner with it."

"And, you cannot even guess who may have been the idea man behind this? The one telling George Lang what to do?"

"Nope. All I cared about was getting my five hundred bucks and the Langs getting their twenty-five hundred to split."

Sarah smiled at him.

"Thank you, Henry. We will make sure the prosecutor knows you cooperated." They returned to the bull pen and Sarah holstered her revolver.

"Think it was worthwhile?" Howell asked.

"It was just something we had to do to close the case, nothing more," she lied.

"Thanks, sergeant. I guess I'll see you in court."

"Will Pope be there?" he asked.

"It depends on how soon it hits the docket. He is

still in the hospital. The bullet breaking his collar bone glanced upwards and came out the back of his shoulder. It made quite a mess. He will be in a sling for some time to come, I'm afraid."

******

Eldon Canfield's fixer, Jack Powell appeared at Wells Fargo the same morning and asked for James Hume. Hume was surprised, but had Powell escorted into his office. Hume wanted to get the most possible out of this visit and had his secretary bring in coffee for both.

"I'm glad it's just you and me, Hume. I can't abide by Morse. We got history from his sheriff days."

Ignoring the opening salvo, Hume poured Powell coffee.

"I appreciate your coming, Mr. Powell. What can I do for you?"

"More like what I can do for you," the tough man said.

"Oh? Then please continue."

"It may not be worth a hill of beans, but I heard some stuff on the street. I heard the kidnapping was more than just the two brothers and the kid. And, it somehow was related to her school. I could not get any more from the guy. I even gave him five bucks. But, he didn't know no more."

"That could be a big help, Mr. Powell. I appreciate you coming forward. Thank Eldon Canfield, too. And, take this for your out of pocket expenses."

Hume gave him a Liberty twenty dollar gold piece.

"I ain't got the proper change," Powell said.

"No change required, it took time and money to get here. Have a nice dinner on Wells Fargo," Hume said as the man finished his coffee with a slurp and stood to leave. Hume shook with him and walked him down to the door.

He checked his gold pocket watch. He had time and scribbled a note on the tip to Sarah and had a messenger take it to the jail to deliver it.

******

As Sarah started the out of the police department door, a messenger flagged her down by Hume's description and gave her a note from the chief detective.

She read it and changed direction, now walking to the San Francisco Girls High School.

As she arrived, a well-dressed middle aged woman was locking the front door behind her.

"Excuse me, Ma'am. Would you happen to be the principal?"

"Yes, young lady, I am. I am Mrs. Smith."

"Thank heavens I have caught you. I am Detective Sarah Watson with Wells Fargo. May I take a few minutes of your time to ask some questions regarding the kidnapping of Mattie Lane?" she said as she showed the woman her badge.

"I have already spoken with two detectives about it," she said with an irritating air.

Sarah switched approaches.

"I am aware you spoke with Chief Detective Hume and Mr. Morse of the famous Morse Detective Agency. Both spoke highly of you when they relayed your information. Which, by the way, helped Detective Pope and me free Miss Mattie and return her home safely. Thank you so much for that!

But, I thought it might be more comfortable for you to go through the final questions with another woman. We can communicate so much better with another woman, can't we?" She saw a spark of agreement in the woman's face and pressed on.

"After all, you and I are pioneers of a sort. How many female school principals are there in San Francisco? Even the whole state of California?"

"I am the only one, I believe," Smith responded.

"Outstanding! What an honor it is to meet you. I am the only woman detective in the area also. I was one of a cadre of us when I was a Pinkerton detective, but here, I am one of a kind. Like you."

"Do come in, detective. I was going out for a quick lunch at the café down the street, but I can delay for a few minutes."

"How about we let Detective Hume buy our lunch? We can enjoy some talk over lunch."

"Yes. That sounds like a good idea. It's just a block down this way," and she started walking with Sarah beside her.

"I just read about a woman detective and that Pope chap in the Chronicle. You were the woman?" Smith asked.

"I was."

"And, you shot the kidnapper?

"Yes, sadly. But, sometimes deadly force is necessary. We are not always as strong as men, so we need an edge. My .44 Smith & Wesson is mine. That, and an open mind."

"Oh, my! And, you saved the other detective?"

"It was mutual. We saved each other."

"Does he talk down to you on the job, or take untoward advances?"

"No. Never. He treats me as his equal. In every respect. He is recuperating from serious wounds in the hospital now."

"Will he recover alright?" Smith asked.

"I hope so. He's a dear. Such a gentleman. You would adore him."

"Here we are." They walked into a hole-in-the wall café and were seated.

"They have some fine teas," Smith mentioned.

She ordered a green tea and Sarah followed suit. Sarah watched Principal Smith, who if she had a first name, did not offer it. The woman was going through some sort of ritual of timing the steeping in the pot brought to the table, then carefully leveling the teaspoon of sugar and balancing the milk. Finally, she had a caramel colored beverage steaming in a thin cup in front of her. Sarah duplicated the effort exactly and held her cup up in a mock toast.

"To successful women!" she said and the older woman beamed.

"I only take thirty minutes for lunch, so we must address the questions while we are both waiting and eating," the principal said.

"Not a problem. I think you know Henry Brown has been arrested as an accomplice. We think there is a mastermind. Someone lurking in the shadows. We think he may have something to do with the school. Do you have trustees?"

"No, detective, as a public school, we report to the school board, but they never come to the building."

"How about parents? Anyone show a particular interest in Mattie?" Sarah asked.

"Mr. Hume asked me the same question. I said no, but I've been giving it some thought.

You are not Irish are you?"

"No, my father came over from Inverness, Scotland twenty years ago. I am not Irish."

"Well, good! Henry Brown was in one of those primarily Irish gangs. The hoodlums, they are collectively called."

"I see, principal. And, the parent?"

"Well! I shouldn't say anything," she said, projecting how much she actually did want to say something.

"Oh, go ahead. It's just us girls here," Sarah urged conspiratorially.

"There is Frances Rose Riordan's father, Patrick. He looks like some sort of criminal to me. All of those Irish are, you know. A big, tough man who looks like he'd beat his wife."

"Has Frances Rose come in with any suspicious bruises or anything?" Sarah asked.

"No, I am sure if she has such they are hidden. But, he used to follow young Mattie with his eyes like an eagle. The look was lecherous. The more I think about it, the more I think he may be behind it. Woman's intuition, you know."

"I do, principal. Intuition has held me in good stead during my career as a detective. And, you deal with lots of people. I am sure yours is honed like a sharp knife," laying it on thick to keep the woman talking. But, she had her say and finished her sandwich with a self-satisfied look and smiled as Sarah paid the bill.

"Principal, allow me to walk back with you and get Mr. Riordan's address. Then, I will take off. I have taken far too much of your valuable time. But, it has been more helpful than you know!" Sarah said, meaning at least the last part.

Sarah left the school and walked briskly to the hospital.

She was disappointed to find Pope having a worse day than the day before. His grandfather was there speaking with him.

Sarah kissed him on the forehead and sat down holding his hand while looking across to Israel Pope.

"Mr. Pope, are you available tonight?" she asked.

"I think it's high time you called me Israel. Not Grandpa. I am far too young and handsome for anyone but sonny boy to call me Grandpa. And, the answer is 'yes,'"

They were interrupted by the Lane sisters flouncing in. Normally, Sarah would be irritated, but their arrival helped the plan she had in mind.

"Here, sit down, Mattie," she said rising and handing a very surprised Pope's right hand to the almost seventeen year old.

"You two are the answer to a dream," she said. "Is there any way you can watch John tonight? He has had a bad day and Israel and I have a surveillance we have to do tonight across town."

"Oh, exciting! Anybody we know?" Martha asked.

"Oh, just a gang boss. Do you know any of those?" she asked in mock seriousness.

"No, I'm sure we don't," Mattie said.

"From the mouths of babes," Sarah though while nodding at her.

"I'm sure Daddy will understand. We all have such a debt to John. And, to you, of course," Mattie said.

"Anything Scout and I have to do?" Israel Pope asked as the hound settled comfortably in Martha's lap eating scraps Millie sent.

"I don't think so. It won't take a disguise. I hope it won't even take a gun, but no guarantee on the gun."

The sisters leaned in for more information. But, since it was about a schoolmate's family, it was not forthcoming. Nor, could Sarah share it with Pope. It did not matter. He was in sufficient pain, the doctor ordered a painkiller and he just dozed off in the middle of the conversation.

Sarah left with Israel and the two sisters smiled at each other, though Martha would rather have gone on a case with the other two. Mattie was happy to stay and hold the hand miraculously placed in hers. She was convinced her handsome savior's hand belonged firmly in hers.

Sarah hailed another hack and could not explain to Israel their operation without screaming above the clopping of the horse pulling them. The operation was no business of the driver's and who knew where his sympathies lay?

Using the type tradecraft learned at Pinkerton's, she had them dropped several blocks away and one street over. They found a bench and she explained the surveillance until the hack disappeared from sight.

This neighborhood was upper middle class. Or, lower upper class. Neither of the non-San Franciscans knew. They just saw all the houses were occupied, the lawns were neat, paint was not peeling off and the size of the dwellings suggested over four bedrooms each, some with more.

They walked past the house in question, casually chatting like a woman taking her father for a walk. It was proof how misleading initial impressions can be.

There was a small park area with a bench a hundred yards down the street from the Riordan home. They took up position there and waited. There were no street lights, so it would be a good after-dark point from which to watch.

Just before dusk, a large, muscular man exited the house and began walking towards the dock area.

They followed at a discreet distance, using yards and trees to block them should Riordan turn around.

After almost a half hour walking, he turned into a small building on the edge of the docks. Israel suggested because of the improbability of finding a hack in his neighborhood, Riordan probably walked to work and caught a hack in the docks for the late night trip back.

There was a small restaurant diagonally across the street from Riordan's building, about fifty yards away. They ordered two cups and a pot of coffee and settled in and watched the building with Riordan Imports emblazoned above the door.

They began to see flashily dressed young men in their late teens approach the building, look around them and duck into the alley beside the building. They would emerge later and disappear into the crowds hanging around the docks waiting for a boat, a fight or Armageddon.

In his hard to see black suit and hat, Israel left his chair in the restaurant and walked past the building and the alley. He peered down the alley. All he saw was a rear door. There were a couple of large trash barrels across the alley from the door. He went over and squatted behind them, repositioning them for better blockage of his form in the dark.

Presently, a group of four boys turned into the alley.

Israel pulled the long barreled Colt and held it ready.

They went to the door and rapped four times, then once. He noticed as the door opened and they were lit by the light within, a couple had bags in hand.

Ten minutes later, they re-emerged. Riordan was visible in the interior light and did not appear happy.

"You little punks ever try to hold out on me again and I will personally fillet you and turn you into shark bait. You got that?" he yelled after them.

Once they were out of sight, he went back to the restaurant.

"It appears they are selling him stuff they stole off people. He was warning them he'd cut them up if they ever held out on him again."

"It has to be past midnight, Israel. Let's go to our respective hotels and meet at Hume's office first thing in the morning."

"First thing like dawn?" he asked.

"No, first thing like eight o'clock," she responded. They left the restaurant and turned towards the docks. Three similar young men blocked their way.

"What's in your coat, honey?" one asked.

"More than you can handle little boy," she replied. He stepped forward and found himself looking at a .44 S&W pointed at his groin.

"You probably want to rethink your intentions. As a matter of fact, my friend with the long barreled Colt and I might want to chat with you. And, you tell us something helpful and you all may remain boys instead of girls. You understand me?"

The leader started to say something and before he could open his mouth, Israel had knocked the wooden club from his hand and had the shiny, sharp blade of his Bowie against his throat. It was firmly enough placed to make a small stream of blood trickle down onto his garish tie.

"Lookie, boys! He's bleeding a bit! Think I ought to just make it right and take his head off? This old Bowie has done it before."

"What do you want to know, lady?" one asked.

"Riordan."

The name evoked instant fear in all three, including the one leaking red on his shirt.

"You boys listen to me. Riordan ain't here. Missy and I are. She just shot a kidnaper. Put two in his chest. They was touching. Me? I lost count. I killed a lot of people who needed killing.

You be smart. Side up with us. I bet there's some money in it and you don't have to roll no drunk to get it. Just talk."

"Riordan is mad. He had a big deal and the Pinkertons or somebody messed it up. He was gonna get thousands. He got squat. He expects us to make it all up for him because he picked some losers to do his job," one of the boys blurted out.

"Was it the kidnaping?" Sarah asked.

"It was something involving a kind of bank paper I ain't never heard of," the nineteen year old said.

"Maybe bearer bonds?" she asked.

"Yeah! That's it. I don't know what they are, but he was going to get a lot and kill the fellas who did it. Some girl he fancied was involved. I don't know how."

"I'm going to give each of you a five dollar gold piece. If you come downtown to the Wells Fargo office tomorrow and tell the same story to the chief detective, he will give each of you one hundred dollars gold. And, I will be there to guarantee it happens," she promised.

"Now, git!" the former mountain man said, cocking the Colt with the distinctive four clicks that represented its name.

They took off.

The detective and the mountain man hailed a hack. It dropped Israel at a modest hotel first and Sarah at a nicer one.

She took off her guns, then shoes, then dress. In her shift, she began to outline the way she began to investigate Patrick Riordan. She listed everything from Henry Brown, including how his and the Lang's expectation was twenty-two thousand below the ransom, Jack Powell's tip, the principal, their observations of Riordan, and the allegations from the three street punks.

All told, it made a pretty comprehensive case against the Irish criminal.

The next morning, by plan, she met Israel at the front door of the Wells Fargo headquarters building at eight o'clock. They went straight to Hume's office. If he was surprised to see them, it did not show.

She laid out her case against Riordan and told Hume the three strong arm boys may show in an hour expecting a big pay day. She told him what she promised and he did not bat an eye on the amount. He knew something neither she nor the mountain man did and quickly explained it.

"During the seventies, Irish strong arm criminals, using pipes, sticks, brass knuckles and sometimes knives took over the city. They were referred to as 'noodlums' which is the reverse of Muldoon, a strong leader of one gang. The papers got it and somehow it became 'hoodlums.'"

The SFPD was overpowered by these roughnecks. This area has a strong, and often not so good, history of vigilante gangs doing what they think the police should do. That happened here. Gangs of citizens with axe handles and clubs banded together and walked the streets. Every hoodlum they found was chased down and beaten. Sometimes beaten to death. Word spread fast and the hoodlums disappeared. Chinese businesses, particularly, could reopen without fear of having windows broken and owners savagely attacked.

But, in the last year or so, it has come back somewhat. The SFPD would love to know who is running the street crime now. I think you just found out for them. Good line of reasoning!

Will it stand up in court as is? Probably not. Will the SFPD get the truth out of Riordan and enough cooperative witnesses from the hoodlums to make his charges stick? I think probably so.

I don't particularly care for the current chief of police. He's a political grandstander more than an officer. But, I do like the mayor who is stuck with him. We should leave right now and have you explain your logic and observations to the mayor. He will take us down to the district attorney and the chief and I believe warrants for Riordan will be issued. Kidnapping, conspiracy, extortion, running a criminal enterprise. He will never see a day of freedom for the rest of his life. Probably. We'll see. Let's go after the hoodlums show up," Hume said.

The draw of gold was too tempting to resist. The

three appeared and gave sworn testimony to Sarah's questions. A court reporter hired by the company documented it and a copy was signed and notarized before the three left with their treasure.

Everything Hume said came to pass when they went to City Hall. The mayor was pleased. The district attorney thought he had enough for search warrants and an arrest warrant. Searching the dock office was sure to find stolen jewelry not yet fenced.

The procession, now including the mayor and prosecutor, trooped down to the chief's office.

He was angry a non-sworn detective force had probably solved the biggest problem facing him. And, solved it on top of solving a kidnaping he knew nothing about. But, he immediately turned it around and began to figure how he could take personal and agency credit for at least part of it.

As they left his office and the door closed, Hume uttered "pompous ass," and the mayor nodded silently in agreement. He decided to check with the city attorney to see how he could replace the chief as soon as possible.

******

Hume had ordered a carriage for the trip to City Hall instead of squeezing into a buggy. They stayed in it and went to the hospital instead of the office.

The girls had left and the doctor had already been and pronounced Pope would be discharged tomorrow.

He was better, cleaned up and looked like his old self except for the sling.

With the boss there, Pope's usual kiss by the striking female detective was postponed.

Hume gave a summary version of how the case had developed and a major crime and fencing operation would be shut down as an adjunct to the kidnaping case.

Over the next six months, Israel Pope shocked everyone by marrying Millie, the housekeeper for the Lanes.

Mattie Lane embarked on a campaign of somewhat romantic letters to Pope. Her sister wrote a similar number of letters to Sarah about being a female detective.

Sarah and Pope developed a training curriculum for the Wells Fargo detectives and delivered it.

She was assigned several cases out of the city and solved them readily.

Pope shed the sling in three months and was as fast with either gun as ever. His grandfather, always looking out for him, presented him with a replacement pair of Single Action Army's in .44-40. He convinced Pope they would shoot 'till the cows come home without cleaning, unlike the tightly fitted Merwin & Hulberts. Pope found he actually could draw and shoot faster.

The edge in skill paid off during the period and his reputation as a fast gun grew.

The company opened a new office in Arizona Territory. Trains and telegraph wires were more sparse than California or most of Texas.

Stage holdups and robberies of the few trains running there, however, were not sparse.

Hume assigned two of his best-ever detectives to the new Prescott Office.

Sarah and Pope loved it and flourished there.

But, the partners were called upon to use their six-guns even more as their reputation as a crime fighting couple grew.

Which Israel Pope, newlywed and former mountain man, would have called "a whole 'nuther story."

A LOOK AT: ARIZONA GUNMAN

A WESTERN STORY OF GOOD OVER EVIL, LAW OVER CRIMINALITY.

County Sheriff James Duncan is fast and honoable. An Arizona lawman who rides rough country, often going up against dangerous men and gangs alone. Dealing with bank robbers, kidnappers and rustlers with his fast gun. Much of his tracking ability comes from his Scottish father, who served as an Indian scout. Valuable experience as a Rough Rider with Teddy Roosevelt, then as an Arizona Ranger.

Outlaws and corrupt government tend to stand in Duncan's way, but he manages to overcome all obstacles with integrity and really fast guns.

AVAILABLE NOW

ABOUT THE AUTHOR

G. Wayne Tilman is a full-time author. He retired from the Federal Bureau of Investigation several years ago. Prior to the FBI, he was a Marine, bank security director, deputy sheriff, investigator, and security contractor.

He holds baccalaureate and master's degrees from the University of Richmond and has been an adjunct faculty member there, as well as the University of Phoenix, St. Petersburg College and Florida Metropolitan University.

Some of his law enforcement subject matter expertise includes threat assessment, continuity of operations, security and executive protection, counter intelligence, international terrorism, and small arms. He has been an instructor in those subjects in a number of training academies, conferences and seminars. Mr. Tilman holds the internationally-recognized Certified Protection Professional board certification, generally accepted as the highest in the security profession. He also earned a US Coast Guard 50 Ton Inspected Vessel Master Captain's license.

G. Wayne Tilman's primary interests are family and writing. His avocations are bushcraft (survival/primitive camping), hiking, boating, kayaking, shooting sports, and travel.

He wrote his first novel over thirty years ago and has now written thirteen novels. Genres include espionage thrillers, mysteries, and Westerns.

G. Wayne Tilman's impetus to write in those genres comes from both personal experience and heritage.

A direct ancestor was a sheriff in Virginia Colony in 1680. Another ancestor was the lawman who brought in outlaw Bill Doolin singlehandedly and helped to decimate the infamous Doolin-Dalton outlaw gang, sometimes known as the Oklahombres. Bill Doolin was the Desperado of song fame. Closer to home, his mother was a counterintelligence agent for what is now the Defense Intelligence Agency or DIA.